ONLY GIRL
ALIVE

HOLLY S. ROBERTS

ONLY GIRL ALIVE

bookouture

Published by Bookouture in 2023

An imprint of Storyfire Ltd.
Carmelite House
50 Victoria Embankment
London EC4Y 0DZ

www.bookouture.com

ISBN: 978-1-83790-188-3
eBook ISBN: 978-1-83790-187-6

My mother once told me, "I won't live to see the first female president, but you will. It could be you." She taught me to dream and the tenacity to go after everything I aspired to be. She is my hero.

PROLOGUE
THE MANIFESTO

Following a revelation to Joseph Smith, the practice of plural marriage was instituted among Latter-day Saints Church members in the early 1840s. For twenty years, the United States government passed laws to make this religious practice illegal. The US Supreme Court eventually upheld these laws. After receiving a revelation, Church President Wilford Woodruff issued a Manifesto banning polygamist marriages. This was accepted by the Church as authoritative and binding and led to the end of plural marriage.

The Fundamentalist Mormon leaders did not agree. This story is the consequence.

ONE

Sliding in behind the man's head while he slept took the killer several frustrating minutes. Trusting in God's command was all that made the nearness bearable. The soft pillow, with its freshly washed case, cushioned the man's head while the killer's legs inched into position for the coming retribution.

According to scripture, to atone is to suffer a penalty for the act of sin, allowing the sinner to reconcile with God. "The man's atonement will be his salvation." These words vibrated within the person sent to deliver the penalty.

The killer lightly inhaled and exhaled into the silence, awaiting God's next command. It came when the man involuntarily moved his leg several inches beneath the covers. Tightening the fingers of both hands, one in the hair at the side of the man's head and the other around the knife, God's judgment became clear.

The blade rose.

With each centimeter, God made the hand steadier.

Jabbing down firmly, the knife's sharp tip punctured the skin below the man's ear. His physical flesh offered no resistance. The body jerked and the killer immediately eased the pressure on the knife, almost releasing it. Unclear eyes opened slightly before gradually closing in peaceful acceptance. The knife slid swiftly through skin, muscle, and tissue, causing warm blood to spray both bed and killer.

Soft sounds came from the man as his spiritual death, caused by his unimaginable sins, gradually turned physical. His hands, rising in objection to his oxygen-starved brain, were easily batted away until they lay still.

Soft gurgles drowned out God's voice for several minutes, the noise a symphony in the killer's ears. The man didn't thrash, and, as God proclaimed, his small jerking movements didn't wake the woman beside him. His heart pumped until the blood stopped flowing and his muscles no longer twitched. Temporal death took him into God's arms without resistance. The killer held the man until his celestial body left Earth and all he offered was dead weight upon the pillow.

Releasing his head, the killer's steady eyes turned toward the woman beside him. She lay farther in the shadows, facing away from her husband, and hadn't witnessed the fate that would also be hers.

The bloodied sheets gave no resistance and the dry spots eagerly awaited their next feeding. Inch by inch, the transfer was made. The woman's soft hair brushed the killer's arm, causing a sliver of doubt. God spoke again, the divine voice echoing loudly off the walls, jarring in the stillness of the room, his verdict in no doubt.

The knife entered her throat. She made no sound nor did she struggle. It was God's salvation and the woman knew her husband, who had fully atoned for his sins, would lift her into heaven beside him to share God's glory. It was the promise made to wives upon marriage. Those worthy would be pulled up to heaven by their husbands.

The minute hand on the bedside clock slowly moved as the woman's blood joined the man's. When the sheets were soaked and thick drops fell to the carpet, steady breathing again filled the room.

The killer left the bed and walked out of the room, glancing down at the blood dripping from the tip of the knife onto the carpet and then the wooden floor.

No regret.

No looking back.

No hesitancy.

Sinners waited for salvation in the next rooms.

TWO

The overcast sky and cold wind were the subtle backdrop for death as Detective Sergeant Eve Bennet prepared herself for what lay inside the house. The urgent call to Utah's special investigative squad gave her and her team a new assignment. The fast-moving storm simply added to the macabre circumstances of the homicides.

Dark clouds rolled over the high rock crests that bordered the northern rim of the Grand Canyon and surrounded the rural community, hundreds of miles from the nearest major city. It was the perfect location for isolation and following beliefs illegal in the state of Utah and the United States.

News of the four murders within the polygamist community hadn't yet reached the media but Eve knew it would. Since the fall of their prophet, the leader of the Fundamentalist Mormon Church in Utah, outsiders couldn't hear enough news about the men with multiple wives and their children. The women and young girls, living like homesteaders in their nineteenth-century-style prairie dresses and puffed hair piled high on their heads, only enhanced outside curiosity.

When federal law enforcement had finally raided the polygamist communities in Texas, Arizona, and Utah, journalists made their private lives available for TV, magazines, and blogs. Viewers around the world were fascinated. Those who didn't live in the Midwest had no idea the polygamist community existed, much less that they lived a way of life that was astonishing as well as perplexing.

Justice was an uphill battle for every case Eve and her team handled. The integrity of law enforcement was compromised within the fundamentalist community and Eve took that personally. From the highest judge in the county to the lowest rookie officer, the entirely male hierarchy supported the fundamental polygamist lifestyle and upheld church dogma even when it didn't coincide with state and US law. Women and children had no rights and nowhere to ask for help. Cut off from the rest of the state, local elections favored the deeply ingrained beliefs of the fundamentalist church, which had been designated as a cult many years prior. The church's rhetoric and extreme doctrine toward any person of color also designated them as a hate group.

Local law enforcement bias was only one of the problems Eve and her specialized investigators faced. Discovering who murdered the man, his two wives, and their child would be difficult at best. Navigating the cold waters of church secrecy would be a nightmare, as it always was.

Eve shielded her face as a bitter wind zipped across the skin of her neck. The gust didn't stop her from hearing a vehicle approaching in the distance. She managed to keep a low groan beneath her breath when she realized who it was. Her worst adversary was about to make his presence known.

"Hell," Clyde, the large man at her side, muttered when he saw who drove the car. He kicked dirt with the toe of his boot and planted his long legs in his *ready for action* stance.

Eve hid a grin at her second in command's muttered expletive. Clyde, a Black man, six feet two inches tall with a muscular frame, resembled a linebacker. His pristine bald head and square, defined jaw added to his commanding presence. Eve was always glad to have him beside her. It helped that he disliked the man pulling up only slightly less than she did. It gave her an added mental boost for what she knew would be a sea of fundamentalist red tape.

Tightening her shoulders, Eve walked toward the car as the man stepped out. His closely cropped hair, dark suit, and hands covered in black leather gloves made him look important. He had pasty skin, blond hair, a prominent forehead, and a large mouth, which gave away his unholy heritage in Eve's opinion. His paleness extended to lips that looked entirely bloodless. His hands, though the long manicured fingers weren't showing, had the same colorless tint. He was the perfect symbol of a pure bloodline, in the church's blessed opinion. He and Eve exchanged mirrored glacial expressions. At five feet eight inches, he stood only three inches taller than her, so she could look him squarely in the eyes: his blue, hers hazel with a slight touch of green that seemed to change depending on the color she wore. Today her blouse was pale peach with three-quarter sleeves tucked into black tactical pants with loads of pockets that helped carry extra forensic gear. She added a light jacket with the state seal to keep her warm. Her black belt held her detective sergeant's badge and her gun along with a handcuff case at the back.

Slowly Aaron's gaze traveled to her hair like it always did. It was secured close to her scalp at the back of her neck without a single stray wisp. She couldn't help an internal shudder. They didn't shake hands. She avoided his touch at all costs.

"Aaron," Eve said using her professional voice.

"Mr. Owens," Clyde acknowledged. He stepped closer and towered over the shorter man.

Clyde knew Aaron wouldn't speak to him unless necessary.

His black skin was an abomination to the fundamentalist community into which County Attorney Aaron Owens was fully indoctrinated. Clyde had worked in the state his entire adult life and could handle Aaron's scorn.

Collin, Ray, and Bina, the remainder of Eve's team, moved forward to stand beside Clyde and show their unity. Eve stifled a smile, squared her shoulders again, and waited.

"Eve," Aaron said with a sharp bark that was his usual tone when dealing with her.

A smug turn of lips was the prevailing attitude of men in the church when speaking to outsiders. Aaron's sneer was specifically for her and Eve knew it.

Their rivalry was buried deeply in church doctrine, or the lack thereof in Eve's case. Even with their unsettled personal history, they usually managed civility. Eve hoped this could continue. Three officers from local law enforcement stepped forward and fanned around Aaron. Another two men from his office who had arrived with him stood alongside him, adding to the threatening vibe.

This would go more easily if Eve quickly settled the chain of command. He wouldn't like it, but then, he never did.

"I want a statement from each person who entered the crime scene from the time the bodies were discovered until now." She didn't stop when pink rose in Aaron's neck and suffused his cheeks. His face took on a darker hue of red as she continued speaking. "I'm not talking only the inner tape." She made eye contact with each man surrounding the county attorney. "If you crossed the outer tape or went inside, you will have a detailed report to me within twenty-four hours."

Hollywood rarely got the simplest of things right and double crime scene tape was one of them. You wanted the outer tape to keep out the public and the inner tape to keep out all but the essential officers and evidence collection personnel. Each person who crossed either tape was required to give a written statement and Aaron knew this. Left to his own devices, he would let the county sheriff or police chief do their looky-loo of the scene without bothering to file a report. This was only one of the many reasons local law enforcement was now dealing with Eve's team.

She brought her gaze back to the county attorney. "That includes your report." His eyes almost bugged from his head and he blustered. She cut him off before he could start his usual nonsensical tirade. "I know you entered the home. I want a written statement about what you touched, moved, everything. You know the way I handle my crime scenes and this is not up for debate."

His attitude was nothing new and Eve was accustomed to it.

"If there is nothing dangerous inside, we're going in," she said abruptly. "After our preliminary findings, we'll review yours." She wasn't doing this to upset him. Eve wanted her team's mental mechanics fresh with no preconceived thinking. She'd told them there was a dead family without additional details. She needed their minds open.

Aaron started to speak again but she lifted her hand in a stop motion.

"You gave me the specifics of the murders on the phone earlier and told me you had no suspects or leads. I want your people and the police moved behind the outer crime scene tape, now." She pointed past the yellow tape she currently stood at to the one approximately fifteen feet beyond. "Before you argue, it's an order, not a request." Her voice carried and several of the men took small steps back. Eve knew if she gave an inch, they would take a mile. A judge gave her this authority and today was not their day.

Inside, she trembled like she did every time she dealt with Aaron. He brought back childhood memories, scars that had never truly healed. If he ever saw her fear, he would exploit it.

Aaron glared at her until he realized it wasn't working. He

then turned his expression on her team. They ignored his hostile display too. Eve knew he was killing time to think of ways to disrupt her job. Aaron's hands were legally tied but he had no problem interfering every chance he could. Aaron, as the county attorney, was the highest law in this major fundamentalist area. He had one nemesis who was court ordered and that nemesis's name was Eve Bennet.

Eve was thirty-five years old. Her olive skin tone came from her father's Italian side and made her different from other men and women who grew up in the polygamist community. Single, she lived with her cat, Daisy, in a one-bedroom apartment completely unlike the large homes of those forced into plural marriages that were all she had known as a child. Seldom-cut long brown hair kept perpetually in a tight bun at the nape of her neck gave her the appearance of a librarian. She knew if she ever needed reading glasses, the look would be complete. With a narrow facial bone structure, Eve looked thinner than she was, though she carried no extra weight and worked out to stay in shape. After attending the police academy, she spent six years on patrol before making detective. Working long hours without complaint and treating even the smallest case with exceptional care took her from property crimes to homicide. It all paid off when she landed her current position. The coveted spot opened because of an overhaul in the way the state government dealt with the fundamental polygamist church.

She turned away from the county attorney, done with this standoff. There would be more conflict in the days to come. With an entire family murdered, Eve and her team would have an extended stay in the community.

Cold air whipped dust and scattered leaves across the yard in front of the house, making a crinkling sound, which conveyed the change in season. Eve shivered then motioned to her team. She unconsciously glanced over her shoulder at Aaron, keeping her revulsion deeply buried.

He couldn't help having the final word.

"Whatever you say, little sister."

THREE

When Eve set foot on a homicide scene, her first thought was always for the ghosts who lingered there, holding on to their secrets for a short while longer. As she paid her respects to the soulless bodies and quietly took in her surroundings, she and her team would begin to make a plan, laying the foundations for the real work to begin.

The brick home in front of Eve, yellowed by time with high, stark outer walls, held mysteries ready to unfold. Her unit was entering a family's inner sanctum and would dismantle their lives in public records for all to see. The yard within the block fence was mostly sand and dust, with no bicycles or toys littering the area. The prophet declared no toys for children and his congregation followed his word to the letter.

Eve shivered again beneath her coat, dreading what lay inside. She'd seen death countless times but the murder of an entire family needed mental preparation.

Aaron and his minions drove away from the scene before Eve and her unit entered the home. Her specialized team consisted of highly trained forensic detectives whose job it was to weed through church corruption and lies to solve aggravated felonies such as homicide. With or without help from the surrounding community, they would discover why a family was brutally murdered.

Tightening her jacket more securely against the dipping temperature, Eve gloved and masked with her team. They spoke in hushed tones because they were accustomed to overeager ears of the community picking up every word they said.

"Your stepbrother was in fine form," her second in command muttered.

Clyde had more overall homicide experience than anyone on the team and he was also their muscle on the rare occasions they needed it. He was not just her right hand; he was her confidant. He knew more about the feud between Eve and her stepbrother, Aaron, than the others. He didn't know it all, though, and she wondered if she could ever open up completely. She guarded her private life, past and present. It said a lot for Clyde that she trusted him implicitly. It was not a trust she gave easily.

Their relationship was complicated. It had changed from friendship to something more during the previous year. Somehow it worked even though she wasn't sure if the team was aware.

As an early mentor, Clyde was one of the reasons Eve became the solid investigator she was today. They had worked a difficult case together and both had walked away with deep respect for the other. Clyde's skin color had made it difficult for him in the white-man state of Utah. Whereas most of the US had a Black population, around twenty percent, Clyde chose Utah and its one-point-six percent to settle down and establish his career in law enforcement. The fact he wasn't Mormon, the dominant religion in the state, didn't endear him either.

"He knows this case will blow back on the church. It's the last thing they need right now," Eve said with candor.

"You think one of the wives went off the deep end and murdered them?" Collin interjected.

Eve gave Collin her famous icy glare and he raised his hand.

"I know. No conjecture before we examine the scene."

"Then why do you say stupid things?" Ray shot back, and smacked Collin on the shoulder like a two-year-old.

Collin and Ray were the team's comic relief. They bickered constantly but would basically take on anyone who looked sideways at the other. They were police-academy buddies who remained friends and applied for the squad together. Exact opposites, Collin Smith, a Mormon, with classic blond good looks, a sweet wife, and four children, had a way of thinking outside the box that often solved crimes.

Ray Gonzales, a dyed-in-the-wool Catholic, attractive, single, and living the good life though his traditional Hispanic mother wanted him married, was able to unwind Collin's theories and turn them into organized patterns.

The pair made a great investigative team and both had forensic specialties.

"Guys," Bina reprimanded in an indulgent voice that could turn abrupt in nothing flat. "For once could you act professional?"

Investigator Bina Blau, short black hair with high prominent cheekbones courtesy of her Indigenous ancestors on her mother's side, was five feet nine inches tall, had long legs, and could make anything she wore look good. Black cargo pants and white shirts were her usual attire. When Bina needed to dress up, she added a turquoise bolo tie that accented her long ancestral throat and oozed class. Even her police boots could look dressy in a pinch.

Bina was the team's Energizer Bunny and came with her own set of specialized training. Like Eve, she could nix Collin or Ray's antics with a look. She indulged them like brothers but hers was a work, work, work mentality. As the team's technical guru, she handled everything from computers to surveillance equipment. If you wanted Bina working around the clock for days on end, you kept her supplied in black tar coffee and gummy bears.

Eve glanced at the overcast sky with little sun coming through the darkened rain clouds, then turned to her squad. Their gloved hands and masked mouths and noses were a sight she was accustomed to.

"We ready?" she asked, and handed out foot covers.

They knew a family was inside and that could mean one or more children. Eve hadn't given them the tally her brother imparted to her. She knew this would be hard. Thankfully, she also knew they could handle it.

They walked to the front door and Collin turned the knob. There was no squeak of hinges as it swung inward. Keeping the door well oiled would have been one of many tasks assigned to the women and girls to keep their hands from being idle. Collin entered first with his video camera. Eve, as their forensic photographer, entered next. She would take photos of the home exactly as they found it while the team stayed out of the way. Clyde, Bina, and Ray placed their hands in their pockets and followed. They wouldn't be touching anything or disturbing the scene in any way.

They entered a mudroom, complete with bench to change boots and shoes. Under the bench, multiple pairs of rubber boots rested as Eve's camera clicked. When it rained in the area, the dry ground swiftly collected water and turned it to thick, muddy soup. Thus, the boots.

Collin pointed the video camera slowly in all directions. They each had a job to do and the team's male–female diversity guaranteed they had different perspectives on each step of an investigation. Their individual gifts uniquely qualified them as vital members of Eve's team.

She looked back before leaving the mudroom and noticed

Bina eyeing what could possibly be a spot of blood about six inches from the bottom of the front door. Eve zoomed in on the stain and clicked while refusing to dwell on what lay ahead. They would encounter the bodies soon enough.

Next, they stepped into a living area, cast in partial darkness by thick drapes covering the room's large windows. The space was tidy and did not appear lived in. This was normal within fundamentalist Mormon homes.

If any would not work, neither should he eat.

The doctrine hung on a plaque by the front door of Eve's childhood home. Idleness was not something she understood as a child and she implicitly knew the amount of back-breaking work that went into keeping a house clean with large numbers of people living in it.

"Eve," Clyde whispered.

He did it on purpose because he knew the similarities between fundamentalist homes spurred thoughts she would rather forget. She and Clyde always seemed to be in tune this way. Eve clamped down on her memories and snapped additional photos. The camera offered a view one step removed from the waiting horror.

"I've got it," she assured him softly so their communication wasn't caught on Collin's sound-recording.

Her camera continued its click, click, click as they walked into a large gathering area usually referred to by outsiders as a living room. This was where the man of the house would summon his family for their twice-daily prayer sessions. Two large black couches made an L shape. Each could sit at least five women who would listen to their husband while holding the smaller children in their laps.

Eve's polygamist family had four couches that held twice that number. It was their respite for sore knees.

Her childhood home, like this one, had no carpets, only bare wooden floors that were swept and mopped daily. She remembered singing hymns to God along with the church lessons. Looking around now, she saw little in the way of ornamentation on the walls. Aaron had told her how many victims were inside and that number said this husband held little power or was young by church standards. Older men were awarded more wives as long as they gave their wealth to the prophet and obeyed the other strict laws set before them.

Gentiles, and non-fundamentalist Mormons, never got this far into the inner sanctum and would be chased away from even entering the outside courtyard. Secrecy, like the bare walls, was key to the polygamist lifestyle.

A large table with ten chairs separated the main room from the women's center of the home, also known as the kitchen. It was large with white cabinets and bare countertops. Unlike the bare walls of the living areas, these were filled with hanging cooking utensils: measuring cups, ladles, items that would not fit in the cupboards or drawers. Above the oversized, six-burner stove were pots and pans in various sizes. Gingham blue-and-white homemade hand towels matched the thin curtains hung over heavy vinyl roller blinds designed to keep out inquisitive eyes. The shadowed inside area held a history of secrets and those secrets were not for non-believers such as Eve and her team.

There was a half bathroom off the kitchen. Approximately five-by-five feet, a toilet, sink, and towel rack with a single white towel hanging from it. No rug or fluffy toilet cover. One at a time they entered then backed out. A large pantry with minimal food also stood off the kitchen. Unlike Mormon food storage where separate households retained enough food for two years, the fundamentalist church kept the coffers in a warehouse for the community and divvied it to the members when they thought it warranted. Eve remembered hunger during her childhood and quashed the thought quickly.

Bina's, Ray's, and Clyde's hands remained in their pockets as they climbed the stairs to the second floor.

They wore soft blue shoe coverings that only slightly diminished the light clunk sounds they made as they went up the wooden steps. A single, one-by-one-foot uncovered window on the landing wall slashed the steps with light that merged with the shadows. The stairwell walls were completely bare, the white paint without a smudge.

She rounded the second set of stairs and the faint smell of death entered her nostrils for the first time. By her calculations, it had been six hours since the bodies were discovered and they didn't know the exact time of death. The cool weather helped keep the odor at bay but not for much longer. The bodies were breaking down and the sooner they could be processed and removed, the better for everyone.

Family members would be clamoring for their loved ones soon. It was hard to explain to civilians why it was important to keep a body's integrity but Eve would try. She also knew they couldn't legally rush her. Each crime scene she investigated within the polygamist community had the same modus operandi. The church, represented by her stepbrother for the most part, would fight her at every turn. The community leaders also wanted them out of the area as soon as possible.

Over a year ago, after a judge ordered oversight of all law enforcement in the polygamist community giving equal justice to all who lived here, not just men, she had had her first confrontation with her stepbrother. He had a dead body removed before calling her. She made it clear nothing would be taken from her crime scene, even a body, and managed to make the statement before the oversight judge. Aaron, who knew better, couldn't argue.

"Master bedroom first," Eve said, directing her team.

She wanted to see the father's body before the others. It always made sense for the killer to take out the biggest threat first and he would be the natural choice. For now she couldn't say this for certain, but investigators based their assumptions on prior experience, and they were usually right. She knew her team's brains were in overdrive looking at details and lining up the puzzle pieces. This walk-through was like putting together the edges of the jigsaw, with the rest of the picture still to be clicked into place.

They passed six doorways, three on either side of the hall, one a bathroom and one a small linen closet. They walked around small dark drops on the wooden floor and barely glanced into the open rooms. Blood had dripped off someone or something, was her guess as she looked down. Eve took photos of the probable blood while the team waited for her at the end of the hallway at the master bedroom entrance. When she reached them, they entered just enough so they could all step inside.

It was hard to notice anything other than the two bodies but Eve made herself wait while she looked at the room. There was one queen-sized bed with a large chest of drawers against the closet wall opposite the foot of the bed. One wooden nightstand was on the man's side with a single lamp on top of it. She noticed a common pamphlet of fundamentalist scripture lying on the floor spattered by blood. She snapped the first picture in the room and allowed her training to take over as she put the bodies in the background of her mind and captured more images.

During her childhood, she couldn't sleep with her mom when it was her mother's time alone with Father. Young Eve didn't understand the reason, she just knew it was hard when she felt little love from the siblings she shared a room with. Seeing this wife in bed with her husband reminded her of those isolated nights. Her deep inhale to evade the memory only enforced the smell and taste of death. She silently counted to five. After she gained control of her emotions, she lowered the camera.

The room was as pristine and orderly as downstairs, if you didn't count the blood or bodies.

Eve lifted the camera and the shutter clicked, the noise calming her. Through the lens, deaths were not as vivid, though the pictures would hold each detail. No matter the images she recorded, they were never as gruesome as the actual murder scene.

"Jesus," Ray exclaimed, which made Eve jump.

Collin shot him a dirty look. They needed to remain silent because of the video camera. The exclamation could even come up in court. Ray wasn't chagrined and offered Collin his middle finger after the video camera changed direction. Collin gave him an elbow in the ribs for his trouble. Their tussle was a way for them to process the brutality in their minds. Most didn't understand but when you saw things like this, you had to find a way to relieve the horror.

Clyde, in pure investigative mode, ignored them and stepped to the opposite side of the bed where the woman was laying with her head on a bloodied pillow. It had once been white. He glanced away and took a slow, even breath, trying to distill the taste of death. His tough exterior was a well-honed mask. Women and children brought out his protective instincts and he was a papa bear when they were harmed. Clyde's commitment to justice would help find those responsible for what happened to this family.

Eve adjusted her lens to zoom in on the man. He appeared to be in his late fifties or early sixties. She then walked to the other side, making sure she didn't step in blood. Clyde nudged her shoulder when she was close and pointed between the bodies. The woman's hand lay beneath the man's. It was highly unlikely they purposely joined hands in death. Eve nodded so

Clyde knew she saw what he did. She captured the image with her camera and continued clicking more photos of the bodies from the new angle.

Steady breathing. Inhale, exhale, don't think of their deaths, only the scene that held the answers to discovering who did this. She cleared her mind, lowered her camera, and looked at the room again without her shield.

Eve always thought in multiple perpetrators until the investigation determined otherwise. The area surrounding the bed was a bloodbath. The covers on top of the man and woman, the same. Her gaze kept returning to the joined hands. The killer made it personal and from her experience that usually meant a single suspect. Maybe someone else had killed the others that they had yet to see. After she forced herself to study the room and the bodies, she pulled the camera back to her eye.

She caught the woman's death in separate frames as she slowly moved around the bed again. She had died exactly as her husband did, the slice to her throat almost identical. Collin stepped closer with the video camera as Eve zeroed in on the wounds.

Blood marked the walls at the head of the bed and because it dripped to the carpet, they couldn't get closer to the bodies and had to stand a foot back on both sides. They would all mentally process this grotesque, surreal scene for many days if not weeks.

A closet door stood open and they looked briefly inside. Suits were on one side, work clothes on the other. Five pairs of shoes in total. The women didn't use this space. After Eve took pictures, she backed out so the others could look inside.

The man and woman in bed together suggested possible marital relations. Had the church removed other wives due to this perceived sin?

Since the fall of the prophet, the rules he dictated from prison had become stricter. Sex between husbands and wives was forbidden. Only a select few chosen men could copulate and father children so pure bloodlines remained intact. These men were known as seed bearers. Just thinking of that term sent a chill through Eve. The evil that permeated this community was the history that she unsuccessfully tried to escape.

She mapped the killer's probable moves in her head and knew her team were doing the same. Ray was mentally unwinding each scene. Collin was imagining strange theories that the others would never come up with. When things didn't add up in Collin's constructs, Ray cleared away the dubious details and got to the truth. Ray had the left brain and Collin the right. That was why the pair were invaluable in helping solve the crimes they handled.

Eve let the camera drop, causing a small pull at the back of her neck from the strap, and took another unimpeded look at the bodies. She blanked her mind and used her methodical investigative brain to examine the scene again. Taking the man out first would be how she would do it. The fact neither the man nor woman appeared to fight the attacker seemed strange but at the beginning of a homicide investigation, most things did. She started putting together a mental list of what they would need in the next twenty-four hours.

Eve had full access to everything the state had to offer. If they needed aerial photography, she had the authority to pull the strings to get it. Her team's uniqueness was partially due to their forensic backgrounds. Hers was photography; Ray's analytics, DNA and fingerprints; and Collin's his artistic ability to draw a scene from memory and include the most minute details. He often mapped out floor plans with a ruler and his grid paper after one walk-through so they could divide work. Clyde held extensive knowledge that included years in SWAT. He trained them in advanced techniques to clear buildings and handle dangerous situations. Detectives were not known for their overall officer safety but Clyde made sure they stayed safe.

Eve also had a fearless secretary. Tamm Mackity was not afraid to make demands on behalf of the team. She was on standby at their office waiting to crack her whip.

Once they completed their observation of the master bedroom, they moved into the hallway, again avoiding the small drops of blood. Eve pointed to the first door on the right. Collin entered, then Eve. It had three twin beds set in a U shape filling all but a six-foot square portion in the center of the room. Each bed had a medium blue comforter, the perfect match to the one in the master bedroom, though smaller. A single white pillow rested at the head of each. The room appeared undisturbed by the killer until Eve walked to the closet. There were two small, dark red stains on the doorframe, the outer edges black where they were completely dry. Both were slightly larger than a nickel. They may have started as fingerprints but they were now smeared. Her camera clicked, capturing the prints for close-up examination later.

Eve carefully pushed back the door to peer inside. A young girl's dresses hung from the rod. Eve counted five. A lower shelf area held religious undergarments, known as holy garments. The clothing was worn next to the skin and defined modesty. It had to always be covered by outerwear when not in bed. A single pair of black dress shoes rested on the shelf along with a plastic bin that held dirty clothes that appeared to consist of one dress and undergarment. They would go through the bin when they collected evidence.

Eve looked at the beds again. This room was used by only one, female child and the girl wasn't in here.

The size of the dresses in the closet did not indicate if she was old enough to be the daughter of the man in the other room. DNA would show the truth. The other option was the father may have had wives and children reassigned to other homes. If a man found disfavor in the prophet's eyes, his wives and children, basically his property, were removed and given to other men. Once this happened, the women and children were told to forget the man who had once ruled them and accept their new husband or father as God's reward.

Three bedrooms to go. Eve's heart clenched again before they entered the room across the hall. She knew there were two more bodies and now she knew one was a young girl.

FOUR

Three beds similar to the previous room were next. None had bedding and the closet was empty.

The dead father, a middle-aged man, was not on good standing within the polygamist organization. Eve knew this because of his lack of wives and children. He only had a midsized home like those that could be found in any residential neighborhood throughout the state. One child did not get you into the highest of the three kingdoms awaiting good fundamentalist families after death. The celestial kingdom was what they all strived to attain. The terrestrial and telestial kingdoms were another two of the three degrees of glory awaiting those who didn't *perfectly* align with God's decrees. The rules could be mind-boggling to outsiders but they had been brainwashed into Eve from a young age. Thankfully she had eventually left the teachings behind after her removal, if not the memories.

Eve and her team moved on to the next room.

The woman's body was in the double bed to the far left, her head tilted downward so her throat didn't gape as the couple's did in the master bedroom. Her chin rested on her fist, propped up by an arm on the pillow. The dark blood looked like a bib with its circled outline on her off-white undergarments. Her long, braided hair lay in two plaits uniformly on her chest, covered in thick blood that was still more red than dark brown.

This room differed from the last by its larger size and the three double beds. Chances are that the woman in bed with the husband in the master bedroom ordinarily shared this room with the dead woman here.

Clyde's fist pounded his other hand in lieu of an expletive. The bodies were stacking up and they hadn't discovered the one that would be hardest on the team. Moving as close as she could, Eve snapped the grisly images for the prosecution. The blood was mostly centralized beneath the body with a six-inch dark red area directly below the bed, on the carpet.

Clyde's shoulder brushed hers once she let the camera drop and they simply stared at the horror of what one human could do to another.

No, the church would not have the outcome they wanted because this case would make national news. Privacy was one of the things most highly valued in the polygamist community. Four grisly deaths in one home would eliminate the possibility of keeping this under wraps.

Eve met Ray's eyes across the room and he, too, did his best to contain his fury. It was the tight set to his jaw that gave him away. One man, two women, and one last horror waited that none of them could prepare for.

The women's closet was larger than the previous one with multiple dresses inside and undergarments folded neatly on shelves. There were two sets of black dress shoes and two sets of mid-calf black boots. The clothing was evenly divided and separated.

The team moved on. Eve tried to prepare herself for what came next.

They stepped out and entered the last room. Same three-bed configuration as the girl's room. That wasn't what they noticed though. The body of a teen male lay on the floor, his head facing the door. Eve's mind jumped to the young girl's dresses in the closet but she reined herself back in so this scene was all she looked at through her lens. She gave her team a quick glance from the corner of her eye and knew they would also wait. They had to analyze this child's death and figure out the discrepancy later.

She turned her camera back to his body. From his size, he had been maybe fourteen or fifteen years old.

He had fought for his life.

Unlike the girl's room and the empty one, his had a small nightstand beside his bed. Several items had been knocked off: A box of tissues, a Book of Mormon, and a highlighter pen. Boys were taught to read so they could control their wives and children with doctrine. Girls had no need for books; they were regulated by men from the moment of birth. Blood saturated the sheets and blue comforter along with spatter, feet from where he lay. Eve caught it all in the lens and slowly prepared herself to grasp the horror of the scene without interference. This time, she kept hold of the camera once she had her shots and simply lowered it slightly. The heavy cold feel grounded her.

His attack started on the bed and moved to the floor where he died, the blood beneath him so deeply red it was almost black. One arm stretched above his head and the other clawed into the carpet where he may have tried to drag himself toward the door. He didn't get far. In his final moments, his head dropped down face first. The garish laceration to his throat was only visible at the edges high on the back of his neck. The amount of blood spray on the carpet, bed, and walls showed how horrific his short battle was.

Eve left the bedroom and quickly walked back into the other rooms for another inspection. Clyde waited in the hall.

"Video camera off," Collin told everyone.

Eve looked at Clyde and they both said the words at the same time.

"Where is the other child?"

FIVE

Eve's childhood nightmare began after her father broke a restraining order and almost ended her mother's life. A young man discovered Maggie at her weakest moment, crying on the courthouse steps, and knew exactly how to help the terrified woman with a young child when no one else could. He'd been trained from the time he could speak that his solemn responsibility was bringing new women into the cult. His words checked each box Maggie needed to hear and she latched onto the promises of safety and community where her ex-husband could never harm them again. With these vows secured in her mind, she carried Eve through the fundamental polygamist doors and straight into the arms of monsters.

With new hope for their future, Maggie became the fifth wife of one of the chosen and Eve became a bride-in-waiting. At four years old, she had more worth than the young man who had accosted her mother on the steps of the courthouse. Shortly after they arrived at the polygamist compound, the man was mysteriously expelled from the church for some small offense. Within a few years, Maggie and Eve understood perfectly. His life had no value to the fundamentalist church where there were not enough women to supply older men with multiple wives. The older teen boys of the community created a problem. An expendable one.

This didn't mean life was easy for women of the church. Endless work and fear of being expelled from their home controlled every move they made, even the young girls. Maggie also had to put up with unexpected jealousy from the other wives. They made her life hell and it wasn't the picture painted by the man who had lulled her into the extreme religious sect. Her new husband adopted Eve within a few weeks of their marriage. She didn't even go to court. Maggie told Eve she had a new father and that was that.

The forced strenuous labor and constant adherence to the whims of the prophet brought Maggie to an eventual understanding that she'd made a mistake. Her new life became cemented in a different fear. She could possibly get away but Eve, as a future bride, could not. Though Maggie tried to obey, she was disciplined repeatedly until finally she was removed from their home.

Eve had a difficult adjustment period without her birth mother. She had never been treated well within the family. When she cried over Maggie's disappearance, they told her to keep sweet and stay in step with God or she would be taken away too. Maggie was a vile sinner. Eve, now eight years old, was referred to as a young woman. She must prepare herself for the future by bringing honor to the family through marriage. Eve's thorough indoctrination continued without Maggie's interference. If she had any hope of becoming the wife of a future God in the celestial kingdom, she had to forget about her mother.

As Eve grew older, restrictions in dress, food, and thoughts made it difficult to adhere to the endless doctrine of the prophet and his son who was the heir to the polygamy throne. Sometimes, Eve doubted her teachings and it left her with a deep-seated fear for her worth in God's eyes. The prophet's direct ear to the Lord dictated the rules that must be obeyed. Filled with the guilt of sin at any small infraction, she felt damned for eternity where she would not be allowed to join her family in heaven. She stopped wanting her mother after they were separated for a year. Eve became ashamed of Maggie for causing problems for her father who did everything he could to secure their place among the chosen. Her father was denied new wives for two years after Maggie was removed. Her mother's sins harmed the entire family and Eve was reminded of it constantly.

The only true break in Eve's church-controlled thinking came at age ten. Her father's second wife gave birth to a baby boy with severe birth defects. His head was large for his body, his muscles weak. A prominent forehead and wide-set eyes made him stand out from the other babies. It scared Eve at first but then his care was given into her young hands and she fell in love. Little Charlie became her world. His blond curls were the sweetest and his blue eyes held trust and adoration. The other wives and children didn't interact with them and Eve knew they didn't understand the sweet love Charlie carried inside his heart. When he smiled, the long nights he screamed didn't seem so bad. For the first time, Eve truly felt loved.

At six months old, Charlie, unable to do more than a newborn, became seriously ill. Aunt Bertha, the midwife, came to check on him when he didn't improve. She'd been present for the birth of the babies, including Charlie's, and Eve didn't like her. These were wicked thoughts but the woman looked at Eve with mean, judgmental eyes.

When Aunt Bertha spoke to her mothers in a low whisper about Charlie, Eve overheard. They talked about *bleeding the beast*, which scared her. She'd heard the phrase before but had no idea what it meant. It would be years before she understood bleeding the beast was taking government aid for children like

Charlie. The money went to the church and did little to help the child.

When Eve became frightened and confused by the grown-up talk, and could not be calmed down, she was locked in her room. She cried for hours. Sweet, beautiful Charlie was gone when they let her out. When she screamed, everyone was angry about her emotional outburst and one of the mothers slapped her. Eve never mentioned Charlie in front of them again. She also never forgot.

A year later, a baby girl, Becky, was born with severe facial deformities that kept her from eating properly. Eve adamantly refused to have anything to do with her because she knew what would happen. Aunt Bertha returned three days later and took Becky away too. Eve didn't cry.

By this time, her young life was full of hard work and complying with whatever it took to be pulled into the celestial kingdom by her future husband. She didn't go to school because the prophet proclaimed girls required no outside education and must only live to serve their future husbands. She needed to study her role and understand her duty as a good wife.

One of her moms sat her down and told her she would be married soon. At age eleven, the women she trusted prepared her for her life of continued submission. Eve knew she could be called to join with a man at any time and she had to be ready. It was even mentioned that the prophet could show her blessings by choosing her as his own. She wasn't sure what turned her into a woman in his eyes but she was assured she would know when it happened. Her only role was to keep sweet for God and to never disobey or question her father or future husband. To keep sweet was to swallow pride, swallow emotions, and suffer silently. Eve worked hard to do her duty and prayed God would find her a young husband. One of her sisters married a very old man with gray, wrinkled skin who walked unsteadily even with a cane. He looked like he was at death's door and Eve didn't want that. She knew her sister would kiss her husband. Each night her own mothers lined up in front of father's door for their nightly kiss. The prophet was also an old man who wore a mask on his face for oxygen and the thought of marrying him scared her too.

Sinful thinking filled her thoughts and she fought against the yearnings for a younger man, knowing she would be removed from her family if they discovered her hopes and dreams. By this time, she had all but forgotten her birth mother.

Their family had continued to grow. Food preparation took hours each day and the clean-up even longer. Washing laundry, cleaning the house, and tending the large garden, which included canning and food storage, was all Eve knew. She didn't remember a time her back or legs didn't hurt from scrubbing floors or being on her feet for hours. She didn't recall toys or other items that would attract children to sinful behavior. Toys went against the prophet's teachings and children should pray not play.

Eve was considered the lowest rung in the household. She was not related to anyone by purity of blood. Lineage was important to the prophet and even the children knew Eve didn't make the grade. Yes, they told her she could be among the chosen, but she knew she would never measure up to the standards taught to her and that her bloodline was unholy.

The one good memory she had was ice cream day each month. Eve's father allowed them to walk into town if they had worked hard and been obedient. She looked forward to the trip with ungodly yearning. Twice, she was left behind after run-ins with one of her brothers. Crying silently while she scrubbed the pots and pans to a high silver shine while everyone else enjoyed time off had an impact. Eve swore she would try to obey every rule no matter how difficult. She wanted the ice cream. That delicious scoop of vanilla made keeping sweet easier. She also hoped her future husband would allow this treat.

On a moderately warm day a few weeks after Eve's twelfth birthday, they left for the ice cream shop. By now Eve had eight moms and twenty-two siblings. The older girls were married and the older boys worked for the church and no longer attended ice cream day with them. Along with several of her young sisters, Eve helped carry the children too small to walk. They also surrounded the youngest in case they ran into people from outside the community, especially journalists. Speaking to non-members was forbidden. Their full, modest dresses created a curtain of safety wherever they went and they used them to keep the youngest away from camera lenses.

In the distance, Eve noticed dust spewing and a large vehicle heading in their direction on the long dirt road that led to their home. They lived in a secluded area with unused empty lots surrounding their house. Little grew in the high desert if it wasn't watered and there were only small shrubs and scraggly trees for cover.

Her family moved farther off the road and surrounded the younger children as taught. Though nervous at the vehicle's presence, Eve wasn't really scared. When the SUV, similar to her father's, stopped and four men jumped out, she didn't have time to comprehend what was happening. A hard grasp on her arm, the baby she carried torn away, and a firm push between her shoulder blades upended Eve into the back seat while her mothers and siblings screamed. Things happened so fast; she hardly made a sound. Arms from the third-row seat came over her shoulders and a voice she hadn't heard in years told her she was safe.

Her birth mother had claimed her.

SIX

Eve took her gloves off beside the front door without stepping outside. The wind made the house rattle and she preferred the warmth while berating her brother over her cell phone. She placed the call on speaker so her team, standing behind her, could hear both sides of the confrontation. After a deep breath, she made the connection. He picked up on the second ring.

"We have a missing child, you asshole. You can't tell me you didn't know."

"It was your crime scene and you had things under control," he replied snidely.

"You should have told me when you called this morning. A missing child is not information you keep from the lead investigator. Do we need to be looking for a body outside the yard?" she demanded, each word clipped while she fought to maintain her professionalism.

"The child isn't missing," Aaron said. "She stayed the night at her aunt's home and is blessedly safe."

Even though she remained angry, her chest untightened a fraction. One child had escaped the family's awful fate. She inhaled to rein in her emotions a step further before she spoke again.

"Is there anything else that you refused to impart that could possibly help solve these homicides?" she asked, her voice stiff.

"I have a written statement from Howard Wall, Bart Tanner's brother. Howard discovered the bodies when he arrived to pick Bart up for work. Bart is fifty-five years old. The woman in the bed beside him was his wife Marcella, age twenty-seven. She was Hannah's mother. Hannah, age ten, is the girl who wasn't home. Tracy, age twenty-two, Marcella's sister wife, was in the other room." A gruff sound entered his voice at the end of his sentence, even though his smugness stayed intact.

Though she considered her stepbrother a huge problem, he occasionally showed compassion. According to doctrine, children belonged to God and were not to be coveted by parents. Women were property and sold as such, holding only the value they could bring through marriage. From his intonation, Aaron was relieved Hannah had survived and he was sad the women had died. Eve had lived with her stepbrother for many years and had seen different sides to his personality. For example, he cared about his mother and protected her from punishment on several occasions. Polygamist families rarely kept secrets from those who ruled the community. Because of Aaron, his mother's worst transgressions weren't reported.

"The boy, age fifteen, was Elijah," Aaron said, breaking into her thoughts. "He worked with his father and uncle at the cement plant. Marcella was his biological mother."

Silence filled the line.

"Is that all you have?" Eve finally asked. "Or are we going to play the same game we always do where you make it as hard as possible for me to solve a case?" Her anger had faded to annoyance. She was able to think more clearly now that she knew there wasn't a missing child held by those who murdered a family so viciously.

"And do your best to get me fired, you forgot to add," Aaron muttered snidely.

"Yes, I forgot that small piece of info." They both knew he was an elected official and firing wasn't a possibility. A judge would need to find him guilty of a felony to get him out of office. "I'll try harder this time," she said anyway. "Where do you want to have a sit-down to go over the preliminary findings so I can read this statement you have? I would rather not do it outside in this weather."

Her stepbrother never took strides to accommodate her team. Because of this they brought a forensic van that held most of what they needed and slept in a local hotel. Tamm, Eve's secretary, had already lined up rooms for them. Eve knew she had a waiting email with the information along with a list of local eating establishments to make their stay easier. The town was growing rapidly with new restaurants and hotels. Tamm assured Eve she had booked them rooms in a hotel that had recently opened. The last time they had stayed in this town, they ran into continuous plumbing problems and nearly froze each time they showered.

"We can use my office," her stepbrother offered.

She accepted graciously though she was still angry over his non-disclosure of the young girl. Eve gave Aaron a heads-up on the next steps her team would be taking.

"My people will start processing the scene during our meeting. The longer it takes, the longer the pathologist's office will be held up because, as you know, I take my own photos and process the bodies myself. The medical examiner's vans for transport should arrive in a few hours."

Eve always tagged the dead, and once the techs bagged the deceased, she secured the closures with tape, and went personally to all homicide autopsies. This kept a clear chain of custody on the body evidence so her cases were never compromised. To do that, she had to make sure the evidence tape with her initials was intact when the pathologist first inspected the bodies. These small details won cases and no matter the problems her stepbrother caused, this case would go by the book.

"Anything else?" His tone conveyed he hoped there wasn't.

"I'll need local law enforcement available to hold the crime scene when we aren't here."

"How long will you need them?" he ground out.

"Shouldn't be more than two weeks." She didn't say seven days, which was the most likely case. If something came up, she didn't want to fight over the extra time.

"Two weeks?" he barked in his usual manner.

"I have four dead bodies inside a home compound. One is a child. If I want the house locked down for a month and need assistance from local law enforcement for that long, you will make sure it's done."

"Are you finished throwing your weight around?" Aaron snapped.

Eve took a breath and then another. Her stepbrother always knew the buttons to push. Though in his youth he had shown compassion for his mother, it didn't extend to Eve. He'd been the cause of her childhood missed ice cream days. He'd punched her in the arms and stomach, shoved her down continually when no one was watching, and kicked her where bruises didn't show. He then lied about her torn and dirty dresses to get her into trouble. As a female, it was Eve's job to stay sweet and not incite her siblings, especially the boys. Aaron's treatment was abusive and controlling. He bragged endlessly that someday he would be Eve's husband and she would suffer for every transgression she'd ever made. He'd terrified her back then and she would have accepted an older man if it meant staying out of Aaron's reach.

"You're in charge of the media," she told him. "You have a

circus coming your way after this makes national news. I know the church prides itself on secrecy but you and I both know lips are already flapping. I also want any household keys you're in possession of."

"How do I speak to the media when you don't tell me anything?" he demanded, his voice rising.

"Don't worry. I'll give you just enough to help you do the job." They didn't bother with goodbyes. Eve hit the end button and called Tamm.

"Have two medical examiner vans sent to my location: four dead. It could be hours before the bodies are processed but I want them on the way."

"Got it," she said. "How are you holding up?"

Tamm was the mother hen of their group. She was fifty years old and a bit of a hippy. Her long red hair streaked with gray frizz accented her heart-shaped face and large mouth. Her glare of green-eyed death was legendary and made you want to cross yourself even if you were not Catholic. She wore gauzy skirts down to her socks with Birkenstock sandals. She had an endless supply of long beaded necklaces that clacked together in a comforting chime when she walked. Tamm had explained her thoughts on life to Eve shortly after she started working for her: Live and let live and die if you want to. After Eve got past the shock, she shrugged her shoulders and accepted Tamm for who she was: a woman who danced to her own drum and one who breathed fire when she had a goal.

"I'm heading to my stepbrother's office to tackle the monster in his den. Does that answer your question?"

"Practice your breathing exercises on the way."

Tamm had a guru response for everything.

"Will do, gotta go," Eve said, and turned to her team after ending the call.

"I'll drive myself to Aaron's office," she said. "While I'm out, I'll check into our rooms. Start processing the scene and I'll get back as quickly as I can. Get my photo markers in place and I'll take the pictures before DNA and print collection." Photographing evidence was different than the photos she took in the initial walk-through. The first images gave a general feel of the entire scene and sometimes the photos showed a larger picture than the ones taken as evidence. She would be reviewing the initial images that evening at the hotel to see if they had overlooked anything.

Eve calculated a few things in her head before continuing. "Does anyone have something they want to say before I leave?"

"Check on the child," Clyde requested.

"I may not be able to physically see her today but I'll set it up with Aaron. She'll be at the top of our interview list and that will begin as soon as we have things processed. Anyone else?"

"Don't kill him," Collin said, deadpan. "We have enough on our hands without adding another homicide."

His comment, meant to be funny, jogged something in her head and she dug her cell phone back out of her pocket.

"What?" her stepbrother barked.

"Have you checked surrounding church members' homes? Could there be murdered families you are unaware of?"

SEVEN

After a short pause, Aaron hung up on her.

"That would be a resounding 'I don't have a clue,'" Bina said. "By the way, making him the media liaison was a stroke of genius."

They all smiled grimly, fully aware that the spirits of the dead listened in too and that now was not a time for laughter.

Eve allowed her own tight smile to convey her feelings. "It should keep him busy. Unfortunately, we need his connections and the media won't keep him out of our hair completely. I'll figure out a way to be nicer or at least try. The man punches my buttons with a steamroller."

"You used a curse word when you called him," Ray said.

"I did?" Law enforcement and cussing went hand in hand but she had never gotten past her upbringing and when she swore on purpose it sounded silly to her ears. This was also a running joke among the team. Collin and Eve, with their Mormon roots—though his were not fundamental—rarely swore. Ray, Clyde, and Bina made up for their lack and pointed out whenever Collin or Eve crossed the line.

"You called him an asshole," Bina reminded her. She'd

removed her gloves and popped a gummy bear in her mouth from a package she kept in her pocket.

"I did, didn't I? I'll say a bunch of Hail Marys tonight or something."

"That's Catholic," Ray said.

"I'm widening my options," Eve replied. "I think the Pope gave permission for Catholics to call assholes assholes. If that's true, I'll convert."

They all knew Eve was delaying the inevitable. She had to face her stepbrother in person once more today.

"They were drugged," she said.

Her team nodded. They had all come to the same conclusion. There was no other way the victims would have stayed still while their throats were slit. Something had knocked them out. "Tag anything that could be the source. I'll take the photos and process the bodies when I return. If there are images that can't wait, take care of it and I'll add your photo log to mine."

Eve took the SUV. The unit needed the van and its contents to do their job. The drive to her brother's office would have taken ten minutes but she wanted him to have time to make sure his community was safe so she drove toward the hotel first.

Thoughts of her mother always came up when Eve was in the polygamist community. They had a tentative relationship and she wasn't sure what she could do to change it. She loved her mother but she resented her choices that had caused so much hurt in Eve's life. She owed Maggie a phone call. How did she get over the damage her mother had caused? Maggie carried so much guilt and it left Eve conflicted. If her mother would talk about what happened to suck her into the cult and the years after she left, it might help. Maggie would rather hide away from life, live quietly, and stay away from confrontation. Eve shook off these thoughts. She would call her mom as soon as she had time.

The hotel wasn't what you would call luxurious but it was

the best in town. Since the polygamist prophet was found guilty of sex with children and imprisoned, new businesses had moved into the area, including a bar. This hotel was one of the improvements. Eve doubted they got business from more than a few truckers and nature lovers visiting the area but it was obviously enough to keep the doors open and this provided nicer accommodations for the team.

She always bunked with Bina. Ray and Collin shared and Clyde got his own room. When they were on a case, they lived in each other's back pockets. Their intense chat sessions discussing the homicides would take place in Eve and Bina's room, away from prying ears.

Much of the evidence would be stored at the closest police department. There were three towns in the county. If it was an unincorporated part of the area, the sheriff handled law enforcement. The police chiefs took care of everything within their town. The county attorney's office prosecuted all crime county wide. Eve knew the men in charge and disliked them all. They were fundamental polygamists and she considered them part of the problem. Having them store evidence couldn't be helped because Eve needed a chain of custody and leaving it in the van was not acceptable. The van had one locked compartment for lab evidence and that was it. Local law enforcement would help whether they wanted to or not. This case landed in city jurisdiction, not the county, so at least she didn't need to deal with the sheriff. He might be the worst of them all.

Eve checked them into their rooms and received five keycards. After dropping her and Bina's luggage off, she steered the SUV toward the county attorney's office for her next confrontation with Aaron. Every other block held a pole camera, which was monitored in the town's security center, controlled by the church. She'd had a warrant for camera footage on one of her past cases. They claimed their entire system malfunctioned and were unable to provide the videos. Everything she did here was an exhausting battle.

She passed blocks of homes much larger than the one where the bodies were found. The farther you lived from the prophet's compound, the lower your church standing. The Tanners were somewhere in the middle because the house held room for more wives and children. She guessed Mr. Tanner could've redeemed himself and one day added to his wife count.

Eve drove past the largest property, located in the center of the community. The prophet's followers maintained it for his return. The building that housed his wives took up two city blocks. He had a large separate home just for himself on the premises. With his seventy-plus marriages, he obviously needed alone time. No privacy existed in prison.

The county offices were located a mile from the compound. They looked dignified with their US and state flags. It was the light-blue-and-white Mormon flag proudly displayed that frustrated Eve. Fundamentalist church members believed their prophet was the true president of the United States and their flag, the one and only.

Again, Eve's thoughts turned to Maggie. She always wondered how her mother allowed them to fall under the fundamentalists' control. As an officer, Eve dealt with domestic violence. Even so, Eve could not reconcile her mother's decisions that cost them so much. After Maggie took her from the polygamist community, her biological father had not returned to their lives. Maggie rarely spoke of him and didn't give her daughter much opportunity to ask questions. Eve had buried so much of her past deep within her mind. She needed her mom to stand up and explain. It ate at her and she wanted that part of her life over and done.

She sat in the county attorney parking lot trying to clear her thoughts and focus on the next fight with Aaron.

She stepped through the smoked-glass doors and

approached the counter. A young woman stared pointedly as Eve drew closer. She must be new. Eve didn't think she could possibly be over twenty years old. The young woman wore a pastel-blue prairie dress with light brown hair swooped high and proud in the front above a plump face. She had a cleft lip that had not been surgically repaired. Cosmetic surgery was an abhorrence under God's rule. The number of children in this area with cleft palates here was far higher than the national average, probably as a result of inbreeding. This had been the reason little Becky was taken away when Eve was young. Her lips were unable to suckle.

Ignoring the woman's contempt, Eve got straight to the point. "I'm Detective Sergeant Eve Bennet, here to see the county attorney. He's expecting me." She'd used her full title to reinforce her lawful authority over this region. It didn't matter that the only law they adhered to was that of the prophet and his twisted teachings from God; Eve had a murdered family who deserved justice.

"He will be with you when he has time." The words were slightly slurred and Eve felt compassion. The young woman knew exactly who she was from the moment she'd entered the office. There was even a chance she was related to Aaron and by that route, to Eve as well. It was hard to forget the teachings she grew up with and she still thought of her stepbrother as a sibling even if there was no blood relation.

Aaron had planned to marry her and even a close family tie wouldn't have stopped him. With that disgusting thought, she really needed this meeting over quickly.

She took a seat and after another harsh glare, the woman turned away. Eve had planned to stare her down the entire time so took the back of her oversprayed, lifted hair as a win. The fact the receptionist worked outside the home showed one of several changes in the community. When Eve lived here, this was unheard of. She hoped the girl wasn't yet married but chances were good that she was. She could also have a child or two by now. Eve shuddered.

She sent a text to Aaron advising him she was waiting in his office since the receptionist had not so much as buzzed his phone. She waited for his reply while she thought about the rules that continued enabling this community.

Utah law stated you had to be sixteen with parental permission to marry. At age fifteen you needed a judge to agree. Judges in this county either practiced polygamy or were the recent descendants of polygamist marriages. They granted permission for the teen marriages and Eve could do nothing about it. Marital unions of girls as young as twelve were illegal but Eve suspected they were still practiced. She herself had been one step away from child rape and to this day, she knew she was one of the fortunate ones.

A ring sounded from the phone on the woman's desk. When the receptionist looked at Eve, she knew her brother was on the line. If he kept her waiting longer, she would leave. He could come to her and they would do the meeting in the cold.

"I'll walk you back," the woman said in her tight, lisping voice.

Eve followed her through a locked door, past offices that hadn't changed since her last visit. Some were occupied, some empty of attorneys. Each held a wooden desk and the back of a computer screen facing the door. Most had one family photo with the man surrounded by many wives and children turned so visitors could see it displayed. The number of wives and children proved their devotion to the prophet.

She entered her brother's personal domain. It was the largest room at the end of the hallway. The woman walked away and Eve didn't spare her another glance.

"Adding women to the justice roster—I'm impressed." Aaron's family photo was also displayed but she didn't look closely at it. His worship of a man who sat in prison for horrible offenses against children made her sick.

Aaron blinked a few times, his bloodless lips tight. "Denise is my newest wife. She has a medical problem and may be unable to bear children. When she's here, it keeps her mind off her failure."

Eve's eyes involuntarily went to his family photo before she could stop herself. His expression turned smug. He sat with his hands steepled in front of him. It was his judgment pose; one he'd trained himself to do since he was a young boy. She couldn't help the chills that ran over her arms.

Her stepbrother had told her that tidbit about his wife to anger her. She placed her hand out.

"The statement," was all she said.

Aaron lifted a manila folder from his desk and slapped it into her hand.

"That's your copy to take with you," he said pointedly.

He probably hoped Eve wouldn't read it in his office. Disappointment would soon be his best friend. She wiggled a bit in the chair to get comfortable. Her brother sighed.

While Aaron watched, Eve read the exceedingly brief statement.

I went to pick up my brother and his son but no one answered the door. I entered the house and found them dead. I called the police.

"You consider this a statement?" she asked, shocked despite herself: this was typical. "You told me more than this on the phone."

"It's what was given to me by Brother Wall. I simply added the personal conversation I had with him. I thought you wanted my help?"

Screaming was not an option.

"I'll interview him first thing tomorrow morning and get a complete statement. Set it up." She gave him a look that she hoped he wouldn't ignore. If things moved more slowly, she would need to call the oversight judge every five minutes. "I want a list of every Tanner family member including anyone removed from the home over the past five years. This includes grown children if any live outside the house. I want the names and addresses of every home in a mile radius. We'll be interviewing the husbands and wives." Eve noticed he didn't write what she said down. "Don't press me or you'll find yourself before Judge Remki, who is not one of your cronies." The original federal judge assigned Remki to handle the heavy work and that was who Eve dealt with. They got along passably well, though in Eve's opinion, he was not hard enough on the interference she always ran into.

Her stepbrother, movements stiff, took out an eight-by-ten legal pad and removed a pen from his desk. He scribbled a few things then looked back at her. Eve was sure this was a job a secretary normally did for other county attorneys but he didn't like others seeing their battles when she had the upper hand. Aaron would never call in his wife because he wouldn't take a chance that she would be corrupted by Eve's apostate ways.

"I need the local police to make their evidence room available," Eve said after a slight hesitation in order to level her tone and not turn this into more of a battle than it already was. "We'll need someone there when we check it in for chain of custody. I'll try to keep it within office hours but I can't make promises. An after-hours cell number too."

Aaron wrote it down as Eve glanced around the stark office. Not a single landscape to add ambiance to the plain white walls. His pride was in the number of women he enslaved and the money he earned for the church. His home and surrounding property belonged to the prophet. The prophet had absolute control over Aaron, as Aaron had over his wives. Eve, even with her upbringing, would never understand.

"I'll arrange for the autopsies to take place as quickly as possible," she continued. "I have Hannah at the top of my interview list followed by"—Eve looked down at the statement—"Howard Wall as the person who found the bodies."

Her stepbrother looked up from the notepad.

"Howard is Hannah's uncle. He says she is distraught and in no position to speak with anyone. Interviewing her may not be possible."

The girl was vital to the investigation. Eve was empathetic to Hannah's situation. They had a murderer on the loose and to keep more people from possibly dying, she had to interview her. It was not optional.

"Make it happen. If you honestly have no idea who killed this family, her testimony is key." Icy resolve was heavy in the words.

"If I knew, believe me, I wouldn't have called in your team so quickly." His hands opened and his pasty white fingers spread in appeal.

Something didn't sit right but she had no idea what that something was.

"You don't have a single suspect? I know you've spoken to the police chief. This family belonged to your church. Did they have enemies, jealousy, any reason four people are now dead?" she asked point-blank.

"Nothing." His smugness remained.

"Is there anything you think I should know or even don't think I should know but it would help with the case?"

"I've shared everything I have."

Eve looked at the folder in her hand with its single sheet of paper. She stood and walked to the door.

"Don't forget my reports from you and the officers who entered the scene. I also need to know if Bart Tanner was

Hannah's biological father. If not, I want the name of the man who provided his seed." She turned at the last minute to see Aaron's eyes nearly bug from his head. She had finally cracked his wall of arrogance. She knew what caused this anger. How dare she mention something so taboo to the outside world? When seed bearers impregnated wives, the husband held her hand and the sister wives helped hold her still while she was raped. Hannah's age and Tanner's lack of wives let Eve know he wasn't a highly valued member of the church. Bart had most likely fallen out of favor over some small transgression. That meant he was not a chosen seed bearer. Eve wanted those guarded details but knew she wouldn't get them. The names of the men allowed to have sex with other men's wives were one of the church's most closely guarded secrets.

Her brother's hard stare didn't let up.

Outsiders could not comprehend church doctrine when it came to the polygamist view on bloodline purity. Eve knew it was one of many harmful laws that kept the women under tight control. Pointing this out to him showed she understood his involvement in the ugly situation. He knew the sex was forced. The wives helped his cause because they did their duty and would never dream of reporting what happened as rape. By the size of Aaron's family and the young children, his wives remained silent to the assault or Aaron himself was a seed bearer and was just as evil as the others.

If, as Eve supposed, Mr. Tanner had once had more wives who had since been reassigned, there was a chance one of these former wives could have committed the murders. If her step-brother would pull his head from his butt, he would know it too. That outcome would be very bad for the church. Eve knew everything she requested would be held up for as long as Aaron could get away with it. This was the game he always played.

She hated that things were this petty between them but she

reminded herself he was brainwashed into everything she found repugnant. His beliefs were a battle she would never win.

"If wives were removed from the home, I want their personal information." It was her last demand before she walked away.

By the time she passed the new Mrs. Owens at the front desk with her sour face and walked outside, she was no longer thinking of Aaron. Her thoughts were on the bodies she would shortly be processing. Head slightly down, she walked toward her car, which was at the end of a narrow cement walkway with small, pebbled gravel on either side. No way would the fundamentalist organization pay to water unnecessary grass. She took a deep breath of clean crisp air before she noticed five men blocking her path about fifteen feet ahead.

They stood in their black dress pants and long pale blue shirtsleeves while wearing identical expressions of disgust. This was nothing new to Eve; the church made it known she was unwelcome. Yet she'd never had them step forward in open confrontation. They usually followed her team in huge black four-wheel-drive trucks.

On closer inspection, Eve recognized the two older men. She'd grown up with them. Each of the five carried the Owen family genes. Their blond hair, blue eyes, stocky build, and short height along with blunt facial features and pale skin were almost identical.

They didn't budge. She looked around the area realizing it was deserted in the middle of the day. Had this been arranged? They spread farther apart, blocking the path and much of the pebbled rock on either side.

Their glares of contempt did not bode well.

EIGHT

Eve had two choices. She could walk around them and hope they let her pass or she could go back inside the office. Her mind clicked to a third option.

"Mark, Patrick," she greeted. "I wasn't aware you were still in town."

Patrick turned to Mark, who was the oldest of the five standing in her way, though younger than Aaron. Mark did not acknowledge his brother's glance. Hatred flared as his eyes traveled up and down her body. He wanted her shame for being improperly covered and she would not buckle under his scrutiny.

Mark whispered something she couldn't hear.

This was their cue to react. As one, they turned their backs to her. Eve, the apostate, was too vile to look upon. Her stomach clenched. One of the three younger men was possibly who she was carrying the day her mother rescued her. Eve couldn't deny the hurt even though she was aware of their backward beliefs.

The staged scene had caught her off guard. She gave the men a wide berth and walked ten feet onto the gravel to get around them. She had always known what her siblings would think of her. They were taught that her wickedness was sent to destroy them. She was evil and even worse than a gentile, Eve had turned her back on God and chosen the devil.

Once she could step onto the walkway again, she did. The heat of their gaze remained on her back and she refused to turn around. She was a police officer and not a woman they could intimidate.

"Abomination," bellowed a deep loud voice, but she didn't know which one said it.

Eve let it go and continued to the SUV. Her family had disowned her many years before. It just hadn't been brought home until today.

She drove from the parking lot and managed to avoid squealing tires. After several deep breaths to gain control and a few blocks between her and her stepbrothers, she turned into a fast-food establishment that had a drive-through. She sent a quick text to Clyde to let him know she was bringing food. While waiting for the order, she pictured her stepbrothers' faces. Foolishly, she had never thought she'd see them again.

She had never known what happened to her siblings besides Aaron. When Eve first left, she'd mourned for them and hated her mother for taking her away. It took several years for Eve's polygamist mindset to change. Wasted teenage years that should have been good memories. She could call her mom right now but this was not a good time. It never was.

Her former life had just joined her present one and there were too many unanswered questions. For now, she would stop thinking about her mother and their pending conversation and concentrate on the murders. She gave herself a mental shake. This was something she had done since her promotion to head of the team. She was getting good at it.

With food for everyone, she headed back to the crime scene. She decided not to mention the interaction or lack thereof with her stepbrothers. The church always staged something for their benefit. They couldn't help themselves. This time, her former family was the weapon. Her stepbrothers were now her adversaries and there was nothing she could do about it.

Her thoughts turned to Elijah's body, and how he tried to escape death. The homicides had to be solved through solid investigative work so the family found justice and others weren't in danger.

By now, the team would be fully into processing the scene. Eve was running behind on her end but they excelled at their jobs and would do whatever was required until she returned.

Their lunch was eaten in the van. They reviewed the steps taken while she met with Aaron.

They were solemn and disturbed by what they'd found, as they always were when a child was involved, especially when there was a chance that others were still in danger.

When they had her up to speed, Eve gave them an overview of her discussion with the county attorney.

"Did he toss you out of his office?" Collin asked between bites.

"He was too busy hoping I'd ask questions about his new wife," she said, and immediately regretted it.

"A new wife?" Bina rolled her eyes. "Be careful." Her expression turned serious. "The way he looks at you gives me the creeps. It's not right."

"No, it isn't," Ray added with the same look Bina had.

"Aaron is a polygamist," Eve said to throw them off the truth. "He looks at all women that way."

"It goes beyond that," said Collin. "He doesn't look at Bina in that manner, nor has he stared at female techs when they've helped us."

Aaron's infatuation was not something Eve wanted to debate. She would not explain his harassment of her as a child. It was enough that her team knew of their mutual dislike. They had learned this on their first case when Eve and Aaron went toe-to-toe. They'd stood by her that day and every time she'd faced him down since. Of course they noticed how he looked at her, his fascination with her hair, his antipathy over her clothing. He did little to hide it.

Eve understood her team's comments though. They usually remained silent about her past. On the rare instances she instigated the conversation, their questions were always considerate even if she saw the incredulity in their eyes. By now they knew these discussions were hard for her and they respected her privacy.

"Aaron Owens is not our concern," said Clyde, ending the discussion.

Relief filled her; he always had her back. It wasn't just Eve and her team who admired Clyde. Clyde's reputation was solid among his peers, his expertise in homicide investigations respected.

When Eve put her team together, she had interviewed more than twenty candidates. She was in the powerful position to enforce equal justice to the entire fundamentalist community regardless of gender or religion and she knew her team would need a diverse background. Two out of three people in Utah were Mormon. Finding the right investigators to oversee felonies within the polygamist community and bring the guilty to prosecution would take an open-minded approach.

She hired Collin for his non-fundamentalist Mormon background. He would be able to deal with male church members who wouldn't cooperate with her. Even though he wasn't a worshiper of the polygamy sect's prophet, his Mormon roots gave him a bit of standing in their eyes. If he abided by the covenants of the Book of Mormon, the fundamentalists felt he would most likely attain one of the two lesser kingdoms of heaven.

Collin and Ray came as a team and she liked that they were friends. The fact Ray was Hispanic and Catholic didn't matter to Collin. She'd heard them arguing about the strange aspects of both their religions. Impartiality was key to her team's success and with the two of them, that was exactly what she got.

Bina's interview for the job was a bit touch and go, but there was something there and Eve couldn't get the young detective off her mind. She mentally chose someone else but, before making the offer, she contacted Bina again and asked her in for one last interview. Eve simply couldn't help herself.

"Tell me why you want the job?" she asked after they sat at Eve's desk.

"You want the truth or the interviewee response," Bina leveled.

"The truth, please."

"I'm tired of not getting recognition for my work. I put in longer hours than anyone in my current division. Others take credit when I solve a case and no one says a word in my defense. I deal with the same shit day after day and I want a change." She shrugged. "That may be the wrong way to put it. I want to work on a team that stands up for each other and where everyone works just as hard."

Eve liked the unfettered reply.

"Why do you think you could work for me?" Eve asked curiously. She knew what it was like to be female in the male-dominated world of law enforcement. Women had trouble getting a leg up. With few opportunities for promotion, competition was fierce among them and they rarely got along with each other.

"Because we're the same. We'll never fit in no matter how hard we try. You'll always be the polygamist girl and I'll always be the Indigenous girl."

Though their state populations were equivalent, there were far fewer Indigenous people than Black people working in Utah law enforcement.

"Your team is taking on the southern district and I want to be a part of it," Bina continued, planting her open palms on

Eve's desk. "I've heard you're an excellent detective and you will make a good leader."

The spark in her dark eyes told Eve everything she needed to know. She made her decision on the spot and never regretted it.

"Give notice to your supervisor. You start two weeks from today. Welcome to the team."

Bina did an air punch and they both smiled.

Eve had been chosen to lead the oversight taskforce because of her background within the fundamentalist church. Outside the higher command personnel, who had read Eve's application where she referred to her history, it wasn't widely known. That changed after her supervisor's supervisor announced her new title and a brief description of her fundamentalist background in an email to all personnel. Bina was the first person to openly address her polygamist past and Eve liked her even more for her candor.

Tamm was stolen from another department and her former supervisor was still not speaking to Eve after a year. Tamm might not fit the normal mold of law enforcement secretary in Utah but she was so good at her job no one cared.

That left Clyde.

Six years her senior, when he and Eve had worked their first case together early in her homicide detective days, Clyde took her by the hand and explained things many would not have taken the time to do.

After the case concluded, he showed up at her apartment one evening with a bottle of wine.

"I'm not interested," she told him, thinking he was coming on to her. It made her angry because she respected him and her cold glare should have frozen him solid on the spot.

He rolled his eyes. "Get over yourself. I came for information and I decided it might be easier if I got you drunk first. One divorce and the hell it caused in my life should be enough for any man."

After another moment's hesitation, Eve stepped back and let him in. "I don't drink," she said belligerently, not sure why she allowed him inside. This was her safe space.

"Not a problem," Clyde said, making himself at home on her couch. "Easier to drink straight from the bottle." He unscrewed said bottle and did just that. "I took a cab and will take one home. Find some snacks and let's get started."

Her small apartment, with its bare white walls and spartan furniture, gave nothing away—or maybe it gave everything away. She had one couch, a comfortable chair, a side table holding a lamp, and a television opposite the grouping of furniture. No wall unit, coffee table, stray magazines, or newspapers. She didn't own a kitchen table. She kept her home spotless but that wasn't hard with only her and a cat that wouldn't come out until the stranger left. Eve knew Clyde would think this odd but if he truly wanted answers, he could deal with it.

It was the best decision she could have made. Clyde didn't pry too deeply but his investigative skills worked on her even though she knew the tactics. By the time he left, he knew some of her secrets. When it came time to build her team, he was the first person she thought of, though she didn't make the call until she had the other members chosen.

"What the hell took you so long?" he grumbled when she finally made the offer. He accepted the position without hesitation.

To tackle fundamentalist doctrine and remove corruption from local law enforcement, Eve's investigators had to deal with current issues. They couldn't change the past or the continued beliefs of the polygamist community. Their job was to see the laws of the state and US followed to the letter. Those guilty, regardless of their standing in the church, had to be held accountable.

"Anyone have some fries they want to turn over?" Collin interjected into Eve's stray thoughts, and again she was thankful for the new subject.

"You can have mine," Bina offered. "My ass doesn't need to grow."

No one said a thing. Bina's ass never changed and she could eat double what everyone else did without gaining an ounce. They'd seen it.

"Does anyone have anything about the scene they want to impart or do you want to hold it for tonight's meeting?" Eve asked.

They agreed later was better.

"Any sign of a murder weapon?" She looked around their group.

"Nothing yet," Collin replied. "Ray did a cursory walk through the yard in case it was in plain sight but we haven't processed the outside perimeter more than that. There's also an attic inside the master bedroom closet I want everyone to see. I think it would be better if you photographed it tomorrow when we're fresh."

They were each building scenarios in their heads and they would all be slightly different. That's how their open-minded-ness worked. Eve counted on those differences. No matter how far out some of their suppositions would be, they shared them without fear of ridicule. Thinking outside the box solved cases. Not allowing mental blinders led to answers.

Until they concluded the case, they would hold a short meeting each morning to set up a game plan for the day and a longer meeting each night to review their findings. As soon as the scene was processed, they would begin interviews.

The polygamist community was three hours away from the nearest crime lab. Waiting on forensic specialists was out of the question. Her team's experience and advanced certifications eliminated that need and kept them on a quicker pace.

Eve and Clyde would attend the autopsies as soon as they were scheduled. The others would stay behind and continue processing the scene. Things would unfold each day and plans would change. That was the complex reality of all homicide investigations.

Eve squashed the empty bag that had held her food with a soft pop and took a last sip of soda. She wanted to get back to work.

"You need the county attorney to sign an affidavit for a cell phone record. The father had one in his bedside drawer," said Clyde.

"I'll add it to my list and give Aaron the request next time we speak," Eve replied. "Package the phone and put it in the van's locker. I don't want it in police custody." If the phone held private church information, it would be too easy for it to disappear. Eve would retain control of the device. "If anyone else has something Aaron needs to handle, speak up."

They smiled as Eve knew they would. Anytime they annoyed her stepbrother it was a win. In the back of Eve's mind, she was always looking for proof of Aaron's corruption in the hopes he would one day be removed as county attorney. In all probability it would never happen, but she couldn't let go of the thought he was involved in fundamentalist illegality up to his eyeballs.

Her phone buzzed and she checked the screen. It was a text from the medical examiner's office. They were twenty minutes out.

"We know they had to have been drugged. Food or liquid would be my guess," Ray said after Eve shared the news. "I've gone through the garbage and taken food samples. I'll lock them in the van." Tamm had arranged a lab tech to retrieve samples each day. It saved Eve's team time, and, with only five of them, they needed everyone working the scene. Those samples would prove their supposition about a sedative and they needed the results as soon as possible.

"I'll get Tamm to schedule the autopsies," Eve said, and made the call.

"Special Investigations Unit, Tamm speaking."

Eve didn't say hello. "We're ready to move forward. Four autopsies. Jump us in front of everyone you can. Three adults and one child with their throats cut. We need answers. If George is available, I want him."

"Anything else?"

"No."

Tamm hung up. Neither of them wasted words when they were in work mode. Eve lowered her phone and glanced at her team.

"I'm ready to process the bodies."

NINE

Eve grabbed her personal forensic bag from the van. Her team had positioned markers for photographs. They would collect and label all evidence samples after the photos were taken. Then, Eve would process the bodies alone.

Her team understood. Since their first polygamist case where a nineteen-year-old seventh wife was beaten to death by her elderly husband in front of his wives and children, Eve took the community deaths personally. When she'd processed the woman's body and saw the faded bruises and broken bones she'd lived with, Eve broke down in front of the team. The circumstances brought too many of Eve's childhood memories to the surface.

She felt conflicted with so many things. She believed adults had every right to follow whatever lifestyle they chose as long as it conformed to the law of the land. But were there really choices within the fundamentalist community? The children were indoctrinated from birth, given no glimpse of the outside world, and taught to fear it.

When Eve thought like this, her mother's mistakes, which placed Eve in the arms of the cult, angered her. Maggie was weak and maybe that was why their relationship had floundered. Forgiving her mother was something therapy encouraged. This was one of the reasons Eve had stopped going in her late teens after she had decided on becoming an officer. Eve did not believe she should suffer because of the sins of her mother, but she did. Forgiveness was something offered by the god you believed in and didn't need to come from victims or survivors.

Eve slowly inhaled to clear the past. She entered the home and located the first marker. This was what drove her. They would find who did this brutal crime and that person would pay under the rules of justice. No one expected the justice system to forgive, so why should she?

Clyde stayed by her side with the photo log. She would say the placard number aloud followed by a brief description of what she was photographing. Clyde wrote down the information and marked the time the photograph was taken. He would then place his initials in the appropriate box to show he logged the written photo evidence to match the image. Eve's name would appear at the top of each sheet as the photographer. They'd done this many times together, which gave them a familiarity that made the job smoother.

Eve didn't miss the warmth in Clyde's eyes when she called out the first number. Their deep friendship had turned into something more. She'd never felt this way about another man. From his sense of justice to his calm presence no matter the circumstances, he was a positive influence in her life. He never expected something she couldn't give. When the squad first came together, she hesitated at seeing him outside of work like they had done for years. She had suddenly been cast into the role of his supervisor. He didn't say a word or seem upset when she turned down his offers to dinner. As with their friendship, their new relationship happened slowly. Seeing each other at the gym turned into sharing conversations over coffee.

She was the one who touched his arm in an overly familiar

way and Clyde took the next step and held her hand. It hadn't progressed much further than that but they both knew what was happening.

Today he wore his usual black cargo pants and black long-sleeved department work shirt that had the state police logo and his title and last name embroidered on his chest. Yes, she noticed how he filled out the clothes he wore. She also knew how it made her feel when he looked at her like he was doing now.

Wanted. Appreciated. Cherished. Not just for the fact she was a woman but for her investigative skills, her leadership ability, and her tenacity. He wasn't threatened by her and she was beginning to see a future that included him on an intimate level.

She wanted to know more personal things about him. Was he naturally bald or did he shave his head? Most of all she liked him working by her side and it was time to stop thinking about him and get the difficult job in front of them started.

She held extra numbered placards in her pocket in case either of them saw something not yet identified as evidence that the team may have missed. They all knew to check over each other's shoulder; it was something Clyde had taught them.

In the master bedroom, her team had tagged two photographs, located in the same drawer with the phone. The first picture showed Bart Tanner standing with three women to either side of him, six total, and seven children standing in front. Eve identified Marcella, Tracy, and Elijah. She wasn't sure about Hannah. There were two girls who looked similar in age, maybe eight. Then she glanced at the next photograph.

This one showed Bart, Marcella, Tracy, Elijah, and a young girl who had to be the missing ten-year-old. Eve was now able to pick her out of the first photo easily. She and Elijah appeared about two years younger than they were now. Bart stood directly behind her, his hand resting on her shoulder. Hannah and her mothers had nearly identical front-swooped hair. The indoctrination began young. Hannah wore a closed-lip smile like the two women. She could tell nothing from Hannah's or the women's expressions. It bothered Eve that she hadn't made contact with the child. She was the only person left alive and she might know if one of her previous mothers could possibly have committed the murders.

Eve looked back at the first photograph. She needed the name of each woman who had lived in the home. It was vital but getting information about wives and children was always difficult.

It took them two hours to complete the photos. The only room Eve didn't capture in her camera's lens was the attic. She would look there tomorrow, as Collin had suggested.

After they finished the forensic photography, Clyde went to the van to speak with the team, giving Eve time to mentally prepare. She re-masked and gloved then placed her bag outside the parents' room and took a moment to collect herself. She'd wanted Elijah's to be the first body she processed because of his age, but since she was convinced Bart was the first one murdered, she would start with him.

DNA evidence still had to be collected and Eve avoided the blood as best she could. Her shoe covers protected her boots. She also had a bio suit made from the same material as the shoe covers to protect her clothing. Sometimes, they still got blood on their clothes and carried hydrogen peroxide along with dish soap in the van. They used the hotel sink or the bathtub to soak the clothes before allowing them to dry. After these steps, they placed them in laundry bags to be washed at home. This was simply a part of their job.

Eve entered the master bedroom. Only the sleeping quarters had the wooden floors covered by earth-tone wall-to-wall carpeting. She refused to think about what she was stepping into as she approached the couple.

She placed paper bags on Bart's hands and taped the bags

around his wrists. Then she carefully pushed the body from his side to his back and examined the wound more fully. She took the body photos and logged the descriptions herself. Bart's holy garments, once white, were covered in blood apart from a few untouched patches, tinged yellow in the glow of the lamplight. She usually checked pockets and removed personal belongings. Dying in bed took that aspect away. Holy garments had no pockets.

She took DNA blood samples from several different locations on Bart's skin and clothing. More would be taken at the autopsies. Her team had handled the carpets and other areas away from the bodies.

Eve stared between husband and wife wondering how someone would cut four throats in a similar manner. Hunter? The similarity of the wounds pointed to a single killer. The evidence would weed out the truth but that always took time unless someone came forward.

Aaron hadn't seemed as concerned about the discovery of four bodies as he should be.

Eve knew it was an act. She'd thought about it after leaving his office and still wasn't sure why he gave her the feeling that something was not as it should be. Possibly he thought the murderer was someone outside the community. She would keep an open mind but she didn't believe that. She didn't think her stepbrother did either. Could Aaron be protecting the killer? If it were someone special in the church, it was a very real likelihood. That thought showed how little she trusted him.

There were other things that didn't add up. It was weird that no relatives had shown up to ask about the bodies. No one hovering near the crime scene. Aaron hadn't even mentioned the outside family. The fundamentalist church buried their dead quickly and at night. They snuck into the county-owned graveyard to do it. Originally the land belonged solely to the polygamist community. The state took possession of it due to mismanagement and now it was a public cemetery. One with rules, where you had to reserve burial plots. According to the fundamentalist prophet, however, God was the only person who could grant permission to bury a body.

Like most petty crimes committed in the county by church members, they got away with it. Eve had also heard rumors that local police kept strangers from entering the area during the funerals. Her team wouldn't touch their graveyard theft with a ten-foot pole and, fortunately, it wasn't their job. It was up to local police to enforce low-level misdemeanors.

When Eve had dealt with the young wife beaten to death by her husband, the father hounded Aaron within hours about funeral arrangements. Eve's number was finally given to him so she could handle his calls.

She checked her watch. They'd been here for more than four hours.

There was also the fact Aaron hadn't called every few minutes to complain. Within hours of coming into town, she usually had text messages and voicemails from him that she had to ignore to get her work done. His having invited her to his office to read a few words on a piece of paper was also odd. Had he set her up for the confrontation with her stepbrothers? He must have. She also didn't have a police chief breathing down her neck and grumbling about her taking over his case. Basically, everything seemed off.

She shook away the strange feelings she had.

Eve walked around the bed to the wife's side and gently bagged her hands. Marcella also wore holy garments with an additional beige nightgown over them.

Eve remembered the heaviness of her fundamentalist dresses with layers of underclothing before the innermost holy garments that went from wrist to neck to ankle. Even in blistering heat, modesty had to be maintained. Eve worked hard to fight the prudishness she still carried. That's what bothered her about her stepbrother's revulsion when he looked at her clothing. She was conservative in her attire, though she would never wear a dress to work. But even fully covered, by the prophet's standards, she was far from modest.

According to their doctrine, the pants, blouse, gun at her hip, and badge at her waist, made Eve the worst of the worst, an apostate sent by the devil to undo God's work. Again, she shrugged these thoughts aside. They got her nowhere.

Eve examined the wound at Marcella's throat as closely as she had Bart's, making more mental notes. She needed a knife expert and would have Tamm locate someone. Since they hadn't found a murder weapon, Eve wanted to know the possibilities so they had some clue on the type of blade they were searching for. There was also the possibility the knife wouldn't be found. If they didn't locate it in the yard, they would do a grid search outside the property. She took a shallow breath. One step at a time and two bodies to go.

Eve did not place Marcella's hand back into her husband's. The murderer wanted it that way and Eve didn't feel inclined to carry on a killer's tradition. Eve removed her bloodied shoe coverings, put on a new pair, and changed her gloves. With a clenched stomach and sad heart, she moved to the next room.

Tracy's hand, propped under her chin, must also have been positioned after her death. Had the killer or killers arranged the bodies like this out of some sense of compassion? Using that word to describe the horrors that happened here didn't feel right. There was one thought Eve couldn't keep from her mind: this was retribution.

She bent at the side of the bed, her boots sinking into the blood-soaked carpet that was nearly dry. She carefully bagged Tracy's hands that were stiff with rigor. Her eyes were murky blue caused by lack of oxygen to the cornea after she died. She took a long look at the blonde, braided hair soaked in blood and arranged over Tracy's shoulders and on her breasts.

The killer knew them. These were added touches. You didn't do this without some connection to your victims. A one-killer scenario was solidifying in Eve's head. The crime scene was too neat for multiple perpetrators. It would be interesting to hear what her other team members thought.

After close-up photos of her body, she rolled Tracy to get the other images she needed for evidence. She finally backed away to her bag at the door and once more changed her boot covers and gloves. She left Tracy with an even heavier heart.

Elijah's bedroom took additional time. Eve stared at the bed, then at his body on the floor. Mentally, she went through what the crime scene revealed. The amount of blood on the sheets suggested his throat was cut there. The trail of blood from the bed to his body showed how hard he had tried to get away. Was the killer still in the room while Elijah struggled to breathe? Did Elijah see who did this? He must have.

The Book of Mormon caught her eye along with the high-lighter pen. Both were drenched in blood and had evidence markers.

She moved closer and examined the dark mahogany stained nightstand. She slowly opened the drawer. Whoever processed this room first would have done it but there were no evidence markers for photographs so nothing in the drawer had been considered vital to the investigation. The drawer held a Holy Bible. Only scripture was allowed for reading. Eve looked at the bed where blood marked the pillow and sheets. It told a story and they would spray the walls, drapes, and furniture with Luminol to gain a more complete understanding. That would have to wait until after the remainder of the scene was processed. They had to take all their DNA samples first.

Eve bagged Elijah's hands and rolled him to his back with a solid push. At fifteen, he was doing the work of a man and was heavy. She would have been more surprised if it wasn't so. She knew he most likely put in a ten-to-twelve-hour workday with his father and uncle.

Elijah was simply too young to die. Like Charlie and the baby girl, Becky, who disappeared so long ago, he deserved justice.

After processing his body, Eve quickly removed her gloves, shoe covers, and bodysuit, shoving them into the plastic bag where her previous used items were collected. She had to go outside and breathe. The smell of death clung to her. The overcast sky echoed the gloom of the house. Three techs from the medical examiner's office, avoiding the cold, waited in one of the two vans she had requested.

She spoke to them quickly and took them into the house, forced to give up her desire for fresh air. She escorted them to each body and watched as they zipped them into bags and put them on gurneys. Eve taped the bags and added her initials with a Sharpie where the tape crossed.

"George said to tell you the autopsies are scheduled for day after tomorrow, if that works?" one of the techs said.

George was her favorite pathologist at the medical examiner's office and she was glad he was on board. "Tell him I'll make it work."

The techs left and Eve went to the van to grab Bina for a bathroom run using the SUV. The guys would go after their return.

Once everyone was back, they began collecting DNA samples. It was always a relief after the bodies were gone. It took two additional hours before they were ready to call it a very long day.

Though tired, they still had an evening meeting to get through and she had photos to analyze.

Eve spoke briefly to the officer assigned to hold the scene overnight. He snapped his words at her, which was normal for law enforcement here. It didn't matter that she was old enough to be his mother. Respect came with your male anatomy and commitment to God and Eve had neither. Women were forbidden from guiding their husbands on any subject and they were to never disagree. A husband or brother's command was the word of God and women were to stay sweet.

Sweet did not go hand in hand with the woman Eve was today.

She left the officer with orders to notify her if anyone tried to get onto the scene or if anything unusual happened. It would be too much to hope the killer would come by but it never hurt to be prepared. Strange things occurred at homicide scenes and they had to be ready for anything.

Ray and Collin picked up their own food using the van. Bina, Clyde, and Eve, in the SUV, went for a salad from the mini-mart a few blocks from the hotel, hoping they would escape without food poisoning.

They met to eat in Eve's room after everyone changed into comfortable clothes that did not smell like death. They each had a sealed bag back in the van for their crime scene laundry so they didn't need to sleep with it in their rooms. They had a special storage compartment they kept the bags in so the smell didn't carry into the van, which was also used for interviews. They had learned to work in this area as efficiently as possible.

"First thoughts?" Eve asked while picking purple cabbage from her salad. "Ray, I know you have thoughts." It was a joke and it received a chuckle from the others.

Ray held up three fingers. "Premeditated, personal, and one perpetrator. I'll stop there."

"Blood throughout the bathroom," said Bina after wiping her mouth. "The killer, and I agree with Ray, was a single person. They showered and cleaned the blood off after the murders. Tossed the towels on the floor and piled them in the corner by the shower. The person knew exactly what they were doing and didn't feel rushed for time. Premeditated and personal, like Ray said. We may be able to isolate the perpetrator's DNA from that of the family, depending on how many people in the house used those towels."

Eve had photographed the evidence placards in the bathroom and reached the same conclusion as Bina. It wasn't a passing stranger from outside the community. This was someone who understood the tidiness of a fundamentalist home. If Aaron didn't know who did these killings, he darn sure knew it was someone local.

"I've got a weird vibe," Collin tossed out, and they all groaned. His vibes were legendary.

"When is being in this county not weird?" Ray teased.

Collin doubled down. "This time things are even more off than usual. Has anyone noticed we haven't been followed since our arrival?"

Within fifteen minutes of entering polygamist territory, they usually picked up a God squad tail. This was a group of unmarried younger men who acted as security for the community. They were to intimidate those who didn't belong and keep an eye on the women given permission to leave their homes. Eve's unit gave little thought to the bullying because they were accustomed to it and it didn't scare them. Thinking back to the trip from the crime scene to the hotel, Aaron's office, and then fast food before returning to the scene, she realized Collin was right: she hadn't been followed. This was exceedingly strange.

It was time for her to add her two cents. "I agree with Collin. Something is off. Where's the law enforcement interference? The chief of police hasn't shown up at the scene. Not a single looky-loo has come by to gape. We have four bodies and no one has asked about them as human beings. My stepbrother is worried about something but is playing it down. Normal should never be attached to any murders, especially these."

"It's personal. The killer is a close family member," Clyde interjected. They fell silent in thought.

From their expressions, this scenario had been nagging at them all.

TEN

The men left and Bina entered the bathroom for a shower. Eve had decided to clean up at the sink. When she washed her hair, it was a long and difficult task. Fortunately, there was a vanity outside the bathroom with what she needed. She was able to scrub her body with a washcloth and remove the last vestiges of death. When she was done, she pulled a long, soft nightshirt over her head.

She hadn't taken her hair down in front of anyone since she was a child. After moving a straight-backed chair to the sink, she removed the large clip and then the pins that helped keep it tightly secured. The brown mass instantly began unwinding. With each twist, the pull on her scalp loosened. Using her fingertips, she massaged her scalp and allowed the stress of the day to fade.

She lifted the brush and pulled it through the strands, relaxing more with each stroke. Once the shiny weight settled around her shoulders and back, she took a deep breath and enjoyed the freedom. Her hair was a natural blend of lighter and darker shades of brown. She'd never dyed it and so far, she'd only found a few gray hairs which didn't bother her. With the small lines at the corners of her eyes, she looked more like her mother with every year that passed.

When ready, she divided her hair into three sections and weaved it until she had one long plait. The braid reached her lower back. She held the weighted length in her hand, hating it, and hating herself for refusing to let such a simple remnant of brainwashing go.

With shoulders back and head high, she said aloud the same line she'd used since her sixteenth birthday. "I am not the property of the prophet and I am more than a vessel for children." Each word rang with resolve in her heart. The fact she recited this after so many years bothered her, but she used the words to ground herself.

Women's uncut hair will wash the feet of Christ upon his return, she'd been taught to believe. Its length proved subservience to the prophet. Women of the church piled their hair high as a sign of their righteousness. They were told pride was a sin, but this was almost an acceptable form of pride. A woman's hair meant everything.

Though Eve no longer followed the fundamentalist teachings, something kept her from cutting it. Her hair was the talisman that preserved the unwanted memories of her childhood. She simply wasn't ready to release the last horrific traces of her abuse. After so many years, she doubted she would ever be completely free of the unholy principles forced upon her.

Swinging the braid over her shoulder, she walked away from the mirror and faced the bed, hoping one day she would be able to leave her hair behind like some of her memories. After pulling back the comforter, she settled against the pillows with her laptop. She downloaded her camera's removable SIM card and reviewed the first series of crime scene photos.

Bina came out of the bathroom with wafts of steam floating behind her. She stood at the mirror and braided her hair too. She'd always respected Eve's privacy and never mentioned the fact Eve prepared for bed when Bina was in the other room. Bina then lay down and fell asleep almost instantly. They didn't speak because Eve was engrossed in the photographs.

Her team would review their taped interviews in their rooms at night once they started that leg of the investigation. The recordings often held small details overlooked when speaking to people. Few had any idea what really went into a homicide investigation unless they were part of it. They were lucky they could see it through the eyes of television shows that had DNA collection, analysis, and the guilty person discovered in one hour.

It took about forty-five minutes to examine the images. Eve didn't find anything her subconscious had previously missed. She expanded the photos of the joined hands and propped chin. The killer held emotional attachment to the victims. Eve needed the list of former wives and the husbands they were assigned to. She closed her laptop and settled down to sleep.

She tossed and turned all night. Bina's side of the room held the same restlessness. It was normal for their first night in a hotel. They woke up early and had coffee waiting for the guys when they arrived at Eve's room with similarly bleary eyes. Tamm always packed a bag of expensive ground coffee and its accompanying paraphernalia and left it in the back of the SUV. She called it her good luck charm whenever they left town on a case.

Evidence collection and a larger outside grid search were at the top of today's list. Bina and the guys would start while Eve contacted her brother. After interviewing Hannah and Howard Wall, she would begin questioning anyone who passed the crime scene tape. She also needed a breakdown of events starting from the brother finding the bodies to the police arriving, in order to form her timeline. This part of dealing with Aaron was always like pulling teeth.

She added the 911 log to her growing list for him. When

she and Clyde went to the medical examiner's office, Bina, Collin, and Ray would go back through the house and reevaluate everything to see what was missed. They needed to get through today first. Locating the murder weapon was also a priority.

They ate quickly, made their game plan, and arrived at the scene a little before seven. Eve said hello to a new officer who had replaced the one from the previous evening. He waited in his vehicle looking bored. He didn't respond before driving away. The media still hadn't arrived and it was one of the reasons they came so early. They drove the van and SUV into the inner courtyard. Eve climbed out and looked at the house. It appeared serene. The sun shone, though a cool wind blew, causing her to grab her light jacket. The storm threatened yesterday had never materialized.

They decided to do the grid search before the media arrived. It took an hour to cover approximately fifty yards around the home. There was nothing but a few shoe-print remnants that were quickly disappearing due to sporadic wind gusts. Eve snapped pictures but it was doubtful they would work as evidence. Though they could see homes in the distance, the Tanner house was semi-isolated with a few trees to break up the barren landscape. No knife.

When they finished the search, the team separated and began the arduous task of listing and collecting the evidence Eve had photographed the day before.

She stayed outside and walked closer to the courtyard wall. She stared into the distance at the rock formations, as tall as some mountains. The sheer cliffs held a majestic quality and she remembered gazing at them when she was young. Her heart had longed for something she didn't understand. Now she did. The pointed top of the tallest peak represented freedom from the endless chores and her yearning to escape. She remembered a feeling of guilt whenever she turned away from them. Keeping sweet was a daily struggle inside her head and she thought she would be damned because burying her emotions was so hard.

Shaking off the memory, she called her supervisor and brought him up to speed. Next, she clicked Tamm's number and gave her a similar update and a new list of what they needed. Tamm had most of it lined up, which made Eve smile. Then, though she didn't feel in the mood, she dialed Aaron's cell.

"What do you need?" he barked.

Eve held back words that wouldn't help the situation. "A list of everyone who entered the crime scene, phone numbers and addresses included, a list of relatives—I gave you all of this yesterday." She snapped her fingers in frustration, which hopefully he couldn't hear. "Add the 911 call log to the list along with a cell phone subpoena for Mr. Tanner's phone found in his nightstand. We'll also need that evidence room. Items will be moved in today." She noticed dust in the distance and after squinting her eyes, realized there was a disc on top of the approaching vehicle. "Media incoming. You need to get here as soon as you can. I'll interview you after you deal with them. Have the police chief lined up next, if he entered the home. I will go to Hannah for her interview; she shouldn't come to the house."

"I've been informed Hannah and Brother Wall are not available today."

It took Eve a moment to process this bit of unwelcome information. "Do I need to call the judge?" She hated using the threat too often, but Hannah and Mr. Wall were essential to the case and the interviews would happen whether Aaron wanted them to or not.

She ended the conversation more frustrated than satisfied. Her stepbrother acted like this was a normal day on the job. It gave her a bad feeling. Whatever happened to this family, Aaron knew the truth, or so it seemed. It was up to Eve to figure out what he and the community wanted to stay hidden. It would be key to the case.

She waited impatiently for the news crew. Two men jumped from a white SUV with their station call letters plastered on the side. She held up her hand to one while the other removed video equipment from the back. "You cross my tape, I arrest you. Don't push it. The county attorney will be the liaison for the media and you're responsible for making sure any other journalists who show up know it," she informed them in her no-nonsense voice. "He'll arrive shortly. I have no statement to give and I won't answer questions." She turned her back as the journalist blustered. She hurriedly walked inside.

This was the beginning. By the end of the day, the area outside the crime scene tape would be full of media and the spectacle in full swing.

"Nice people skills," Clyde said from the doorway. His lips tipped ever so slightly upward but even if the journalist noticed, he wouldn't know it was Clyde's way of smiling when they were at a scene. The small dimple that appeared on his right cheek was all that gave it away.

"We don't have time for their bull crap."

He raised his eyebrows and she realized even the words bull crap went across the cussing line she'd always kept. It was this county.

"I need a word with you," Clyde said, his dark eyes intense.

If Clyde wanted a word, she would give it to him. Eve knew the whole team had been affected by the deaths, particularly Elijah's. They could mostly turn it off but some images lingered no matter how hard they tried to put them aside.

"In the van?" she asked.

"That works."

Eve didn't like the tight lines between his brows. They entered the van and Clyde closed the door.

"I agree with Collin's strange vibe. There is something odd going on and I can't place my finger on it."

She massaged the tendons of her neck. This was the intuition officers were taught to listen too but putting it into words wasn't easy.

"You're right. Something is off. We need eyes in the backs of our heads whenever we're in this county but this is stranger than usual."

He grunted in a pure Clyde way, his frustration clear.

He rubbed his head. "Collin just told me about the attic. We need to take a look. Grab your camera."

Eve did not have a good feeling about what lay in store.

ELEVEN

Collin led them through the gathering area and up the stairs. The bad feeling in Eve's gut did not diminish. In the master bedroom, Collin went to the closet and grabbed a pull-down rope that she didn't remember from her pictures. The stairs made a slight creaking noise as they lowered. There was plastic, wrapped and taped to the wooden steps, that someone from her team had secured. Eve would have time to ask questions later.

The stairs were wobbly but held. She climbed then stepped onto a floor made of stained wood, rougher than the ones on the first floor and the upstairs hallway. This room wasn't spotless like the rest of the house and that was odd. The floor was dusty and multiple sets of footprints littered the area. There were cobwebs in the corners of the ceiling. She remembered going into the attic where clothing was stored when she was a child. Hand-me-downs were a way of life. It also held extra cribs when they weren't needed. Like the remainder of her childhood home, the room was kept clean and free of bugs.

This attic was entirely different.

There were smudges that looked like dirt on the cracked and peeling walls. At the back of the room, a small octagon-shaped window with translucent glass gave the area its only light. There were no electrical fixtures. The dark shadows made the room feel more like a dungeon than attic. She removed her flashlight from her pocket and observed the empty area again until the light rested on the only furniture, which was tucked in the corner to the right side of the stair opening.

A single metal bedframe with a bare, thin mattress stood out in the large, nearly empty room. The yellowed mattress with thin blue pinstripes had various visible stains. Stacked at the foot of the bed was a folded beige blanket resting on a set of white folded sheets. The wall behind the bed was empty of anything but peeling paint and the same dirt smudges. Eve moved her flashlight.

Three feet from the bottom corner of the stacked bedding was a wooden, straight-backed chair with spindled legs facing the bed. It was what was on the chair that drew Eve's attention. A partial roll of silver duct tape lay on the seat. To make it worse, a wide black, leather belt hung over the back.

Serial killers and rapists used duct tape.

Eve ran her gloved hands over her arms. Weird wasn't exactly the word that came to mind. The items in front of her were more unsettling than anything. She turned to her team who stood behind her.

Bina shrugged, her eyes on the chair and duct tape, not Eve. "Is this fundamentalist ceremony shit that you can explain?"

Eve understood why Bina would say this. During their work together, her team had learned of certain polygamy practices that made no sense to them and Eve had to explain. In some cases, such as women holding down other women for their first marital bed, grasping the weird concepts accepted inside the community was difficult. Her team saw much of it as a crime and didn't like the fact it wouldn't be charged.

"Why a ceremony?" Eve asked Bina curiously while her eyes went to the bed again.

"This is strange, creepy weird. I thought it could possibly be part of a secret, unknown ritual."

The single bed and chair were bizarre. Add the duct tape and belt and even creepy weird didn't describe her personal feelings. Her fight-or-flight response was kicking in and she wanted out of the attic. If any of the murder victims had been abused, as the room led her to believe, it would be discovered at autopsy; she never undressed the bodies.

"There were traces of possible blood on the stairs so I preserved them after collecting samples," Ray said.

Eve's eyebrows rose.

"They are also some on the bed and chair," added Bina. "We need to Luminol the entire room to get the full picture. Maybe Luminol will clarify what we're having trouble seeing."

What they were seeing was a room of deeply held secrets within the family. Horrible secrets.

"Do it Friday," Eve said. "I want to be here. We have the autopsies tomorrow."

"Believe me, I don't mind waiting for you," Bina told her. "I don't want to be up here alone under any circumstances."

They were spooked because this room did not fit the narrative of the dead family. It fit more of a case of abduction and torture.

Eve thought about the overall investigation for a moment

"We need to keep working and more things will add up." She looked around at each of them. "Are you good to go?"

"Yes," Collin said. Ray and Bina didn't question her. They all felt the eeriness of the room. Clyde gave his nod of agreement.

"I'll photograph up here," she told them, and saw Bina, Ray, and Collin's looks of relief.

Clyde stayed with her while she took still images of the attic. Collin had videotaped the room the day before. Bina was right: the Luminol would show a clearer picture.

She received a text message from Aaron shortly after she'd climbed down the attic stairs. He'd dealt with the media and had an officer stationed at the home around the clock until Eve finished processing the scene. This type of cooperation from him was strange but she didn't question it. He asked if he could be interviewed in the early afternoon and she agreed. He would bring the responding officers and police chief with him.

That works for me. Please call Mr. Wall and ask about his and Hannah's interviews. I will make time to do them today no matter what is on my plate, she'd texted back. Eve hated asking please when dealing with Aaron, but those interviews were vital. As a child, she'd begged him to leave her be because please didn't work. He took satisfaction in getting her into trouble. She finally learned to stay quiet and accept his bullying. Keeping sweet was no longer in her vocabulary but she needed to interview Hannah.

I'll make contact, Aaron assured her. She wished she trusted him.

Over the next two hours, several more media vans arrived.

Eve called Tamm and requested an expert who could identify the type of knife used in the homicides. Tamm had accomplished everything from Eve's earlier list and was one step ahead of her.

"I have a forensic expert out of Texas on standby. He works in federal law enforcement," Tamm said.

Eve would be able to send him the images that evening and get his opinion on the murder weapon. When dealing with civilians with expert knowledge there were hoops to jump through. The expert's certified status made it much simpler.

"Is your brother causing trouble?" Tamm asked.

"Not as much as usual," Eve told her. The strange feelings she had were not something she could put into words.

After the call ended, she walked to the front door and looked outside. The wall and their strategically placed van blocked the media's line of sight into the courtyard and home. She decided her team could continue gathering evidence and she would use this time to put her mental notes on paper. Mostly questions. She used the kitchen table inside the house, which had no evidence tags on or near it.

Sometime later, Clyde sat down next to her. She looked up from reviewing her notes and gave him a soft smile. It was natural. His steadfast personality calmed her and she'd learned to appreciate him during the cases that seemed endless. She had a lot of pressure on her back from those who gave her this position and Clyde knew it.

"I have something you need to see," he told her. "We found this in the very back of the drawer in the bedside table next to Bart Tanner's body."

He opened his hand and she saw a small, unframed picture. It wasn't weathered with age. Eve closed her eyes. The baby appeared to have the same genetic disorder as little Charlie. They had found no evidence of a baby in the home, not even an old crib in the attic. Things were simply too strange in this case for her to take chances. Her cell rested beside the legal pad. She lifted it and hit Aaron's number.

"Was there a baby in the house?" she asked after he answered.

"He died last year."

Anger exploded inside her head.

Had the child died naturally or had he too disappeared?

TWELVE

Eve's adoption by her polygamist father had been illegal, just like his marriage to her mother. With no entitlement to child support, the only money Maggie had after leaving the community was what she brought home from minimum-wage jobs. Reprogramming Eve's brain was the hardest part of her rescue. For a long time, she thought of her mother as the devil's apostate and wanted the comfort of what she referred to as her true family. It didn't matter that her stepmothers and siblings had never been overly nice. The poor treatment by her fundamentalist family was all she knew and her life with them revolved around entering heaven, even if the top tier was out of her reach.

Clothing, daily prayers, and everything else about her life changed after leaving the fundamentalist sect. It terrified her. She had been due to marry soon and her mother tried to explain it was against the law. Maggie did not understand those laws did not apply to Eve. Only the laws of the prophet did.

Two things changed Eve's perspective and let her see around the church doctrine that had been brainwashed into her. Maggie gave Eve a kitten for Christmas. Worldly holidays were something else she wasn't accustomed to and pets were not allowed within the community. It was a wonderful feeling to have Whiskers' soft fur against her while she slept. The cat's sweet disposition and willingness to be held helped open Eve's heart to change.

The second gift brought Eve a new beginning. A camera. It was not expensive but to her, it was priceless. Her fears of the sinful world looked different through the lens. The camera protected her from prying eyes as she spied through the filtered view with the click of the shutter. She became the girl in school who always had a camera to her eye.

Her mother had a hard time communicating with Eve. She tried to apologize but it pained them both more than it helped. When Eve did ask questions, they were evaded, which Eve didn't understand. Maggie finally sent her to a therapist where she could talk through her emotional difficulties. After meeting with one woman for several years in high school, law enforcement was mentioned as a possible career. Eve's strong sense of injustice over living within the cult was something the therapist helped her with. The more Eve thought about it, the more she realized law enforcement could help her right the wrongs done to women and children.

Maggie had married a violent man, then given her daughter to an abusive society. Eve felt she needed to protect other women and children from the same scenario. These thoughts spurred her forward.

She graduated from high school at nineteen and signed up for community college, majoring in justice studies. After receiving an associate degree, Eve attended the police academy at age twenty-one and went to work for the State Police in Utah.

The prophet who ruled during Eve's time in the church was dead but his son, a bigger monster, was isolating the community even more. Eve read every scrap of information she could find, from news articles to memoirs of those who got out.

While working on patrol full-time, she returned to college and earned her bachelor's in criminal science and then her masters. It brought her to where she was today. The promise she made herself years ago about never forgetting little Charlie spurred her forward still.

During her second case within the polygamist community, a young mother mentioned the loss of her child and then Babyland. It was a chance discussion but one that wouldn't leave Eve.

She brought it up when she met Aaron at his office to review another case she had in his jurisdiction. His expression immediately closed and he glanced away. When his eyes returned to hers, he gave a tight-lipped response.

"It's none of your business. Let the children rest in peace."

She had already discovered that giving an inch with her stepbrother got her nowhere.

She planted her hands on his desk and leaned forward, an image of little Charlie alive in her mind.

"Tell me about the babies or I will make your life a living hell and the media will get all the gory details even if I'm fired," she ground out. She then sat with clenched teeth while he gave a very short explanation.

"Some babies die young. It's the way of God."

"How many babies die young?" she asked, her fury growing.

"I don't understand why you won't let this go." His face was red and his clasped hands so tight, the fingers were blue.

"You had a brother," she told him. "He was my brother too. Aunt Bertha took him away. Where did he go?" she demanded. Even though she knew little Charlie was most likely dead, deep in her heart she hoped he had been given to another family to raise. Aaron was making her face that lie head-on and she hated him for it.

"God takes the children with the purest blood," he said without blinking.

"What does that even mean?" She was close to losing her temper entirely.

"God decides who we marry. Cousins, nieces, or sisters; it is not up to us. The pure bloodline is wanted by the Lord and sometimes he takes them early."

Eve leaned back against the chair, trying to absorb what he'd just said. In the back of her mind, she'd always known this horror. She knew Charlie had a genetic disorder. She'd thought him an anomaly. Babies were born throughout the world with cleft palates like Becky's. Why hadn't she considered the inbreeding she herself witnessed when her father's brother married one of her sisters?

Trying to sort the horrible questions running through her mind, she asked the one she had to know: "Where. Is. Babyland?"

Aaron was furious now too, or maybe embarrassed. She wondered how many of his wives he was closely related to. He'd insisted Eve belonged to him when they were children and he would marry her when she came of age. She saw him as a brother and his sick thinking had disturbed her even when she lived with him. He wouldn't have cared if they had blood ties. None of the men did. They took what they wanted and women were property.

"There is nothing you can do," Aaron said stubbornly. "Uncle Todd died years ago. Aunt Bertha is an old woman and a judge already decided not to prosecute."

"Not prosecute what?" she yelled, coming out of her chair.

"The death of the chosen children." He didn't look at her when he said it.

Chosen.

Murdered.

All in the name of God.

Her memories of little Charlie swelled inside her head, his

loss, and years of not knowing what happened to him, making her hands tremble.

"Tell me where they are buried."

He finally gave her directions and she left the office before he saw her tears.

Her team finished their case and they returned home. Eve was eventually able to put a name to Charlie's condition: Fumarase deficiency. Large head, high, pronounced forehead, wide-set eyes. These babies averaged an IQ of 25 with lifelong difficulties. He was the sweetest, most loveable child and the polygamist church built him with their years of cousin-to-cousin and niece-to-uncle marriages.

How dare Aaron? How dare the men behind this evil?

Eve finally came across a blog post that mentioned Babyland. The babies with the worst defects were taken by Aunt Bertha and Uncle Todd, who ran the cemetery. Those children were laid to rest in unmarked graves at the back. The prophet himself, fully aware of what happened to these children, called it Babyland.

She took the information to the state prosecutor and then the judge. She got nowhere. The deaths were a thing of the past and Eve's job was to oversee law enforcement in the here and now.

Alone, Eve had made a special trip to the graveyard. In the middle of nowhere, with nothing to identify the barren landscape, Eve found the children. She'd walked from her car to the rickety wooden fence and pushed through the broken gate.

Rows of marked baby graves dating back more than fifty years had family names. Their birth and death documented on the stone. All under twelve months old. These were the children recorded under state law. Some of the graves were well maintained and had plastic flowers showing care and marking the tragic loss.

The farther she walked, the less well-kept the area was, with weeds scattering much of it. A long stretch of graves at the back of the site were unmarked. Plot after plot of Charlies and Beckys. Eve went to her knees at the last two. They weren't her sister and brother but in her mind they were. With handfuls of soil she collected from the two graves, she sobbed until she had no more tears. Brushing the dirt from her knees and off her hands when she stood, Eve felt the heavy weight of despair.

Aaron had shown no compassion for his biological siblings. What happened to them was proclaimed by God and even though the babies were without sin, God's judgment was harsh.

Someday, Eve vowed, she would find justice for her brother and sister.

THIRTEEN

They took an hour's lunch break away from the scene. They didn't talk about the murders in the local diner because of curious ears. Everyone knew who they were and why they were there. A few reporters sat close to them, hoping to catch some small tidbit they could run with. They were accustomed to journalists eavesdropping and spoke about mundane subjects from weather to sports.

They were back at the Tanner home shortly before Aaron arrived. Eve began her interviews in the front seat of the SUV. She had a recorder and a notebook. Her brother was the lucky one and was first.

"Do you have a copy of the 911 tape for me?" she asked.

"There isn't one. Howard called the police chief's cell phone directly."

Eve knew he meant Chief Jackson. She was interviewing him in approximately an hour.

"What are you hiding?" She wanted him on edge so tossed it out there.

He smiled. His bloodless lips pulled slightly upward and his eyes zeroed in on her. The only way to describe the expression was calculating.

"You have an overactive imagination," he said, his voice a low grumble.

Eve knew something was going on. Her entire team did. She wanted badly to ask him why Bart Tanner was out of favor with the church but something held her back. She wanted more information before she broached the subject.

"Has family called about the bodies?" she asked, not allowing him to break her stride.

"Of course. They are very upset." He looked away and then peered back at her. He was not a good liar.

Eve continued, "I'd like names."

"Too many to run through."

He thought he was so smart.

"Try."

He twisted in the seat and faced her fully. She was slightly sideways and the SUV seemed smaller. His gaze went to the bun that peeked out from the back of her neck and Eve resisted the need to place her hand over it. Aaron gave her the creeps.

"What's this about?" he demanded, without giving her a single name.

"There are four dead bodies, one a child. There's been little excitement except from the media. No one seems concerned that you have a child murderer running around. Care to explain?"

"You're being overly emotional. Elijah was nearly a man and your use of the word 'child' does not help your investigation."

This infuriated her. He was a child. He deserved to have hopes and dreams. With the fundamentalist preference of casting young men from the community, Elijah may have had the opportunity to attend college and have a life that would have taken him far away from the pathetic doctrine that controlled him. He deserved a chance but he didn't get it.

"Nice try, brother." She leaned closer. "Your face is red and I'd bet your palms are sweaty. A sure sign of nerves and another sign things are not as they seem."

"You're crazy." He looked away then swung his eyes back.

Eve rolled hers and didn't respond to the statement. "Have you arranged an interview with Hannah?" she asked instead.

"Hannah is distraught and her aunt would like to wait a day or two." He moderated his voice, his words precise like they'd been rehearsed.

"I will handle Mr. Wall's interview first then. After his, I would like to interview the aunt and any sister wives in the home. They may have knowledge about the Tanner family that would be helpful," she said, tamping down on her temper again.

"He is out of town for work," Aaron continued without changing his expression. "He'll return in a few days. I'll need to check on Linda Wall. I doubt now is a good time to leave Hannah's side."

Why would the Walls avoid interviews, she silently asked herself? She would make a list of things that did not add up. Maybe if it were in writing, something would make sense.

"I have autopsies tomorrow; I'll interview Hannah the following day along with the Walls," she told him sternly. "Make it happen." She put a touch of threat in the words. Aaron had no respect for women and even less for her. The only way to deal with him was with force she could back up.

The interview went downhill from there. He stormed off after he answered the majority of her questions. The ones he didn't answer were marked in her notes. He'd also told her he had sent her the subpoena for Bart's phone and it would be in her email. This meant he wasn't afraid of anything that would be on the phone.

Eve interviewed the three officers next. They'd all entered

the home. Again, it was pulling teeth. They'd been trained to give her as little information as possible. Her questions were thorough and would land them in trouble if they lied. It was the best she could do until they were further into the investigation and she had more information. They each handed her a one-paragraph written report that was useless and left out all pertinent information. This was expected and didn't raise red flags. Finally, something normal.

The chief had to wait an extra hour. He wasn't happy when he sat down beside her. She would not apologize; it was the fault of his stubborn officers.

Jackson's shortly cropped hair and stiff, large-going-on-fat body screamed lifetime cop. The shiny stars on his collar and immaculately pressed uniform added to her assumption. In his sixties, he and his family were lifelong polygamists. He was part of the problem and held a great deal of power.

"Chief Jackson, may I have your full name?" Eve knew the interview would be a disaster because the chief was friends with Eve's polygamist stepfather, who now lived in Texas.

"Chief Manny Horise Jackson," he said with little mouth movement.

Being questioned by a woman was an act against God. She'd had several cases in his jurisdiction but they hadn't touched him or his department beyond glacial stares from his men. Aaron had mentioned the chief's relationship with her stepfather as a side note to irritate her during one of those cases. It hadn't worked like he'd hoped and she was using that information. She didn't bother with more than a cursory kindness because it would bounce off this man's brick-wall persona.

Eve slowly wrote the name in her notebook, dragging out the time he was in the vehicle with her. She finally looked up.

"Why did Howard Wall call you directly and not 911?"

He shrugged.

Eve lifted her recorder and spoke into it with a bland expression that matched her voice.

"Chief of Police Jackson shrugged his shoulders at my question."

He tried staring her down while Eve put the recorder back in the middle console. She had no problem playing games if he insisted. His attitude was that of every man she dealt with in the community and she was not intimidated. She simply held eye contact, her expression unchanging.

"We sit on the same church council and we're related, as is most of the community," he replied at last.

"You know each other well?"

"Yes." He folded his arms over his pooch belly.

Aaron had mentioned this man had ten wives. He was a rising star within the church. Not being able to have sex with them must be difficult. It was a snide thought and she used it to keep her defenses in place. She expected him to bring up her stepfather and she wanted to be ready.

If he knew Howard Wall, he more than likely knew Mr. Tanner. He would know why he only had two wives.

"Did you know Bart Tanner well?"

"No."

"He's part of the church—why wouldn't you know him?"

"We had nothing in common."

"But you know his brother?"

"Yes, I know Howard. I've already answered that question. Move on."

"Do you have any idea who killed the Tanner family?" She hid the fact she was grinding her teeth and kept her tone level. It practically killed her. She could tell him she didn't answer to him but like Aaron, he was trying to get under her skin. Just the fact he was sitting here being questioned by her got under his and she needed to be satisfied.

"Uh, no." His small hesitation said a lot and it was Eve's job to figure out what was behind it.

"Have there been rumors?"

"It happened yesterday," he snapped with a look of disgust.

Eve knew what he thought about rumors, especially among women. They weren't just frowned upon; women were not allowed friendships with other women outside their home because it was thought they gossiped too much and relationships needed to stay in the family. This was simply another way the men controlled their wives. His disgust wasn't an act but the rest of his interview most likely was.

"Did the murders happen yesterday?"

This had bothered Eve. What was the actual death timeline? With how cold it had been there was the small possibility the bodies were there longer than Eve thought?

"Yes, the murders happened yesterday. Bart Tanner was at a brief church meeting the evening before." he snapped.

She scribbled in her notebook, which irritated him, if his fisting hands were a clue.

"Why did Bart and Howard have different last names?"

"You lived here. Is that question necessary?" he grumbled.

"It could come up in court. So yes, it is."

"Howard and his mother were reassigned after his father died. Bart had moved out by then." Relocated wives and children took on the name of the new father.

"Thank you for the interview." Eve smiled as sincerely as she could manage. "I'll try not to bother you again but that may be impossible. Thank you also for the use of your evidence room. The state lab will have all items collected and out of your hair as soon as possible. We should have the scene processed within a week."

He climbed from the car before she finished, though he did wait to slam the door.

FOURTEEN

A state tech arrived and picked up their DNA and fingerprint evidence before five. Her team loaded the van with the items going to the police department. Collin and Ray dropped the packages off while Eve, Bina, and Clyde drove to the hotel. Ray and Collin picked up dinner but they showered before bringing it to Eve's room. The mood was a somber one once everyone was together. They had no leads, no murder weapon, and no idea what the outcome of the case would be at this stage of their investigation. It troubled them.

"I can't get the attic out of my mind," Bina complained. "Whatever happened within that family, it was evil." She stood and began pacing, her hand going involuntarily to her pocket for a gummy bear. "I've tried to think of another explanation besides the obvious one of sexual abuse. Nothing makes sense. No one is even screaming about funerals. We're always treated as pariahs but this time it's like we aren't here."

The confrontation with her stepbrothers popped into her head and once again Eve decided not to bring it up. They had enough to deal with without muddying the waters with her family history.

"They're hiding something," Clyde stated emphatically. "We need to be prepared for this to be a high-ranking church official. It's the only thing that makes sense."

"They're always hiding something," Eve said in frustration. "I agree with you though. They've got to be protecting someone important to them or maybe one of his past wives. A brainwashed woman committing these murders would cause this reaction. It would make it more newsworthy to reporters and that's the last thing the men of the community want. Or, for all we know, their prophet could have said something that instigated murder and it backfired. I'll have Tamm check to see if he's changed a rule from behind bars again."

The prophet was notorious for writing long revelations in prison, given to him by God, that changed the doctrine for his congregation. Some were simply crazy, like the seed bearer dictate. Who knew what his insanity would come up with next?

The meeting ended and the guys left to get some sleep. Bina showered, then Eve. She had to wash her hair even though she was exhausted. She did it in sections, pulling a wide-tooth comb through the tangles after adding conditioner. After her hair, it was a relief to scrub the residue of the crime scene with the spray of hot water and a lot of soap. She towel-dried then braided her damp hair before leaving the bathroom.

Sitting up against her bed pillows, she reviewed the photos she'd taken earlier in the day. The same creepy feeling filled her when she went through the images from the attic, her gaze resting on the chair. It made her angry. It wasn't like her team hadn't seen or handled sexual abuse cases before. They just hadn't resulted in the brutal death of four people. She knew in her gut the room and the deaths were connected. She put her laptop aside when she could no longer keep her eyes open. Sleep was a blessing.

. . .

Eve and Clyde left before the sun rose. The trip to the medical examiner's office took three hours. It was the first stretch of time where they were able to speak without the others.

"How are you holding up?" Clyde asked her.

"Confused, upset about the attic, and angry at Aaron for covering up whatever it is he's trying to keep us from discovering." She was in the passenger seat looking over her notes, hoping something made sense.

"I have the same thoughts," he said. "We all do. You're the one who interacts with him the most. I've always felt he was too smart for his own good."

"He's too smart to follow an insane prophet who says he speaks directly to God." Eve put her notes aside and closed her eyes. "I don't understand how intelligent people fall for this."

"It's manipulation by the man who leads them. The prophets are always charismatic with huge egos. The more fear they create, the more people follow blindly. If it made sense, we could easily fix the problem."

She had studied the radicalization of these groups in college and the fundamentalist Mormons were not alone in the outrageousness of their belief system. Direct communication with God or believing the leader was some type of messiah seemed to be the common denominator. The polygamist sect was her history though and it weighed her down when she was here. Childhood memories dogged her and she often wondered if she were the right person for this job.

When they entered the next county, she gave a huge internal sigh of relief. It was always like this. The demons of her past haunted her worse when she was in the fundamentalist lair.

She skimmed through her text messages, found the information Tamm had sent for the knife expert, and hit the number. He answered on the first ring.

"This is Detective Sergeant Eve Bennet. You spoke to my assistant, Tamm Mackity, and I emailed the images we have."

"Yes, I've been expecting your call. You have an interesting group of homicides."

"That we do. Any chance you can identify the type of knife used?"

"A skinning knife would be my guess, one with a sharp tip. Some skinning knives have a short, wide blade. That fits with the photographs. To work for skinning, it needs to be exceptionally sharp. I would also say the person had some knowledge."

"Thank you," Eve said. "Would you send your report to Tamm when it's ready? I appreciate your help. If we locate the weapon, you'll hear back from me."

The call ended.

"We're looking for a skinning knife and since I don't know what that looks like, I'll text Collin and have him email some pictures."

Collin was their hunter. He took off once a year for man time without his wife, and went out in the wilderness with several of his brothers.

She fired off a text to him. Fifteen minutes later, she had several images to look over.

"Have you spoken to your mother recently?" Clyde asked after she lay the phone in her lap.

"No." Guilt shot through her. "I need to call but like always, I delay." She looked at him and saw no judgment in his expression. "I think of her more when I'm in this community. I have so many questions and, like you know, she never answers them."

"I can't help thinking there's a reason," he said softly.

"What would be so bad she would keep it hidden for so many years?"

"I don't know. Something gave your mother enough backbone to get you out. I hope one day, you learn the truth."

So did she.

"I'm tired and wired at the same time," Eve finally said.

"Close your eyes and try to nap. I'll wake you when I stop for coffee."

Eve did something she'd never done during a case before. She rested her hand on Clyde's. He twisted his over so he could squeeze her fingers, letting her know he was alright with the simple touch. His warm grip grounded her and she relaxed. He didn't let go. She only half nodded off but it gave her brain the additional rest it needed to face the long day.

They made good time on the trip. The medical examiner's offices were off the highway in a large white building with huge smoked-glass windows near the local university. They had ten minutes to spare when they entered. Eve took a quick restroom break and when she came out, the receptionist showed them to the prep room. They placed paper medical gowns over their clothing and grabbed gloves and masks they would put on when the autopsies began.

George entered with a smile for Eve and Clyde. The pathologist had a headful of dark brown hair, a triangular face, green eyes, pointy chin, and large glasses with thick lenses that made him appear as smart as he was.

"Tell me what you have," George asked after they sat down at the table directly outside the autopsy area.

"Four bodies. Father age fifty-five, two sister wives ages twenty-two and twenty-seven, and a male child of fifteen. Their throats were cut," Eve told him.

"Murder weapon?"

"Still missing, but I have photos of possibles. I'd rather keep those to myself until after you examine the bodies."

"Anything else I need to look for?" he asked. "Cause of death appears straightforward."

Eve studied him for a moment. "Please, make no assumptions. The fifteen-year-old was the only one who put up a fight.

They had to be drugged and it will show in toxicology. Keep an open mind on everything."

"Got it, let's get started."

They masked and gloved before entering. Eve examined her tape on the bagged bodies and took pictures showing they were not compromised and the chain of custody had been kept intact. The examination room was sterile with steel cabinets and the steel table the autopsies would take place on. A huge industrial bottle of common yellow store-brand dish soap sat on the countertop nearest the sink. Eve never purchased the brand for her apartment because it reminded her too much of dead bodies. George thought it funny when she'd told him this early in their work relationship.

"Best cleaning product on the market," he'd quipped. "We use it because it works."

Bart was up first. George said he would perform the juvenile autopsy last. Eve and Clyde moved around the table, giving George access when he needed it. Eve had learned a lot about death from him and he didn't mind spending extra time explaining things to her if she had questions.

Bart was stripped, the paper bags removed from his hands, and his body taken by the assigned tech to be weighed. It only took a few minutes before he was wheeled back into the room. The tech then manipulated the joints to release rigor. Eve always found the sounds of the procedure, bending the limbs almost to the point of breakage, nerve-racking.

George unpacked the sterile items he would need for the autopsy while this took place. Just as Eve's team operated, George and the tech worked in unison, having performed these same steps many times. George also took his own photos along the way and kept a small digital camera around his neck.

When the tech finished, George walked around Bart, speaking his observations into a recorder. He picked up the left hand, examining it and the arm closely, followed by taking fingernail samples. Then he did the right side before moving to the legs and feet. He took hair samples from the scalp too.

He studied the throat carefully before glancing at Eve.

"The tissue at the cut is too thick for the weapon to have been a scalpel, but the blade was very sharp. Knife went in directly above the zygomatic bone at the ear. I would guess prior knowledge on slitting a throat."

She glanced at Clyde. He was deep in thought. Her gaze went back to the table. Photos came next, followed by extracting fluid from the eyes with a long syringe inserted directly into the pupil. If the family was drugged, it would show in the vitreous gel.

The Y incision was made and the organs removed one at a time to be weighed. Small slices were then cut from each organ and placed on slides for examination by clinical lab experts. Stomach samples were also taken. They would show a sedative if it were in the food.

It took another forty-five minutes before George finished the first autopsy. His tech began sewing closed the Y incision with a large needle and heavy yellow cord.

"Nothing strange that I could see with Mr. Tanner," George told them. "Cause of death was definitely the cut to the throat and not drugs. No contusions or hematomas to the brain that would cause unconsciousness. The incision was too clean and he was drugged to the point he didn't fight."

Her team knew it, but it was always nice to have it validated by the pathologist.

Bart Tanner's body was moved to its original gurney and he was zipped back in the same bag. The table was scrubbed and George was ready to continue.

Marcella was next.

After her clothes were removed, it was impossible to miss the tape residue on her wrists and ankles. Thoughts of the attic filled Eve's head. She couldn't see the expression on Clyde's face behind his mask but she knew he was speculating about the same things. George stopped his examination and turned his green, quizzical gaze on her.

"The crime scene matches this," she told him. "We have a room in the house that makes us think something more happened."

The autopsy continued. Eve usually added to her notes when George examined private areas on the bodies, unless it was a sexual assault case. The duct tape on the chair and evidence of it on Marcella changed everything. She also had several bruises on her back and upper thighs that fit the width of the belt. George snapped photos after he cataloged them in his recorder.

"From what the examination shows, she's been sexually assaulted," George said. "She has bruising and—"

Eve's gaze snapped to George. She barely registered the rest of what he said. Could Bart Tanner have been a seed bearer? It made no sense. His home was small and he only had two wives living with him. He was not in good standing with the religious sect. He couldn't be. Your worth was defined by your female property and the number of children you had. It made more sense that a seed bearer was brought in and the women fought against what was happening.

"I'm taking semen samples," George told her. "I know they are from the polygamist community and it would be nearly impossible for the women to cheat on their spouse but I'm doing as you asked and treating this like a case I know nothing about. It will be interesting if the DNA did not match her husband."

The team knew about seed bearers but it had not come up in a case before. Fundamentalist polygamy information was disseminated to law enforcement and Tamm was in charge of advising them on anything new that they might encounter. When the prophet established the doctrine given to him by God that children could only be fathered by the men the prophet selected, Tamm had been livid. Eve and her team hadn't reacted much differently.

Like so many of his revelations, this one was unimaginable.

There was a metal folding chair in the corner of the autopsy room. Eve walked to it and sat down. The cold from the seat traveled through her clothes and she crossed her arms in front of her. She needed time to think. Could the deaths of his family be punishment for Bart's sins? Was having sex with your wife, against the prophet's orders, enough of a sin?

"Continue." She waved at George and Clyde. "I'm thinking. Let me know if you find something else." Sex was one of Eve's personal and emotional hang-ups. The polygamist church was directly responsible for how she felt. It embarrassed her that she would have fallen in line like Marcella and Tracy. She would not have questioned Bart no matter what he had done. It was not the role of women.

Keep sweet.

She hated that phrase.

Would George find the same evidence with Tracy? So many questions. She was unable to wrap her head around the unwanted thoughts this case evoked.

"God will inform the prophet when you are ready," one of her mothers had told her when she was eleven years old. "Your only job will be to keep sweet and do as your husband commands. Your sister wives will be with you when your subservience is tested. Rely on them and do not fight your husband."

None of it had made sense at the time and she had looked forward to marriage. Now she knew that sister wives stayed with the very young brides on their wedding night and helped pacify them for their new husbands. The entire practice was abominable. Eve knew she held on to a lot of guilt over the fact she would have gone along with everything in order to attain the lowest rung in heaven, which Aaron had convinced her was the only shot she had.

"I'm starting on the second Mrs. Tanner," George said, breaking into her memories.

Eve walked back to the autopsy table and watched as he began the same methodical examination of Tracy. Tape residue was also found on her wrists and ankles. She had much heavier bruising on the backs of her thighs. George again found signs of sexual assault. Eve stood there throughout, trying to remain focused and not allow her mind to wander to the attic.

It was finally time for Elijah. He had the same tape residue but his physical injuries were far more pronounced. Elijah's hips, thighs, and legs were covered in belt marks. Some had broken the skin and healed, while others were open sores. He had been severely beaten. It was hard for Eve to hold her anger in.

He had suffered so much more than his horrific death. George's next pronouncement made it hard to hold back a scream. Elijah had been sexually assaulted.

Clyde's eyes held pure fury. He and Eve were standing on the edge of a very steep cliff. George made it clear the bruises and sexual abuse were not a one-time thing. His tone had changed and his cheery disposition was gone. Marcella, Tracy, and Elijah were all subjected to an unimaginable monster.

George saw more tragic abuse and death than Eve could imagine and he was having as much trouble with this as they were.

Bart, the person who held absolute power over this family, the most likely source of their torture, was dead. It didn't make her feel better.

When the autopsy was over, the tech wheeled Elijah's body away. Eve and Clyde followed George out of the room. He ripped off his face mask and turned to them.

"I don't know who is responsible for what happened to this

family. Obviously, the deaths were not caused by the man lying in the refrigerator. He could have been the one to blame for all the other pain, maybe not. I don't often ask for follow-up but I do want to sleep at night. Find out what happened and let me know."

He assured them he would email the toxicology results as soon as they came in.

Eve had never seen George upset. Clyde rested a hand on the other man's shoulder before they walked out. George's chin jerked and Eve could read the emotion behind his thick glasses.

Before they got into the SUV, Clyde walked over to the passenger side and pulled her into his arms. She allowed his warmth to settle against her body. Like her taking his hand in the car on the drive here, they needed this comfort.

Eve wished suddenly she was a different person and the mountain of baggage she carried was not between them. This man, with his intelligence and compassion, was what she needed. It had simply never been brought home like this. They were friends. Best friends. She was more determined than ever to make their new relationship work.

"Our thoughts are in a bad place," Clyde said after he turned out of the parking lot and jumped on the freeway.

"Shouldn't they be?" she asked.

"We need to keep an open mind. Even though we think your stepbrother is covering for someone, the only way we discover who did this is to find out the why." He stopped for a moment.

Eve waited.

"You lived within the community. You hold possible answers. Maybe it's time you accept your past and stop being angry over what you were unable to change."

Eve turned her head and looked out the window at the darkening sky. They hadn't eaten and she was not hungry.

"Eve?" he asked, and she turned back to him. "You are not

responsible for the time you spent with them. You were a child. You will never be able to forgive yourself because there is nothing to forgive. You would have left even without your mother. I know you. Those monsters could not have kept you under their delusional control. It's not who you are."

FIFTEEN

"Your hair is ugly," nine-year-old Aaron had jibed, pulling on the front so it fell from its high swoop. With his other hand he made sure the mess could not be easily fixed.

Eve had lived in the house for one year. She was now five. She had many siblings and most of them ignored her. Not Aaron though. He liked to tease and make her cry. Crying was forbidden and she was sent to bed without supper if she were caught. It was easier to remain silent, like now.

She avoided him whenever she could. He scared her and the rules confused her. She wanted to play; she remembered going to the park. They didn't have parks at her new home. She scrubbed pots and pans with steel pads that cut her small fingers. She helped strip the beds and remake them after the sheets were washed. She was told that idle hands were a sin.

Occasionally she would look down from an upper window and see her brothers being lazy, sitting on the yard's fence doing nothing. It wasn't fair. There was always work for the girls to do. Everything she did to have fun was a sin, but not for the boys.

"You must keep sweet," her mother told her after she complained about Aaron pulling on her hair.

"I don't want to," young Eve said stubbornly while they stood in the bathroom, her mother with a brush in her hand. At least now Eve wasn't waiting on her sisters, like she did in the morning, for her turn to get her hair done.

Her mother gave her a look that Eve was accustomed to. Maggie did not like it when she spoke out.

"It is a sin to complain," her mother said. "God watches you always. Heaven is only for those who are pure of heart."

Eve stomped her foot and crossed her arms.

"Eve," her mother said harshly. "You will be punished if you act out. We cannot leave here. This is where we're safe. You must keep sweet," she repeated.

She jerked on Eve's hair as she brushed and secured it so the front puffed up again. She then adjusted Eve's dress over the layers underneath it. The material was hot and uncomfortable. The boys could wear pants and shirts. They could run.

She didn't know why they had to stay here. When Eve asked, her mother would say it was where they were safe. Maggie was afraid of the man who hurt her before and Eve didn't understand. The mean man was only a vague memory.

Right now, she hated Aaron, even though it was a sin to hate your brother. She would try to keep sweet if anyone watched. She had to pretend she was worthy for God. She wasn't very good at it and she wanted to run away.

The day after Aaron pulled out her hair, he pushed her down.

"God punishes you because you are beneath everyone in this family. You are an apostate."

Eve knew that was a very bad word and it scared her.

"The devil is in your soul," he continued, and kicked her down while she was trying to scramble up, her long dress getting caught in her legs.

"I'm as good as you," she argued back, even though she knew she shouldn't. "I hate you," she yelled.

Aaron was chosen by God. He had natural righteousness that Eve did not. She didn't even know what that big word meant. She did know she was the sinner because Aaron never got into trouble for the things he did.

She was trying to push up with her hand but he shoved her back again and then stomped down on her fingers. She screamed and he ran away. One of her mothers came into the room. She gave Eve a look of disgust, bent down and lifted her hand.

One finger was crooked and it hurt. She continued crying.

"Stop bawling, you wicked girl. God is watching you."

The threat didn't work. Her pain was worse than God's punishment. Maggie arrived and sat on the floor with Eve.

"It's broken," Maggie told the other woman, her hand wiping Eve's tears away, trying to comfort her.

"It just needs to be straightened." She reached over, grabbed Eve's hand from Maggie's, and jerked her finger.

Eve screamed and Maggie carried her upstairs to the bedroom she shared with another of Eve's mothers.

"I'm sorry, baby," she said, and held Eve in her arms. "I'm so sorry."

Her mother could not keep sweet that night and she cried after she thought Eve was sleeping. Eve didn't like seeing her mother upset. Her finger throbbed but she promised God she would try harder.

Eve glanced down at the finger that had been broken so long ago. She rubbed it with her other hand. They were in her hotel room with the entire team, going over the autopsy findings.

"We know it's Bart Tanner," Ray said, his expression controlled, his anger only showing in his hard gaze.

Child molestations were always difficult cases. The sum of

horrors done to the women and Elijah was something they needed time to grasp.

Clyde stayed quiet while Eve finished explaining the autopsy findings. Collin paced. Ray clenched his fists.

"How did you live this way?" Bina asked looking straight at Eve. "I'm sorry," she added before Eve could reply, "I shouldn't have asked that."

"It's okay," Eve said, rubbing her finger again. "I ask myself that all the time. I was a child and had no choice. At least I got out before I was an adult and didn't have that excuse."

She turned away from Clyde's sudden frown. She'd listened to what he said in the car. It was hard to hear, but what Clyde said was the truth. She wouldn't blame a child in one of her cases for believing in the fundamentalist lifestyle. She couldn't blame Elijah for what had happened to him. She needed to accept that she was not to blame for her earlier life.

It bothered her that she didn't think she would have left if Maggie hadn't rescued her. Clyde's faith that she would have was something she needed to think about. But not now. They had to discover what or who Aaron was protecting.

"They're evil," said Ray.

Clyde grunted.

"Where do we go from here?" Bina asked, and finally slipped a gummy bear into her mouth now that she was a bit calmer.

"Hannah, the one person who wasn't home." Eve's voice was clipped.

"Oh God," said Bina, understanding that Hannah was also a victim of Bart Tanner.

"Do you think she's in danger?" Clyde asked.

"We need to assume she is." Eve thought about how strange the case was. "We shouldn't take this to Aaron. He knows something. It's the same with the police chief. I wouldn't be surprised if the officers are aware too, possibly every man in this community."

"Family Services needs to take Hannah into custody," Clyde said.

"I agree." Eve nodded. "But you know how difficult that is and it takes time. Hannah is with family and we cannot prove she is in immediate danger. I have an idea."

Eve left the team and walked to the front lobby of the hotel. An East Indian woman worked the desk with her husband. She spoke heavily accented English.

"Are you aware of the murders that happened two days ago?" Eve asked with the proper amount of curiosity and decorum.

"Yes, I heard they died. Very sad," she said. "Very sad for the little girl who lost her family." The woman appeared to be in her fifties, a few inches shorter than Eve. She wore a bright-colored gown that represented her heritage. Eve thought it beautiful. It could not be easy for them to live here. The fundamentalist church would consider them abominations sent by the devil simply because of their dark skin.

"I'm trying to find the young girl," Eve told her. "Do you know where her aunt lives? She is taking care of the child."

"You are investigating, yes?" the woman asked.

"I am. Any help you could give would be useful." Eve smiled hopefully.

The woman made a phone call and spoke briefly to someone, asking about Hannah. She smiled after she disconnected.

"I'll write it down," she said. She handed a piece of paper to Eve when she was done.

If this hadn't worked, Eve would have asked at the convenience store a few blocks away. The last resort would have been getting the address from Aaron. He was blocking their investigation and she couldn't trust him at any juncture from here on out. She knew he was aware of the horrors that happened inside the Tanner home. The church had to be protected at all costs and Aaron was, at the very least, guilty of the silence that allowed the abuse to happen.

"Take Collin with you," Clyde said after she returned to the room and shared the information.

He was right: Collin needed to accompany her. With his Mormon affiliation, he was their best bet for cooperation from Mr. Wall.

They'd discussed their chances of having Hannah removed from the home. Family Services would need to be called in. It would take all night and they might not take custody. This was a delicate situation with the church and the law was not clear-cut.

Hundreds of children had been forcibly removed from their parents in Texas when the atrocities of the fundamentalist prophet became clear. The removal was horrendous for the children and, like the rest of the nation, Eve watched it unfold on national television. Most of the children should never have been taken away, but at the time it was a tough call. The secrecy in the church meant federal officers had no idea the extent of the child molestations. Utah took note of what happened in Texas. They were unlikely to remove if Eve could not show a clear and present danger. Hannah was with family and the county attorney who would carry weight in Family Services' decision was not on Eve's side. They decided to try and make contact themselves.

The home was fifteen minutes from the hotel and a little over a mile from the crime scene. Collin parked the SUV in front of the block wall. The house was the largest in the immediate area, three times the size of the Tanners' and even larger than the homes on quarter-acre lots around it.

It was after eight and there were no outside lights turned on. They used the headlamps from the SUV to see their way through the gate of the courtyard. Eve noticed a glow from two second-floor windows that she hadn't been able to see from where they had parked behind the outer wall. Collin activated his flashlight. The front of the home was almost identical to the Tanners' except this one had a separate garage to the right of the entry.

Eve knocked on the door. No one answered and after a full minute, she did it again. They waited. It required a third knock.

The man who finally answered was dressed in slacks and shirtsleeves. Howard Wall was unattractive, tall, and thin, much like their prophet. She didn't know his age but he appeared to be in his late forties. She knew he was younger than Bart. His pitted face was stark and angular. As a middle-aged man of the fundamentalist church, his looks would not concern him. Wives were assigned based on what God told the prophet, which was dictated by the amount of money a man handed over each month.

"What do you want?" he demanded angrily.

For now, Eve put aside the fact Aaron had lied to her about Mr. Wall being out of town.

"Mr. Wall," Collin began after Eve stepped back slightly. "I'm Detective Smith and this is Detective Bennet with the state's special task force. We need to speak with Hannah," Collin said with authority.

Eve was not someone the man before them would respect and she had to let Collin handle this. Mr. Wall stood straighter, his shoulders squaring. He quickly gazed at her, his expression reflecting exactly what he thought, and turned back to Collin.

"No one will be speaking to that child," he ground out.

Eve took note of the words, *that child*. It was another oddity she would add to the list. Children belonged to God. After the prophet was in prison for a year, he gave the command to kill every family pet. The men of the church took their dogs and cats into the street and executed them. If the prophet said God wanted the children in heaven with him, the men would gather the children and do the exact same thing. That was how their sick minds worked.

"We have reason to believe she's in danger. We're not leaving without speaking to her," Collin insisted.

"The child is sleeping." He looked at Eve again and placed his right hand on the doorframe, blocking them completely.

Collin didn't back down. "A visual would work."

Eve watched Mr. Wall closely. Something about him made her skin crawl. It could have been the revulsion he showed when he looked at her. For a moment he seemed to be considering Collin's request.

"No!" He forcefully slammed the door in their faces.

"I need to call Aaron," Eve said after they returned to the vehicle.

Her phone chimed and she looked down. Speak of the devil. *Call me*, the text said.

Collin's eyebrows rose when Eve showed him the message.

"They hate gossip, or so they say." She was trying to find humor in a humorless situation.

"Not gossiping travels fast here." He looked out the window. "Some days, I hate this job."

They were all worried about Hannah but there was little they could do. After a deep inhale, she dialed her brother with the call on speaker.

"Why would you bother the family?" Aaron bellowed as soon as she answered.

"You lied to me about Howard Wall going out of town." She didn't wait for his reply. "We have information that Hannah could be in danger. We need to at least see her even if she's sleeping."

"That won't happen. Her uncle said Hannah is distraught and hasn't spoken a word since she found out about the murders. Seeing a stranger would upset her worse. She also hasn't slept until now and Howard is not disturbing her. He wants to consult a doctor before she's interviewed. I guarantee she's safe."

It sounded plausible for anywhere but here. Going to a doctor took money out of church pockets. The hairs on the back of Eve's neck stood up.

"You can make that guarantee?" she demanded.

"I can."

"If something happens to Hannah, I swear you won't walk away with a job." As far as threats went, it would gain her nothing, but she couldn't help herself. "Do you want to explain why you lied?"

Her brother laughed without humor. "Everything is a conspiracy theory with you. He came home early." Aaron disconnected.

"You gave up too easily," Collin objected as soon as Eve glanced at him.

"I had my reasons. My stepbrother didn't ask about the evidence we have that would make us think Hannah was in danger. He didn't ask because he knows who did this."

Collin internalized his thoughts while heading back to the hotel and Eve did the same. They shared what they had with the team. No one felt Hannah was safe. The problem was Aaron would give plausible reasons to Family Services not to remove her. There was very little Eve could do at this point.

They knew Hannah possibly held the secrets that could unlock this case. Eve couldn't get rid of her fear that Hannah might not be alive long enough to share those secrets.

SIXTEEN

Before they left for the Tanner home the following morning, the team had a quick meetup in Eve's room. Ray had grabbed donuts so they promptly got high on sugar and caffeine before heading out. All but Clyde, who ate a protein bar. Collin drank a Red Bull to abide by the Word of Wisdom that didn't allow coffee. He shrugged his shoulders when they teased him about the hypocrisy.

Eve, on the other hand, was thankful the fundamentalist sect had split from the Mormon church before the Word of Wisdom was strictly followed. She craved coffee and had since she was a young child. She figured it was one of the reasons polygamist wives and children were able to work all day.

Feel exhausted, here, have another cup.

Eve reluctantly ate a donut, knowing her butt was nothing like Bina's and would not remain small on a steady diet of junk food. Her team stayed in shape but during a case, their diet was fast food and their exercise minimal. Eve longed for a home-cooked meal and a round at the gym. Soon.

Tamm called before they left.

"The news doesn't have much. On a brighter note, they're

making the fundamentalist church out to be almost as bad as they actually are. At least they got something right."

"Anything we need to know for the case?" Eve asked.

As embarrassing as it was, the media had a way of ferreting out information when people wouldn't talk to cops. She didn't worry about the news because she knew Tamm was a fanatic and would record every station.

"No, they're running on misinformation juice," Tamm replied.

"That juice could change today. Be ready." Eve didn't say why and Tamm knew not to ask. Some conversations were not appropriate over cell phones or even hard-wired lines. The molestation of a teenage boy and sexual assault of the wives would be big news. The autopsy passed through too many fingers and this information could be leaked at any time. Since she firmly believed Aaron knew about the assaults and abuse, Eve could only contain the knowledge with her team. If it worked in the church's favor to release the news first, her brother would do so.

"I'll let you know if things change," Tamm said.

The call ended and once again, Eve was grateful she had someone back at base in their corner.

The drive to the house was even more somber than it had been the day before. Media swarmed and photographers came close, placing their cameras against the tinted windows. One of the officers, now at four for crowd control, lifted both tapes for the van and SUV as they slowly rolled through the courtyard entrance.

First on their list was Luminol. The evidence had been packaged and delivered to the police department the previous day by Collin, Ray, and Bina. Spraying the Luminol on doors and walls would show a clearer picture of the crime. They had also lifted fingerprints from the home for comparisons with the ones taken at autopsy. The prints from the house were locked in the van along with the DNA evidence.

They sprayed room by room, beginning downstairs, where the only blood they thought they had found was on the front door jam. It was most likely a speck of ungodly dirt with no plausible explanation in the spotless house. When everything at a crime scene added up perfectly, there was a good chance it was staged. They were not dealing with that in this case. Too many dots did not connect.

The violence took place upstairs and the killer didn't track the blood to the lower floor. That made sense, with evidence the killer took a shower. Taking the time to wash the blood off their body showed they were unworried about being caught in the house after the killings and that they didn't want the evidence seen on them after they left. Chances were good that they had brought a change of clothes with them.

After meeting Howard Wall, a horrible thought nagged at Eve. What if he were the killer? They had so many unanswered questions. It left a ten-year-old girl in danger and they didn't have enough evidence to prove that danger came from inside the Wall home. Eve was impatient to discover the truth. For Hannah's sake, they had to solve this case.

They began spraying upstairs in the same order they approached the bodies. Bart's bedroom door and frame had partials of bloody smeared prints once the Luminol lit them. The fluorescence caused when Luminol and the oxidant reacted to blood only lasted for thirty seconds. Eve had her camera ready with a long-exposure lens to catch the images correctly.

A blood trail went from the parents' room to Tracy's and then to Elijah's. In the fluorescent blue glow, Collin, their blood spatter expert, saw a clear pattern. After Elijah, the killer had backtracked to Hannah's room. The blood drops on the far side of the hall floor showed the progress along with longer smears of blood most likely from shoes or feet. It would have been nice to have a full shoe or footprint but they weren't that lucky.

They followed the specks of blood straight to Hannah's closet. The killer still carried the dripping knife and the Luminol made it easy to track. It also showed body fluid on Hannah's closet door. The reddish-brown color, after the chemicals wore off, identified it as blood.

The killer was searching for Hannah. Because of her age, she would be the least likely threat. Her body size would also mean the sedative would make her sleep harder. The killer was not afraid of Hannah and took out their victims accordingly.

Shivers ran across Eve's arms when she photographed the bright glow smeared on the sleeves of two of Hannah's long dresses. The killer's search made Howard Wall less of a suspect because he would have known where she was. Eve hoped Hannah was safe. Living in this community, she knew it wasn't a good bet.

Luminol showed no bodily fluids in the unused bedroom. The killer knew which rooms were occupied, making it more probable it was someone who had once been a family member. Now Eve's thoughts once more turned to the possibility one of the wives, removed from the home, killed them out of revenge. Maybe Marcella and Tracy, though they were mistreated too, helped Bart Tanner in his abuse. The fact women kept other wives calm during their first sexual encounter, though horrifying, made this less of a stretch than it should have been.

Once they had the list of names and addresses from Aaron, they would need to make contact with any prior wife who remained in the community. She needed her stepbrother to come through with that list.

They finished the bedrooms and hallway and moved to the bathroom. The spray showed blood on the floor, shower walls, and rim of the tub where fluorescent marking outlined the horror. The towels and shower curtain had been bagged previously for evidence and were already at the police department. The killer only seemed to care about removing the blood from their body and not the room.

Ray packaged Hannah's dresses with the dark stains on them. They'd taken DNA the day before.

They saved the attic for last.

"We doing this?" Ray asked when he finished packaging the dresses and met them beneath the drop-down stairs in the master bedroom closet.

They knew the attic would be the worst room in the house. They'd all felt the evil in the walls and air. It wasn't a scientific response but it was a human one. Eve had also chosen her team for their empathy. This wouldn't be easy.

They removed the plastic and sprayed the stairs first. Blood showed on the steps of the ladder. Was it caused from the beatings? Eve had to clear her mind and focus on her job to continue. All their expressions were frozen by the time they climbed into the attic.

Spraying in sections made it easier for Eve to capture the needed photos. Luminol showed blood and other bodily fluids such as urine and semen. They didn't need lab work to know sperm was mixed with blood and they were looking at a scene out of a horror film. They'd taken previous samples for identification and DNA and they were fairly certain what they contained.

The attic was a torture chamber of punishment and humiliation. It made Eve sick. Children suffered in this room. The wives suffered. Even to Eve, with what she knew of the church, this was unimaginable.

They had to wait on labs for positive DNA found where it shouldn't have been on the bodies, but she knew Bart Tanner was responsible for this atrocity. He had absolute power over their household, which gave him an opportunity no one else had. There were six wives in the photograph from the drawer.

Were four of them removed because of his actions? When the details of the case became public record, the media would have a field day. Marcella and Tracy were the two women not removed. Had they threatened to speak out?

So many questions but the biggest one in Eve's mind: Was this reason enough for the church leaders to murder an entire family?

SEVENTEEN

"I want to do a complete walk-through the scene. We need to mentally picture the crime as it happened and see if it leads to anything we've missed," Eve told them after they finished with the Luminol. "We'll grab lunch from the van first and I'll print photos of the bodies as we found them."

Bina, Collin, and Ray entered the van but Eve lagged in the courtyard. Clyde gave her a questioning look.

"I need a moment," she told him.

"Do you want company?"

She nodded. He closed the van's door behind the others and stood beside her. She rotated her shoulders, hoping to relieve some of the stress. The warmth from the sun helped. She was desperately trying to drive away the demons after what she'd photographed in the attic.

Her fundamentalist father from childhood referred to demons as unclean spirits that entered the bodies of women who did not obey men. Men carried the words of the prophet who carried the words of God. These unclean spirits were one of his favorite topics during his daily prayers and teachings. She remembered holding little Charlie in her lap as he squirmed through the hours-long monologue while her father looked at her as if she was the demon. At age ten, thoughts of her wickedness kept her from sleeping many nights as she lay there expecting God to strike her down or send men to kill her. Maybe her father.

Clyde remained by her side while her thoughts kept her from focusing on the case. He was always the solid force she could lean upon. He deserved more than a psychologically damaged woman with a past that kept her from moving forward in a relationship.

He touched her side for only a moment, his hand warm and grounding. She was no longer the little girl. She oversaw a team who battled the evil of the fundamental polygamists. Without a word, Clyde followed her into the van with the others.

"Download the photos from your camera and I'll make the sandwiches," he said, and moved toward the cooler.

"Thank you, appreciated."

The others were already eating.

"Be sure to print a few from Hannah's room," he reminded her, "and Elijah's bed."

She transferred the images to her laptop then chose the ones she wanted to print.

They spoke quietly, aware the press still waited close by. Bina, Ray, and Collin finished their meals quickly, cleaned up and went back inside the home. After they left, Clyde walked over and placed his hands on Eve's shoulders, rubbing gently. He'd noticed her stress. It was hard to think of not having him as part of the team. It was something that bothered her about their new relationship. If it didn't work out, he might leave.

"Feel better?" he asked close to her ear a few minutes later.

"Yes, thank you."

"This case is getting to us all," he said. "Even Ray and Collin haven't been as irritating as usual."

Eve grimaced. He was right. They weren't bickering like a

married couple. The team had all handled homicides that included abuse and sexual assault before. They came from different regions of the state's homicide divisions. Bina had transferred from Salt Lake City Police two years before she joined Eve's team and had worked several cases that made headlines. This case with the Tanner family felt different. If it was driving Eve nuts, it was affecting her team the same way.

"How are you doing?" she asked.

"I want to know who did this. I just don't think it will be that simple." He grabbed the other chair and brought it closer. "This is a church cover-up and I don't trust what they might do to keep their secrets."

"I agree. I'm going to send Lieutenant Crosby an email outlining what we have. We may need assistance from another special crimes unit. I want him prepared for the request." The lieutenant was her supervisor. He mostly stayed out of her way and rarely commented on her cases. She kept him apprised of what they were doing and he made sure no one from the state police got in her way.

The printer stopped and it ended their conversation. She grabbed the stack of full-sized images and gave Clyde a brief smile before they left the van.

"Thank you for the neck rub."

His teeth flashed and Eve wanted to hug him so badly. It was times like this that she needed his quiet strength the most. The moment passed and she was sad she hadn't.

Collin, Ray, and Bina waited inside, ready to get started. They had re-created crimes like this before and it helped give them a clearer picture.

"I need a minute to line up the photos," Eve said, and shuffled them into the most likely order. If it changed, they were easily rearranged.

"No forced entry." She glanced at the others. "Nothing to

tell us if they used the front door or back so we'll assume the front." Everyone nodded. "Direct path upstairs. Let's go."

They climbed the stairs and reached the hallway. They looked closely at the dried blood left behind on the floor. There were maybe twenty drops in all. The blood never came close to the stairs, which led them to believe the killer went from room to room and ended at the bathroom. There was another door in the hallway that was a linen closet. The Luminol had shown no bodily fluid inside. The killer had used towels from the bathroom after they showered. This might have been in order to avoid leaving clear DNA traces.

Television was unheard of in the community so they didn't watch forensic shows. Eve still wouldn't count out that the killer knew not to use recently cleaned towels. It was one more thing that didn't quite add up.

"Does anyone disagree that Bart Tanner was killed first?" Eve asked.

"It's the most likely scenario," Collin said. If anyone were to disagree it would be him.

"Okay, master bedroom," Eve told them.

They entered the room and spread out around the bed. Eve stood at the foot, toward the middle, taking the position from where she shot the images of Bart and Marcella that encapsulated the scene best.

"The killer had to get behind them," said Ray. He walked to the side of the bed and crawled onto it. After the bloody sheets had dried, they were removed and packed as evidence. There were still dark spots on the mattress. "The easiest way would be to put my knees beneath the pillow and grab his head."

"Agreed," said Bina as she moved closer.

"They were clean cuts, both from left to right," Eve said, repeating what George had told her and Clyde. George had also clarified that the cuts were performed by the killer using his right hand, the deeper cuts to the throat on the left side of the neck.

Ray made the motion with his right hand. "He would have waited for him to die before moving over. Tanner didn't fight. Would he walk around or slide across?" he asked.

Eve didn't correct the use of *he*. Her past and what Bart had done to his family brought a woman to the forefront as the suspect in her mind now that she was fairly sure Howard wasn't responsible. Her team would have their own conclusions and each would have a chance to enlighten the others. *He* was also commonly used as reference when they didn't know the gender.

"I'd slide," said Collin. "No visible spatters on this side of the bed, just blood that came from his throat. It could cover drops from the knife but there isn't a trail." He walked to the opposite side where Marcella's body had been and squatted down to look closely at the carpet. "There are some here." Collin stood. "The direction of the spatter shows the killer didn't walk around. He got off the bed on Marcella's side and walked to the foot then straight out the door. Slide over," he said when no one argued.

Ray moved and repeated his gruesome movement with the knife once he was in place.

He waited a minute and climbed off the bed holding his fist upward.

"He would have carried it low, at his side," said Collin. "The directional spatter is minuscule, which means the knife was closer to the carpet. He had to have carried it with his hand down at his side or the spatters would have shown they came from a greater distance. I noticed the same thing in the hallway."

Ray lowered his hand and they followed him outside the bedroom door.

"Tracy's room next," Ray said, and they followed.

He entered the room and crawled onto the bed. He

repeated what happened in the master bedroom. They trailed him to Elijah's room. There were still bloodstains on the wall behind where the boy's head would have been.

"The cut to his throat wasn't clean like the others," Clyde said. The autopsy evidence matched the crime scene.

Elijah being killed last meant the suspect's clothes were already covered in blood. When the return came in on the DNA from the bed of each victim, it would most likely show a combination and would pinpoint the order of the murders precisely. The house would be released by then but they could walk through it in their minds using Eve's photos if the scenario changed at all. Hopefully they would have a suspect in custody but they still had to have an airtight case for trial.

Ray got on the bed, his back to the wall.

"He started fighting, which caused the blood behind the pillow," Collin said. "The killer would have moved with Elijah to keep the knife at his throat to try and finish the job."

"Did he wrestle his assailant to the floor or did the person get off the bed and watch him bleed out?" Eve asked.

"Could have gone either way but we don't have footprints with blood on them, which is strange. Nothing close to the other two beds, either."

They thought about it for several minutes.

"Could he have been pushed off the bed?" asked Collin.

"More likely fallen," said Clyde.

They examined the images and moved to the bathroom next.

Bina stood looking in the bathroom. "The killer brought clothing. It's the only explanation."

No one could disagree.

"Any other scenarios?" asked Eve, moving beside Bina, each with a shoulder touching the doorframe.

"The blood trail is all we have to go on and how we just

walked the scene is the most likely scenario," Collin said, looking at the spots in the hallway again.

"Let's go back down to the table and lay out the photos in order," Eve told them now that they had an outline of the homicides in their heads.

She started laying them out from the left end of the table, then began again below the first picture to make a second row. Her team spread around the table, pulling in their chairs so they could get a closer look.

A few seconds after Eve laid down the last photo, Bina turned to the front door.

"Did you hear that? A woman's voice?"

Bina was up and moving before they understood what they were hearing. She threw the door open. A police officer, inside the inner crime scene tape, had his arms wrapped around a woman in a yellow dress. He was trying to carry her out of the small gap left between the wall and the van. Her feet and arms flailed and she yelled out again.

"Let her go," Bina demanded, and ran toward them.

The officer ignored her and didn't release the woman. Clyde grabbed the uniformed arm. The media was looking through the same small gap and Eve wasn't sure how much they could see.

"Stand down," Clyde told the officer.

The woman wrenched herself away and the officer's attention turned to Clyde, his hand going to his gun. "This does not concern you," he sneered. "She needs her husband."

Eve's hand moved to her side, closer to her own gun, as Collin and Ray stepped between the woman and the officer, blocking the view of the journalists. Clyde dropped his arm and stepped back, his eyes going pointedly to the officer's hand. Slowly the man relaxed his grip and his fingers slid from the holster.

The woman, breathing heavily, backed toward Eve, then turned.

"I must speak with you. Please," she begged.

She looked familiar, blonde hair in its high front poof making her prominent forehead stand out even more. It dawned on Eve: she was an Owens. It took another few seconds to register it was her stepsister Sheila, who had married before Eve left.

"I don't want to live with him," Sheila had cried to Eve the day before she was taken from their home. Her mother had only told her of the marriage that morning. "He's old. I don't care what the prophet says. I'll run away." She'd stayed even though she cried all night.

Her husband-to-be was their Uncle Thomas and he was older than their father. He had squinty eyes and walked hunched over slightly. Eve dreaded her sister leaving the house and she didn't think their uncle would be nicer than their father. The two men were very similar.

Her stepsister left the following day. From then on Eve only saw her in church and never saw her smile again. Sheila was not allowed to speak to her siblings and had to stay loyal to her new family. Eve shivered internally at the memory of her stepsister's fear that long last night and moved closer to Sheila, giving her a quick nod.

Another officer crossed the inner tape and joined the first. Was this the reason Aaron had arranged extra scene coverage? Was he trying to keep the women from speaking to them? It wouldn't surprise her.

"This is my crime scene," she told the officers. "You have crossed the inner tape against direct orders. I want a full written report of this incident within twenty-four hours. I will also call Chief Jackson and inform him of what happened here." She said it loud enough for the media to hear. The officers had no choice but to back down. They didn't blink over her threat to call their chief. They knew he wouldn't care. The fact they hadn't stopped Sheila would cause more trouble for them than disobeying orders.

"Please step into the van with Detective Blau. I'll be right behind you," she told Sheila, purposefully not using her name, hoping against the odds that the officers didn't know who her husband was. The color dress she wore would identify her and her sister wives as belonging to the same man.

Collin, Ray, and Clyde stood beside her until the officers returned to the outer perimeter. This was another reason Clyde was on their team. He kept his cool in violent situations and he was always prepared when a threat escalated. She would send the report of this incident to Judge Remki. Maybe someday the reports would be enough to get rid of local law enforcement and start over in this entire area.

"Clear everyone fifty feet beyond the second tape while I speak with her," she told the guys. "There's a reason they don't want her talking to us and it's time to discover why."

Before Eve stepped into the van, muscle memory moved her hand to her pocket and she flipped the switch that turned on her recorder.

"Detective Blau, please stand outside the door and see we aren't disturbed." This was said for Sheila's benefit.

Behind the front seats, there were two bench seats along the sidewalls facing each other. Overhead cabinets were high enough that even Clyde could sit comfortably. Eve sat beside Sheila and offered a gentle smile.

It was the first time she'd seen her stepsister in over twenty years. She was one of Eve's few siblings who had been nice.

Sheila was disheveled. The back of her hair was half out of its braid. The front swoop was sticking out in odd places. Her dress had dust on the hem and she had a smear of dirt on her face. They were the same blue eyes, though time had given her soft lines at the corners more prominent than Eve's. Her jaw was clenched and her rapid breathing showed how upset she was. Standing up to the officers, men of the church, went against everything she'd been taught.

"I didn't know if you would remember me," she finally said, joining her trembling fingers together.

Eve smiled again. "You wiped my tears enough times. I don't think I could ever forget you."

Sheila had been nice to everyone. She made keeping sweet appear easy. Eve may have been a little jealous. They both had hopes and dreams of marrying one of the boys they saw at church. Neither had any idea what marriage meant back then. It was a way out of the house. They'd hoped their husband wouldn't be as strict as their father, whose only allowance outside their structured life was monthly ice cream day. Her stepsister had not gotten her wish.

Sheila closed her eyes for a moment. When she opened them, the strain still showed.

"The entire community hates you," she said softly. "I don't know why you came back."

Eve swallowed, finding it surreal to be talking to her. "I came so what happened to little Charlie and Becky would never happen again," she said honestly. Sheila had wiped so many of the tears after Charlie was taken. There was more Eve wanted to tell her but she couldn't risk alienating her.

Her stepsister's attention turned to Eve's hair, then her clothes. Eve's pants and blouse were far from modest. Condemnation changed Sheila's expression.

It hurt but Eve hid the pain. After the run-in with her stepbrothers, she shouldn't be surprised. They were fully indoctrinated adults and no longer impressionable children.

Sheila glanced away and her eyes skimmed the inside of the van, looking at the drawers and cabinets that held their evidence supplies.

"When I heard you were taken," she said, the criticism

strong in her voice, "I thought they would find you and bring you home. When that didn't happen, I hoped you would escape and return."

Eve had never considered that the church would look for her. It was something she needed to ask her mother about. It might explain some of Maggie's continued fear after she had Eve back with her.

She had a quick flash of Maggie after Eve had run from their small apartment one day and hidden in the bushes across the street for hours. Her mother was shaking when Eve had finally come out and Eve hadn't understood.

"You cannot leave the apartment," Maggie had yelled after they went back inside. "You are not safe out there." To Eve, this was a way her mother, an apostate, kept Eve from keeping sweet. The apartment had too many worldly items such as a radio and television.

Eve closed down the memory.

"What was there to return to?" she asked Sheila. "You were the only one who was pleasant to me and you were gone."

"Devotion to God and the prophet," was her stepsister's quick reply.

Their conversation today would not change Sheila's beliefs. It took years to overcome the brainwashing. Sheila had to want out first. She had spent her entire life within the community and quite possibly would never leave. Eve had to accept that.

"Why are you here?" Eve asked bluntly.

Her stepsister inhaled deeply then released the breath, glancing down and not meeting her eyes. "One of my sisters came from this home. She's been upset about the deaths." Sheila looked up at Eve. "More than upset. She thinks the person who killed them will come for her. My husband, Craig, punished Candace for acting out and she's remanded to her room. This isn't like her. My husband said what happened here is God's retribution for the Tanners' sins. Speaking of their family has been forbidden."

Sheila's husband knew what Bart Tanner had been doing. And, if he did, the other men of the church did too.

"I need your address and your husband's full name," Eve said. She couldn't help feeling glad that Sheila was no longer with Uncle Thomas.

Sheila's shoulders stiffened and she shook her head.

"I'm investigating four homicides," Eve said, her voice firm. "If you live in the area, we would be interviewing your family eventually."

This was their first lead and Eve needed this information.

"Craig Wilson is the third husband God granted me," Sheila said, giving in. "He will know I came here. I knew I would be punished when I made the decision to speak to you."

"How old is Candace?" Eve asked after writing down the address.

"She is twenty. She's terrified of something. I—" She stopped and looked down. "She's had trouble since she was married into the family. She has nightmares."

Eve couldn't imagine what it would be like to live within the Tanner home. Eve's stepfather was strict and his punishments harsh. Nothing he did to her or Sheila compared to the atrocities Bart Tanner committed.

"I need to leave," Sheila said, and abruptly stood.

"I know what you've risked by coming here," Eve told her.

"Do you? My sin may be forgiven." The hardness entered her eyes again. "You walk beside the devil and do his bidding. You will be condemned to the fires of hell."

Arguing would not help at this point. "How far is your home?" Eve asked wearily. Fear brought her sister here. A greater fear for Candace than that of Eve's damnation rubbing off on her.

"A few miles," Sheila said.

"Did you drive?"

"No."

Walking several miles explained her disheveled appearance.

"I need to interview Candace. We don't know who did these murders. She could be in danger."

Sheila gave a small nod. Her sisters would condemn her for coming to Eve. Her husband would punish her. The church might take her children away and reassign her to another husband. She'd taken a huge risk. Even though Sheila's attitude hurt, Eve appreciated that she came.

"You should interview her now before my husband returns or before someone from the church arrives."

"Thank you."

They stepped out of the van and Eve opened the door of the SUV for Sheila. She gave her team a quick narrative of the conversation.

"Bina, I want you with me in the vehicle. I don't expect a warm reception and it's likely her husband will show up if he isn't there already." She looked at Clyde. "Thank you for keeping your cool."

"They're on edge. We need to figure out what's going on. Hopefully, you'll get answers."

"The media will follow when I leave. I want someone staying here inside the house. Two of you follow in the van to hold the media back."

Clyde volunteered to stay behind. Ray and Collin had media control. Eve climbed into the passenger seat. Bina drove. It didn't take long to reach Sheila's home. They pulled up to a house that she pointed out. It was also larger than the Tanners'. Bina drove through the open double gate of the courtyard. Ray and Collin would keep the media behind the white brick.

Maybe they would finally have answers.

EIGHTEEN

"How many sisters do you have?" Eve asked.

"Ten."

Sheila made eleven wives total. There was nothing Eve could do about Sheila's perspectives on marriage or anything connected to the polygamist church. She kept her feelings to herself.

"Who will give us the most trouble?" she asked. The hierarchy of women would save Eve time.

"Sister Kathryn."

"Do you have advice to deal with her?" From experience, Eve knew forcefulness when dealing with the women got results quicker but it never hurt to ask.

"Insist on speaking with Candace."

Bina stayed in the vehicle with Sheila. Collin and Ray were keeping the media back but the men from the church would show up eventually. There was no way they could stop them from entering the courtyard.

When Eve's team spoke to women in the community, the men always objected. Everything the women did was monitored to keep them in line. The fear of damnation was also used. The men didn't want the women speaking to anyone outside their immediate home. Talking to Eve or members of her team caused punishment, sometimes severe.

A woman, maybe in her early forties, dressed exactly like Sheila, opened the front door and stepped outside before Eve climbed from the SUV.

"That is Sister Kathryn," Sheila whispered.

Kathryn had left the front door open behind her. Eve closed the car's door and stepped forward. The older woman tried to see behind the SUV's dark windows.

"I'm Detective Sergeant Eve Bennet. I'm here to interview Candace," she said. "I need her out here immediately."

"What have you done?" the woman shouted at the car. Eve walked past her to the front door. "You can't go inside. Leave at once," the woman called.

Eve spoke loudly so her voice carried inside the home. "I'm here to interview Candace Wilson about four homicides. I can get a court order or call the county attorney to intervene. Will that be necessary?"

It took less than a minute before a small woman stepped to the door looking nervously past her to Kathryn.

"Are you Candace Wilson?" Eve asked.

"Yes."

"Candace, do not speak to her," Kathryn insisted.

Eve turned and lifted her hand to Bina. She stepped out of the vehicle at the same time Sheila opened the back door.

"Detective Blau, stand between the house and the SUV while I conduct the interview." She turned slightly to Sheila. "Do you wish to stay out here or go inside?"

"I'll go inside," Sheila said, not looking at the older woman. It surprised Eve when she stopped where Candace was and spoke to Kathryn. "I had to do what was right."

"Your sins are counted; you know the punishment. How could you?" Kathryn's anger needed an outlet and unfortunately Sheila would receive the brunt of it.

Eve pointed Candace to the SUV and closed the doors against the argument. Threats against Sheila would not help this interview. Eve needed her to talk openly. Sheila was on her own when it came to punishment and Eve could not interfere. Her stepsister knew there would be a penalty. Eve had to get Candace talking before her husband arrived. If he forbade her cooperation, Eve could walk away empty-handed.

She checked to be sure her recorder was on before climbing into the driver's seat. Candace worriedly watched the interaction between Kathryn and Sheila, their voices faint through the glass. Eve could see her panic building and needed to get her attention off the women.

"Candace," Eve said, which made the young woman turn. "This isn't the greatest place to do an interview but it's vital I speak with you. You were married to Bart Tanner, correct?"

Her large eyes held tears and her hands shook as she nervously fluffed her dress. Her gaze darted to Kathryn and Sheila again. She looked younger than twenty, her round face very unlike Sheila's. She had strawberry-blonde hair and green eyes. Her front teeth were slightly crooked.

"I need your help," said Eve calmly.

"My help?" Candace finally asked, her attention fully turning to Eve.

"You were removed from the Tanner home and I need to know why."

Candace stared at her as she decided what to say. Eve had interviewed too many women from the polygamist community not to see the signs. She wanted to talk but church rules were getting in the way. She did not have her husband's permission to speak with Eve.

"I desperately need your help, please," she implored.

Candace's expression changed slightly. "The church reassigned me and several of my former sisters. Our children too. God knew what was best for us."

"Why were you reassigned?"

Candace stared at her for a long moment then dropped her eyes to her lap. "One of my sisters complained to the bishop," she finally said.

Keep sweet ran through Eve's head. Women accepted what God gave them to bear. It didn't matter what Bart Tanner had done.

"What did she complain about?" Eve pushed.

Candace shook her head without looking up.

"We will need fingerprints and DNA swabs from you to compare with what we found in the attic."

Candace panicked and for a second, Eve thought she would leave the car. Instead, she pulled her dress up to her mouth and screamed into the material. It was a sound Eve would never forget. Fundamentalist women were taught to never show emotion. The attic was a terrible memory and this young woman had suffered unimaginable horrors in that room.

Candace stopped screaming and pulled her legs up, curling her body inward, rocking within the confines of the seat.

"Candace?" Eve asked softly. "Do you know who killed the Tanners?"

She continued rocking, Eve's words not getting past her misery.

"I should have killed him. I hated him," she finally said.

Husbands held the priesthood and only they could attain heaven. A wife must be pulled up by her father until she was of age and then the decision went to the man she married. Candace's admission showed the horror Bart's wives suffered.

"Were you there when he died?" Eve asked.

Candace shook her head.

"Where were you the night he was killed?" Eve needed to establish if Candace had an alibi.

She didn't answer.

"Four people died. Two were your sister wives. Elijah was a child. I need your help but I need to know where you were the night they were murdered."

"I was home," she whispered, her body still moving back and forth.

"Do you have someone who can confirm that?"

"Yes."

"Was everyone accounted for on the night of the murders?"

Candace stopped rocking and turned her face slightly toward Eve.

"I don't know," she whispered.

She was lying.

"You do know. Elijah needs me to find who murdered him."

Candace cried into her dress again. "Elijah was guilty too," she said angrily when she glanced back up.

Eve had not expected this. Did Candace not realize Elijah was forced into whatever he did? When you interview someone, you keep your expression neutral. Eve's mask slipped.

"You know what men are capable of," Candace accused. "Don't act like you don't. I know you were one of us. You know what it's like here."

"You can leave. Is that what you want? I can help you."

Candace shook her head. "I have two babies. Bart can't have them." The statement didn't make sense.

"He can't hurt them now," Eve said softly. "He's dead. If you want to leave, there is a way out."

"Is he really dead? Did you see his body?"

"I can't go into detail but he was murdered along with Marcella and Tracy. I did see his body." Eve didn't mention

Elijah. "Help me, please. Was everyone accounted for on the night of the murders?" Eve repeated.

Candace took a deep breath and interlocked her shaking fingers. "Kathryn left the house after our husband went to bed. I don't know where she was but she came home around three."

"Was Kathryn one of Bart's former wives? Would she have reason to kill them?"

This fit the scenario in Eve's head that the crime pointed to a woman. However, she needed a motive.

"No, Kathryn is my husband's first wife."

"Is there another reason Kathryn would have hurt the Tanners?"

She stared at Eve. Her eyes darted out the window. Sheila had gone inside. Kathryn was glaring at the vehicle but Bina's presence kept her from approaching.

"I had a nightmare and I told her what happened in that home. It was two days before they died."

Eve now had motive at least for Bart Tanner's death. Revenge for harming Candace. It was weak but they had nothing else at this point.

"Did you see her leave the house that night?"

Candace shook her head. "No. One of the children had a nightmare and I couldn't calm her down. I went to find Kathryn and she was gone."

"What time was this?"

She shrugged her shoulders. "Around midnight. She came home shortly after three. She told me to go to bed when I asked where she went."

"What time does your husband go to bed?"

"Ten, every night after prayer."

"Do you think Kathryn killed them?"

"No." She shook her head sharply. "She was angry Marcella and Tracy hadn't left when they had the chance. She wouldn't hurt my sisters. Kathryn said it was our sin, not Bart's, but I was smart to leave."

Eve pushed back her memories. It was always the women and girls who carried sin.

"Did you notice anything strange about the way Kathryn was dressed when she returned to the house? Did she carry any type of bag or other clothing?"

Candace shook her head.

Eve did not have enough to make an arrest at this point or even obtain a search warrant. Could Kathryn have taken food to them that had been drugged? It was possible but Eve couldn't see them answering the door and eating something brought that late at night. It was more likely the sedative was placed in their dinner. Eve tried to work it out in her head. Evidence showed one person murdered the family but it didn't rule out somebody else helping with the drugs.

Candace interrupted her thoughts.

"Kathryn did not kill them," she fervently stated.

"Why do you think that?" Eve asked, puzzled.

"She knows my previous husband's sins do not belong to him. He must have gotten in the way and that's why he died."

"Kathryn left the house the night of the homicides and you don't think she's involved?"

"No." She looked away and Eve could feel the lie.

"Sister Sheila told me you were afraid. Is that because you feel you should be punished?"

"He said it was our sins that made him do horrible things. I—"

Two vehicles pulled into the inner courtyard and interrupted Candace. A man got out of the first car and Aaron stepped from the second. Eve knew the officer at the Tanners' home would call someone up his chain of command. It took them longer to get here than Eve expected.

"Is that your husband?" she asked.

"Yes."

"Is there anything else you can tell me?" She wanted to ask about the attic but with her previous reaction and her husband's arrival, she couldn't.

"I think Kathryn knows who killed them."

NINETEEN

Aaron was furious, which didn't surprise Eve. Candace's husband immediately ushered the women inside the house. Bina approached her quickly.

"Be the eyes and ears," Eve muttered, and turned to her stepbrother.

"You have no right to be here," were his first words. His jaw was locked in anger, his blue eyes pinpoints of displeasure.

Eve remembered the disquiet in his gaze when they were children. She'd suffered the consequences repeatedly. She was no longer that young girl without recourse. She was standing within her stepbrother's church domain with the judge's authority behind her and she was tired of his never-ending interference. If she allowed anger to lead, she would lose this battle. She bit her tongue and reined in her resentment before speaking.

Mr. Wilson stepped back outside but it didn't stop her.

"I am conducting a homicide investigation and have every right to be here. I will interview the women of this home." She stopped and turned to Mr. Wilson. "Those interviews will take place immediately." He simply glared. Wearing a suit, he obviously worked something besides a contracting job. He was somewhere in his forties, which was young for such a large family. She looked back at her brother. "I also need that list of Tanner's prior wives so I can interview them too."

A huge truck roared into the yard. Aaron didn't look at it so he knew who it was. Eve stopped speaking and watched two men climb from the vehicle. They were backup for Aaron.

"Brother Owens," one of the men greeted her stepbrother.

"Brother Hammond, Brother Bockstater," Aaron acknowledged, and they shook hands. The two men wore suits and ties. Both appeared to be in their sixties. Eve wondered where they stood in church hierarchy. She didn't recognize the names.

The seed bearers would be middle-aged to older men. The thought disgusted her. Everything about these men did, even if they weren't the chosen. She shouldn't carry this preconceived dislike but this case was bringing out the worst in her.

"Detective Bennett was just leaving," Aaron told them, which brought her focus back to him.

Eve stepped closer to her stepbrother and addressed the two men who had not bothered to look at her. It gave her reason to believe they were involved in whatever the church was covering up.

"I'm investigating the Tanner murders, as you're aware. I have full authority to go where the investigation leads. I will be interviewing each woman in this home." She turned and shot Aaron a cold look. "I will say when I leave." She then gave her attention to Mr. Wilson. "We'll start the questions now and do them in my vehicle. They should be short and not disturb your household more than necessary."

Mr. Wilson looked over Eve's head and addressed the men.

"I'm sure you can handle this from here. My family needs prayer." He turned and entered the house, closing the door solidly behind him.

Eve caught the angry flash in Bina's eyes. It wasn't the first time something like this had happened. It always pointed to church cover-up that Eve's team was unable to prove.

The man addressed as Brother Hammond turned his gaze to Aaron and gave a small nod. Aaron moved back a step.

This shocked Eve. She realized whoever these men were, they held power over the county attorney and Aaron did their bidding without hesitation.

Hammond turned his head only slightly in Eve's direction. He didn't meet her gaze, treating her as a lowly apostate who wasn't worth his regard. He had no problem speaking as long as there was no eye contact.

"This house and the believers inside are off-limits to you. The community has suffered a tremendous loss and it has affected us all. A good family died and they deserve justice. Someone from outside our community did this and if you do your investigation correctly, you will discover the truth. Now you will leave this home."

The man's tone held fanatical belief that every word he said was that of God. He did not understand that Eve, as a lowly woman, did not answer to him. Her recorder was still on and the audio file would be emailed to the judge as soon as Eve left. She also knew the chances were high that the women would disappear. It was what the church did best. This moment was not hers. Without another word, Eve gave Bina a small nod and they both went to their vehicle. They drove away quickly.

Collin and Ray followed, the media trailing behind.

"I shouldn't wear my gun when I'm around those people." Bina's words broke the silence, though Eve's glare continued burning up the road in front of them.

"Their views will never change," Eve said after a deep inhale.

"Do we have a lead now?" Bina's question finally calmed Eve's nerves.

"Kathryn Wilson was not home the night of the homicides. Candace thinks Kathryn knows who committed the murders."

"Okay." Bina drew out the word. "Is there a possibility the murderer is Kathryn Wilson?"

"Maybe. She only has a slight motive. Candace told Kathryn what happened in the attic two days before the homicides. It's weak. We still have a child alive from the Tanner home who we haven't interviewed." Eve took another slow steady breath. "If it was Kathryn, we need to find out if she has been inside the Tanners' house. With the rules against friendships outside the family, she shouldn't have been. We'll need a warrant to obtain her prints and DNA. I doubt they are on file. Knowing she wasn't home the night of the homicides is likely not enough to gain that warrant."

"We've been here before," Bina said. "We need to break it down as a team." She was right. Looking at ways around impossible situations was what they did best.

"If the church is involved in the Tanner deaths—at the very least, covering who did them—they will remove the women out of state or the country. It's the only duck and cover they know." Eve was thinking out loud. Maybe she could get the judge to call Aaron and put the fear of the court in his prophet-worshiping head.

"When I compare this to past cases," Bina added, "nothing about this makes sense. We don't have a tail and haven't had one since we arrived. I know we've been over this but it's bothering me more and more. The church does everything they can to impede us and the intimidation squad, or God squad, as you call it, follows us everywhere. They never let up and make sure we know their authority comes directly from God. On this case, we'd been left completely alone until the suits arrived on the Wilsons' doorstep. It's like they think we're bumbling fools and if they just give us space, we'll stumble our way to the wrong conclusion."

Eve's thoughts were racing. Everything Bina said was true. When Eve first took the job, she saw a conspiracy around every corner. She'd had to remind herself to keep an open mind for the sake of her cases.

Now her brain was filling with conspiracies that could be true. She didn't see how a simple man from the church committing these murders would cause the cover-up. They would hang him out to dry, allowing the media stories to die as quickly as they started. If, on the other hand, one of the wives, put through years of abuse, killed the Tanners, it could cripple the church again. The last thing they wanted were journalists taking notice of their atrocious practices in the name of God. They'd been down that road before and practically lost everything. Or another possibility was someone high up in their organization. A seed bearer, maybe, or the bishop. The team needed to think the possibilities through.

"The county attorney was afraid of Hammond. Maybe he's the bishop," Bina said.

"That wasn't who Aaron was staring at. Once Hammond started speaking, his eyes never left Bockstater. It was a bait and switch. He was the real threat."

Bina pulled up to the Tanner home. The media who had stayed behind swarmed their vehicle. Thankfully, an officer moved the tape aside. Eve's cell rang just as she was stepping from the car.

"It's Aaron. I'll be inside in a moment," she told Bina.

"Hello." Keeping her anger in check wasn't easy. She watched Collin and Ray walk into the house after they parked.

"We need to talk," he said.

"We are talking." He would not walk all over her. She was tired of the crap that went on at the Wilson home. Aaron understood the lawful authority of the judge and how close law enforcement, including his own office, came to being prosecuted. The men of the church did not care. Their authority came from God, or so they believed.

"The women in the community are distraught over what's happened. They are afraid for their families. They are gossiping and making it harder on themselves. You know how things work here," he declared, his demeanor exactly as it was during their childhood. He excelled at manipulation and bullying.

Eve knew exactly how things worked. No gossiping and no friendships outside the family, at least for the women. Secrets and illegal activities were kept to minimal discussion so the men didn't do jail time.

"Is that all you have for me?" Eve asked calmly, even if she didn't feel it.

"These women aren't like the worldly ones you know. They will say things to start trouble for us because they have difficulty abiding by God's commands."

Eve's mouth dropped open. He was trying to pacify her. Did he have a clue who he spoke to? Eve had lived this life. She knew what the men thought of women. It was as if her stepbrother thought he could appeal to her fundamentalist side. There wasn't one, and she needed to make that clear immediately.

"I'm contacting Judge Remki. I have recorded conversations from two women that make them part of this case. I have reason to believe someone else in the home may have information. If those women disappear, the judge will know why and you will be held accountable. We will interview all the wives tomorrow and Mr. Wilson too."

His heavy breathing filled the line.

"You have no idea who you are messing with. You do not want to disobey me." He disconnected the call.

TWENTY

"We need to get out of here," Eve told them once she was inside the house. "Let's take a ride. I don't want to be overheard."

They took the van and remained quiet while Ray drove to a deserted parking lot and shut off the engine. Two media vehicles parked and sat watching the van. At least the press were acting normally, even if the fundamentalists were not. Eve told her team what had transpired since she had interviewed Sheila.

"Are the women in danger?" Ray asked when Eve finished.

She shook her head. "Candace thinks she is safe but that means nothing. These women do not understand what danger means unless it comes from outside the community."

"We still haven't seen or interviewed the only Tanner left alive," said Clyde.

Eve had the same thought. She was trying to keep hold of her fury at not being given contact with Hannah. She needed the judge to act.

"I have the same concern and she is my top priority. I'm sending everything we have to Judge Remki. I'm including my conversations with Sheila and Candace. My recorder was running when the church suits arrived. We must have access to Hannah, at least a short interview."

"The county attorney knows the judge will put a stop to the interference," Collin stated.

"We're not seeing the bigger picture," Eve told them. "Something is missing. Treachery runs the church and always has. It's possible Kathryn is a set-up. I don't feel Candace was lying but if her husband told her to, she would."

"Do you still think the killer is a woman?" Bina asked. They'd discussed it again in the room the night before.

Eve shook her head in frustration. "It makes sense the church would cover up a woman because the media would go crazy and it would impact the church negatively. That said, what if it were one of the seed bearers?"

"Just that phrase gives me the creeps." Bina rubbed her arms.

"I think we can all agree on that," Ray said.

Eve glanced at Clyde who was remaining quiet during the exchange. He had his thinking face on and would speak when he was ready. Eve knew the fact they hadn't been able to physically check on Hannah's well-being bothered him. He did better inside his head and Eve would let him work.

The rest of her team had more luck when they talked through events and quashed the non-working ideas methodically. The one thing they could all agree on at this point was the strangeness of the response from the church. As their conversation wound down, Clyde finally spoke.

"We handle this completely by the book and double-check everything. Get the judge involved immediately so we can begin interviews. No matter what the church is covering up, they won't be able to keep every person silent. We do our job and stop allowing them to call the shots."

With everyone in agreement, they prioritized their list of what needed to be done and helped Eve draft the information for the judge. Before they returned to the scene, she sent the email along with the audio recordings.

A mile from the Tanner home, they picked up a tail. The God squad in their large black lifted truck had arrived.

They locked the Tanner home and returned to the hotel. While Bina took a shower, Eve braided her hair and climbed into bed. She didn't feel like being sociable and exhaustion caught up to her and she fell asleep. The following morning, she was groggy, her sleep disrupted by running thoughts in her head each time she woke up. She needed extra caffeine to start the day.

First, they planned the final walk-through of the Tanner home. Afterward, the house would remain on lockdown with police security. Eve's team would not go back inside unless they had to find evidence that matched something discovered in the interviews. Usually, the home was released to family as soon as their initial investigation was finished, but no family had come forward and the longer they controlled the scene's integrity, the better. There were too many unanswered questions.

They entered the silent house, its walls keeping the secrets the home still had. The downstairs wasn't the pristine area it had been when they arrived. Dark gray fingerprint dust stained the walls and other surfaces. They were here to collect the evidence markers, Sharpies, and tape. Someone else would clean the blood from floors and walls. Carpet would be replaced. She wondered if whoever lived here next would feel the evil that Eve did. It wasn't the house's fault, but she didn't know how someone could live here.

"Room by room," she said.

They began their final walk through the house of horror.

Looking at the beds and the dried blood one last time, Eve tried to keep her childhood memories at bay without succeeding.

She remembered entering her bedroom when she was around eight and finding a dead mouse on her pillow. She'd screamed and been sent to bed without supper after her mother removed it. This was one of the last memories she had of Maggie before she left the home. Maggie was not upset for Eve; she was terrified about something.

Eve had no proof Aaron placed the mouse on her pillow, but his eyes gave him away. He liked when she didn't keep sweet. He excelled at torment.

The team stayed quiet for the most part while they walked the Tanners' house. Usually, their last walk included conversation about the next stage of the investigation.

"Why am I creeped out right now?" asked Ray when they entered Elijah's room.

"He fought. He knew he was dying and still he fought," said Clyde.

They silently closed the child's door behind them. Last was the attic.

"I don't even want to see the pictures when this case is over." Bina looked up the stairs and Eve felt the same dread. "This entire house is evil."

Eve ran her hands over her arms, wanting to get it over with.

The attic, with its bed and chair, remained as they had left it. The chair disturbed Eve the most. It represented a horrible monster and what was done to those inside these walls. Did he sit in the chair and torment them?

She glanced at her team, all dwelling in their own thoughts. The climb down the attic stairs and then to the front door was done in silence, each carrying a supply bag where they'd placed the items they'd gathered.

Eve gave a soft sigh of relief when they finally walked outside. She called Aaron before they left.

"I'm heading to the Wilson home for interviews. Should I expect trouble?" she asked.

"Those women know nothing about your homicides and this is pure harassment."

Eve cut him off before he continued. "The judge has the recordings of what happened yesterday including my interviews. I will be calling him next. The interference in this case stops today. I'll ask again. Should I expect trouble at the Wilson home?"

"No."

The line went silent. Aaron had disconnected, again.

Eve dialed the judge's office. It was early and she was hoping she caught him before he took the bench. She spoke to his clerk.

"We received your files and the judge will review them today. If you could call back this afternoon, I should have more for you."

It was frustrating, but there was nothing she could do about it. They drove the van and SUV to the Wilson home. Sheila's husband answered Eve's knock. He was wearing dress pants with a white button-down shirt and tie. It had taken time but Eve had finally recalled the Wilson name. The men were high in the hierarchy and several married to the prophet's daughters. One had taken the brunt of a federal investigation into welfare fraud. He had willingly given up five years of his life. The others responsible were let off the hook by his confession. It was how their system worked.

It also explained why Mr. Wilson, younger than most with large families, had so many wives.

The Wilson men were considered easy on the eye. They held a certain charisma. They had good facial bone structure and somehow eluded the appearance of inbreeding that many families couldn't escape. Mr. Wilson had dark, almost black hair, with deep blue eyes. This was another family trait. Eve had admired several of the Wilson boys during church when she was young. She and Sheila giggled about marrying one of them.

The Wilsons had the direct ear of the prophet and believed his was the voice of God. If the prophet told them to kill, they would.

It made this man very dangerous.

TWENTY-ONE

"Mr. Wilson," said Eve with a slight nod, relieved her brother had taken her warning seriously and the family was still here. "We need to interview the adults in your home." She was careful to let him know they would not be speaking to the children. "If you would like to start, Detective Smith is waiting in the van. I will interview Kathryn first. I was unable to speak with her yesterday."

Eve did not want to give away the information she'd obtained from Candace. If she chose to tell her husband, she could. Each person in the home would be interviewed and asked the same list of questions her team had decided on. This was standard procedure to pin everyone to a story. It allowed the team to cross-reference answers.

Kathryn was a lead at this point. No matter how strange it was in the polygamist community for a woman to leave her home at night, it did not mean she killed four people. If the interviews uncovered more threads leading to her, they would reevaluate quickly.

"I do not want you in my home," Wilson said with a condescending sneer.

"We have the van and SUV," she replied calmly, knowing what was coming next.

"I will be present when you interview my wives."

"That is not possible," Eve told him, leaving no room for argument. "This is a homicide investigation and my team is speaking to everyone privately." She ignored the instant fire in his eyes and hard press of his lips. "Please have Kathryn step outside and we will begin."

He wanted to argue. She was sure he'd spoken to Aaron and was aware Eve had every right to interview the women. Their male arrogance was impossible to control when they spoke to women and this man would push at everything she said even if he knew the eventual outcome.

After a full minute, without saying a word, he backed away and closed the door behind him. A few minutes later, he walked outside with Kathryn. Her hair was at least an inch higher than it had been the day before. Eve was unimpressed by her righteousness. She knew from the look on the woman's face the interview would not go well. Her husband had most likely forbidden his wives from sharing any information. Mr. Wilson went to the van where Bina and Ray waited. Clyde would monitor the recording equipment in the back of the van.

Collin sat in the back seat of the SUV with his recorder.

Eve opened the passenger door for Kathryn before walking around and sitting behind the wheel.

"This should not take long," Eve assured her. "We have the same list of questions for everyone. This is the routine part of our investigation to be sure we cover all bases. How well did you know the Tanners?"

"I request my husband be present for my interview," Kathryn said stoically.

"You are an adult and may have information that helps us solve the deaths of four people." Eve intentionally left the word "innocent" from in front of the Tanner name. Mr. Tanner was far from innocent. "We need your help," she implored.

"I am requesting my husband be present."

"That will not happen," Eve said point-blank.

"I will not speak to you without him." She glared at Eve showing all the revulsion she felt.

"You are interfering with a homicide investigation. If any woman in this house tells me you are involved in any way, I will arrest you on the spot. I will arrest anyone who refuses to answer simple questions if I discover they had any knowledge that would lead to solving the homicides. I am not part of your church and I do not live by your rules, I live by the laws of our state and the laws of this country. Help or don't help. The consequences will be on your head." Eve repeated her first question. "How well did you know the Tanners?"

Kathryn stayed silent for more than a minute. Eve breathed slowly and simply waited her out. Silence made others uncomfortable and could be a detective's best interview tactic.

"I did not associate with the Tanners."

Eve went to her second question.

"Are you aware of anyone in your household having a friendship with the Tanners?"

This was a trick question. Eve knew about Candace's tie and wanted to see if Kathryn would answer honestly.

"One of my sisters was removed from their home. You spoke to Candace yesterday." Her expression said she knew Eve was trying to trick her. It didn't matter. Eve just wanted to lock Kathryn into a story.

"Did she have any association with them after she left the family?"

"No."

"Do you know if any women in the community had friendships with Marcella or Tracy Tanner?"

"Women do not make friendships outside their sister wives. I know of no one who would do that."

"Was there gossip about the Tanners?"

Her chin came up while she looked straight ahead. "I do not listen to gossip."

"When was the last time you were inside the Tanner home?"

Her hard glare snapped to Eve. "I told you I did not associate with the Tanners."

"I asked about their home, not the family. When was the last time you were inside the home?"

"I have never been inside that house and I hope never to enter it," she said with a frustrated shake of her head.

This was the question Eve really wanted answered. They now had Kathryn saying there was no reason they would find her prints or DNA at the crime scene.

"Where were you the night of the homicides?" Eve kept the same tone with each question.

"I was at home," Kathryn replied.

Her hands clenched into fists when she lied. A good tell Eve would remember when they interviewed her again.

"Do you know of anyone who would want to harm the Tanners?"

"No."

"Are there questions I haven't asked that could help us solve this case?"

"No."

"We will ask this next question of everyone we interview. Would you agree to provide DNA and fingerprint samples?"

Her gaze went to the side window. Eve didn't look at Collin but she knew they were both thinking the same thing. This was a simple question and there should be no hesitation in answering it.

"If my husband commanded me to provide those things, I would," she finally answered and glanced back at Eve.

"Do you have any boys in the home who may have associated with Elijah?"

"No."

"Thank you. Those are my questions. Would you please send out one of your sisters? Your husband is providing their names. I do not have the list yet."

"I will send Meredith next."

Eve saw her relief. They had kept the questions simple for this reason. It laid their groundwork to uncover lies. If Kathryn had been inside the Tanner home, they could prove she lied. They still needed enough evidence to gain her prints and DNA with a body warrant. Eve was far from convinced Kathryn committed the murders. Eve also needed another woman to back up Candace's story.

Slow and steady would get the job done. She took a breath and prepared for the next interview.

Meredith looked like Kathryn, though younger. She was possibly Kathryn's blood sister or some other close tie. Eve asked her questions and then went to the next interview

Two hours later, they left the home. They stopped by the closest convenience store and grabbed junk food that passed for lunch. They went back to the parking lot Ray had stopped in the day before and ate their food in the van while discussing the interviews. The God squad stayed about fifty yards back. The media, which had tailed them from the Wilsons', parked near the black truck.

"Craig Wilson said he had no contact with the Tanners outside of church. He said Bart Tanner was not someone he wanted to associate with but would not elaborate." Collin rolled his eyes. "He knows what's going on. I can feel it."

"You interviewed four wives. Did anything seem off?" asked Eve.

"Yeah, four wives," answered Clyde before Ray could.

Eve shook her head and gave a small grin. It broke the tension.

"We interviewed five. That's a total of eleven once we add in Candace and Sheila," Collin said with a slight quirk to his lips.

"Christ." Clyde rubbed his hand over his bald head. "This is getting to me. We need to check on Hannah."

"I'll call Aaron right now and tell him we will speak to her today or get a court order. I can't return the call to the judge until after three. We need him to put some teeth behind our request."

Eve clicked the number to her brother's office. She was transferred to him immediately.

"We are ready to interview Hannah and the other adults in the home with her. We will begin the interviews at two."

He cleared his throat. "I spoke to Howard Wall this morning. Hannah remains distraught and she is under a doctor's care. Your interview will not take place until the doctor gives his okay." His smug tone ground on Eve's nerves but she hid it in her voice.

"Have you physically seen Hannah Tanner or spoken to her?" Eve asked.

"I have not but I know she is safe."

"We are investigating four brutal murders with one surviving child. We have not seen or spoken to her. It ends today. Hannah may have information that would help this investigation. If you can't guarantee the interviews will happen before the sun goes down, I'll alert the judge when I speak to him this afternoon."

"Let me make a call," Aaron said with a weary sigh and hung up.

Eve looked at her team who were listening to the exchange. "Interviewing the Walls will take us the rest of the day. Let's go through our answers from the Wilsons and see if anything stands out."

Bina and Clyde had taken written notes so they wouldn't need to listen to each interview and they could do this quickly. The oral interview would be transcribed but that took time. It was almost two when her stepbrother called back.

"Hannah and several of the wives are ill with the flu or some other nasty virus. It will be impossible for you to interview them today and I can have the doctor speak to Judge Remki if needed."

"That may be necessary," Eve told him. "I doubt the judge will be happy with the interference we've run into since arriving."

"I'll look forward to speaking with him," Aaron said with his earlier tiredness gone and his arrogance fully restored.

The line went dead and Eve wanted to scream.

Clyde glanced out the window before speaking. "We need to keep interviewing neighbors in the surrounding area, beginning with the homes closest to the Tanners."

"I agree." Collin said. They were all frustrated but still had a job to do. "No time like the present."

They split into two groups. Clyde and Eve took the SUV with Bina, Collin, and Ray taking the van. No one answered at the first home when Eve knocked. This was another tactic used to impede investigations. They got lucky at the next compound where two women were returning from the grocery store. Six women were interviewed. One was pregnant and ready to give birth and one brought a newborn infant into the SUV with her. They learned nothing new. They'd asked the exact same questions as they had of the Wilsons.

Eve was beyond frustrated by the time she called the judge's office after their last interview. She desperately needed his help to get the murderer caught and put away. She spoke to the same clerk. He went straight to the point.

"I'm incredibly sorry to tell you this but the judge is having his appendix out in emergency surgery. I was unable to speak with him before he was admitted."

Eve's eyes flashed to her team who had gathered in her hotel room. They knew how much this hurt their investigation. Going to an outside judge was impossible. Remki was in charge of oversight and there was no one else with his authority. They needed Judge Remki's bite to back them up.

"If you speak to the judge, please relay my hope that he makes a quick recovery," Eve said; she wasn't without sympathy for his circumstances, even though her gut twisted with the news.

"I will be sure he's aware of your entire situation as soon as I'm able to."

"We're screwed," said Ray after the call ended and ran a frustrated hand through his dark hair.

She gave them a small pep talk. "We're going to get good food and not the junk we had for lunch and review everything we have. Put your thinking caps on and be ready to throw out the craziest ideas you can think of. This wall will come down, one brick at a time."

Eve put this team together for a reason. They were the best at their jobs and they would solve this case with or without the judge. Interviewing everyone was where it started. They would circle back to anyone they missed but they would continue until they had something solid.

They decided to go out of town to eat. The God squad turned around when they crossed the county line. They found a small diner with a decent menu and homemade pie to die for.

They felt slightly better after taking a break and for a short time spoke about life in general. Collin kept them laughing with his kids' antics.

"Ella is just like her mother and I have no idea what to do with her attitude."

"Tell her you'll sell her to the fundamentalists," Ray told him in a quiet voice in case someone around them was listening.

"Bad joke," scolded Bina, after taking another spoonful of the apple pie à la mode she'd ordered.

"It was, and I don't give a shit," Ray replied. "I'm tired and unhappy. I'll do better tomorrow."

"Order more pie," said Collin.

Ray lifted his hand to the waitress and did exactly that.

Clyde said little but he did surprisingly order apple pie without the ice cream. Eve knew his only concern at this point was Hannah. It was hers too and she couldn't allow this to continue. The church did not want them speaking to the child most likely to have answers. In her opinion, this placed Hannah in danger. Eve couldn't help wondering if Hannah had somehow survived the attack by more than simply not being home, and knew who killed her family.

Getting to Hannah could mean life or death for the ten-year-old.

TWENTY-TWO

At the hotel, Eve shut the SUV's door on Clyde's glare after she had taken the driver's seat. He was not happy she was going to see Hannah alone. Eve pulled rank, which upset him even more.

"Explain what I'm doing and tell the team not to worry. I'll text as soon as I'm at the house."

She drove straight to the Wall residence. It was now dark outside and a slight breeze made the few tree branches sway as her headlights passed the polygamist houses. The moon wasn't visible yet. There were no street lamps and the only lights came from upper windows. She planned to demand that she lay eyes on Hannah. That was it. A block from the hotel, she picked up a tail. It wasn't the normal God squad truck but her gut said the car belonged to the church. Eve ignored it completely, sick of their intimidation tactics.

She parked in front of the Walls' home outside the court-yard and sent Clyde the promised text. The vehicle behind her drove past, turned around, and parked a block away facing her with the high beams on. She ignored it and entered the unlocked gate. The house appeared deserted and Eve used her phone's flashlight to see the ground after the wall blocked the bright headlamps from the SUV outside the courtyard.

She knocked on the door, stepped back, and stared up at the second-floor windows. All were closed, no lights shining outward like she'd seen the previous time she was here with Collin. She rubbed her arms, wishing she had taken the time to grab her jacket. The thin material of her blouse with its three-quarter sleeves was doing nothing to keep her warm. She knocked again after no one responded.

The light from her cell did little to dissipate the shadows but it was enough to see. The homes and their courtyards to keep out curious eyes always gave her the creeps and tonight was no exception. She had a weird feeling in her gut. Before she figured out what was making her apprehensive, she heard a sound behind her and turned.

Five men entered the courtyard. Dark masks covered the lower part of their faces. They each carried a medium-sized cloth bag. One of the men held a gun pointed at Eve. She didn't miss the significance of there being five. It matched the number of her stepbrothers waiting outside the county attorney's office. Their shorter height, like Aaron's, was about right too. She had her weapon on her hip, but one thing people never speak of—if someone has a gun pointed at you, it's too late to draw yours.

She lifted her hand away from her holster. This wasn't good and whether she survived or not, Clyde would never forgive her. One of the men stepped forward suddenly and she instinctively turned away and tried to draw her gun. The first punch hit her stomach and a heavy grip on her right arm stopped her from falling. She dropped her phone when his fingers dug into the muscle and, at the same time, bent over slightly, trying to catch her breath.

"Don't move and keep your hands up," said the man holding the gun. Given she was doubled over, his directions were impossible to follow.

The one holding her arm removed the gun from her holster and stepped back while Eve gasped for air. It was not a time for laughter but for the strangest reason that was what she wanted to do. These were the children she had grown up with. It was nerves. They were adults and dangerous no matter Eve's connection to them.

They slowly fanned out around her. The shadows cast by the house and the outer wall made what they did appear more ominous. She prepared herself to be beaten half to death. She knew how the church worked, or thought she did. They stuck their hands in the bags and she didn't have time to think about the oddity of their actions before the first large stone hit her in the back of the head.

At the stinging discomfort, she turned and the bombardment started from all sides. She was struck in her arms, stomach, and upper torso. They threw the sharp rocks with as much force as they could. They hit with dull thuds then made a clunk when they bounced off her body and fell at her feet. She used her arms to shield her head. A rock got through when she protected the back and hit her forehead. She cried out, feeling pain everywhere.

The barrage continued and more rocks dug into her skin. She shouted for them to stop but her voice sounded small to her. Then, she could do nothing but groan. She lowered an arm in agony after a rock bounced off her elbow. A larger rock hit her head, sending her to her knees.

The men repeated one word in a low steady tone, while they stoned her.

"Abomination. Abomination. Abomination."

The pain took over and she could no longer defend herself. Eve curled into a tight ball, hoping it would simply end. She had no idea how long they pelted her. Her whimpers were soft now as consciousness slipped away.

A voice broke through her foggy brain. Everything hurt and

she was disoriented. It took her a moment to understand until he repeated the words.

"Let's get you into your vehicle." It was Aaron.

She cringed away from his hand, not wanting him near her.

"I need to help you," he said urgently, refusing to back away.

She cried out when he touched her arm.

"Wait," she whispered.

She took a few deep breaths. Once she felt steady, she tried to stand. Aaron caught her before she fell. He slowly steered her to the SUV, his voice coaxing as they walked. Each step caused pure agony in her head and she felt sick.

Aaron opened the passenger door, and she leaned against the seat, her legs shaking, her head pounding. She could now see him from the glow of the inside light. She didn't need to see the dirt and blood that covered her, she could feel it. Her head was the worst of her injuries. Nothing felt broken but her skin was no defense against stones meant to seriously injure. They had tried to kill her; she was sure of it.

"I can't take you to the hospital," Aaron said when she finally focused on him.

Her thoughts came together slowly. She was still in danger. He was the enemy. Her hand went to her waist, checking for her gun. It wasn't there and she remembered one of the men taking it.

"What are you doing here?" she asked shakily. Shock was setting in and she'd never felt so cold in her life. She knew she could be badly injured. Her trembling hand rose to her cheek and came away with blood. She felt it on her forehead too. Something wet rolled over her eyebrow and blurred her vision. Or maybe it was the head injury. Her thoughts were frantically scattered.

"I know you won't believe me, but I'm here to help."

"Help who?" she demanded.

"You," he insisted, though Eve didn't believe him.

"You knew what they planned. Do not try to deny it. Where's your mask?" Eve accused sharply then gasped for air, her stomach rolling. She was going to throw up. With a slight turn, she managed to keep her insides outside the vehicle.

"You and your team need to finish your investigation and leave," Aaron said, barely waiting for her last heave to end.

"Not happening." She coughed and wiped her mouth, not caring what her stepbrother thought.

"You have no idea who you're dealing with," he said desperately.

Eve looked at him and saw fear. It had been in his eyes the first day when she arrived at his office. Someone controlled him.

"I know exactly what I'm dealing with. I grew up in this mess you call a church," she said, while breathing through her nose to try and stop another round of vomiting.

Aaron stepped back, his hands going to his waist. He didn't look away as they stared at each other.

"You are an apostate, sent by the devil. He controls everything you do. You live an abominable life and turned your back from the prophet and God," he accused harshly. She remembered this arrogant tone and posture from her childhood.

Fog and pain shifted through Eve's brain, but she understood him perfectly. He would never bully her again like he had when she was a child. He might think he held the power right now, but he was wrong. As messed-up as she was, she would fight.

"What you mean," she ground out, "is that I turned my back on a child-molester old enough to be my grandfather before he raped me. You have no idea how long it took to undo the brainwashing I suffered at the hands of your cult. You and your beliefs disgust me." Her gravelly voice underscored her pain and she wanted to cry. She wanted to tear his eyes out and stomp on his face until he was unrecognizable. She wasn't a violent person, but that's what she felt at this moment, and her fury was giving her strength.

Aaron didn't say anything for a moment. The contempt returned to his expression. He didn't like the truth.

"Finish and leave. I can no longer help you."

Eve laughed, the sound vibrating through her head in a steady pound. Her brother stared with his tight-lipped arrogance. When her laughter faded, she put her own glare into action.

"You've never helped me. This is how you threaten and intimidate. You'll lose your legal license for this and there will be nothing your high and mighty church can do about it." Eve knew she wasn't helping herself. Her hand went to her waist again. "Where is my gun?" she demanded in frustration.

"I didn't see it. I came to talk to Howard about the interview with Hannah. Put your crazy thoughts out to pasture. I found you after you were assaulted. I saw no one and simply offered assistance. I'm still here, I haven't harmed you." A look of innocence took over his expression. Eve saw it as pure evil.

"You lying sack of shit," she said. Her stepbrother made her swear again. He seemed to be the only person with that unique ability.

"Finish and leave," he blared suddenly, his patience at an end.

"What about Hannah?" Eve demanded. "She's in danger. She needs help."

"That child will be fine." He walked away.

Eve held onto the side of the SUV as she made her way around it. She needed to check for her gun, but she'd never make it to the courtyard then back to the vehicle. It took everything she had to climb into the driver's seat. She started the engine and rested for a moment. She had to get away; she knew she was still in danger. Her phone was missing too and she couldn't call for help.

Sitting up straighter, she turned the vehicle around. Her brain was too foggy to figure out the seatbelt so she let it go. She slowly headed toward the hotel. She needed a doctor but Clyde was all she could think about. He would keep her safe.

A vehicle's lights appeared in the distance and she stopped breathing. She had no weapon, no way to call for help. She could barely drive.

Had her stepbrothers returned?

TWENTY-THREE

Eve picked up speed. If all she had was the vehicle, she would use it. She released the breath she held. If she blacked out, this was over. She had trouble controlling the steering wheel and her stomach wasn't doing well.

The vehicle drew closer and she saw a van's outline when the road curved. Clyde's bald head in the driver's seat was impossible to miss.

She slammed the brakes and the SUV skidded on the asphalt before she brought it to a stop. She rested her arms on the steering wheel, laying her head on top of them. *Deep breaths*, she thought to herself, trying to keep from vomiting again. Her body's aches and pains were one sensation with no end.

She would live. That was all that mattered right now.

Her stepbrothers had openly attacked her. Stoned her according to the Bible.

And thou shalt stone him with stones, that he die.

The verse from Deuteronomy ran through her head. Her

fists clenched and she wanted to cry. A knock on the window made her glance to the side. Clyde's familiar face pushed the verse from her mind. He immediately realized something was wrong and tried to open the automatic locking door. Eve managed to push the correct button, though she wasn't sure how she did it. She fell half out of the vehicle and Clyde caught her. Collin also grabbed her and they took her to the ground so her back was leaning against the side of the car.

"What the fuck?" Clyde demanded.

He appeared above her as a dark avenging angel.

"They stoned me." She covered her eyes, emotion taking over, and began crying softly.

"You need a doctor," Collin insisted while Clyde said words that were unrepeatable.

"Not in town." There was a health clinic nearby, but Eve didn't want the record there. It was probably closed anyway. If emergency services were called, they would medivac her to who knew where. They were working a homicide case and there was no way she was leaving the area.

"The hospital is an hour's drive away," Collin said.

"Hospital. I need a record." That probably didn't make sense.

They helped her into the back seat. Clyde slid in beside her while Collin drove. She rested her head on his shoulder, allowing his warmth to seep into her skin. She didn't think she'd ever been this cold.

"Bina has an extra van key so I locked it. They're at the hotel."

Eve thought he might be talking to her.

"Clyde, can you call them?" Collin asked a moment later.

Now she was confused and decided it would be easier if conversations took place without her. She examined what she could of her right arm that she could barely see even with moonlight shining in the window. The outline of round circles was

visible below the sleeve of her blouse where bruises were form-
ing. It didn't seem real.

Clyde spoke into his phone with one hand, his other arm
keeping her close to his chest.

"We're taking Eve to the hospital; she's been assaulted.
She's conscious but other than that, we're unsure of her condition." He hesitated and then answered, "With rocks, we're
assuming, but we haven't gotten much out of her."

"Rocks," she whispered, finally managing to get the correct
word past her lips. Clyde looked at her and she knew his anger
was for who did this. It was terrifying. She lay her hand on
his arm.

"I'll be okay." She didn't hear much after that and dozed off.

Things happened quickly when they arrived at the hospital.
She was placed in a wheelchair and rolled into a small cubicle.
A nurse removed her clothes and put her in an unattractive
gown. She was covered with a warm blanket. It felt wonderful
against her freezing skin. There was a knock and the curtain
was pulled aside. It was a uniformed officer.

"I need a statement," he said.

The nurse turned to Eve.

"Let him in." She'd rather have the interview without Clyde
and Collin in the room. She couldn't deal with their condemnation right now for not telling them about the run-in with her
stepbrothers.

He introduced himself as Officer Gilbert. He was young,
late twenties maybe. His short, perfectly cut chestnut hair
screamed police officer. His deep brown eyes were kind and he
smiled gently after introducing himself.

"I was dealing with a case around the corner and was asked
to swing by and get your statement."

Eve sensed Tamm at work but it could have been anyone
from her team. Clyde would have notified Lieutenant Crosby
immediately, so it could have been him. She'd been here ten

minutes and usually getting an officer took a while. Law enforcement took police assault seriously.

Her head still pounded but some of the fog had cleared and she was able to give a statement and answer questions.

"You mind if I grab my camera and get some shots of your injuries?" he asked after he finished writing in his notebook.

"No problem," she told him.

He left to get his camera.

Eve assessed her condition and took a moment to gain her bearings. She knew she looked terrible but there was no mirror. The nurse had cleaning supplies ready but waited for the officer's return. She was familiar with assault procedures. He came back in and snapped his pictures. He assured her he would request a copy of her medical record to cite her injuries in the report. He also said a detective would most likely take over the case.

As soon as he walked out, the nurse went to work, carefully cleaning her wounds. A few minutes later the doctor entered and gave her a thorough examination. The worst injury was the cut on her forehead, which required two sutures. It was directly beneath the hairline and the doctor assured her it wouldn't leave a noticeable scar. The blood from that cut had dripped into her eye and she was able to see clearly now that she was cleaned up. He still ordered a CAT scan. The bruises on her arms were mostly superficial. The one on her cheek only required a butterfly bandage. Her arms needed cleaning and there were a few scrapes. The back of her head had been cushioned by her thick hair. She was exceedingly fortunate.

Collin and Clyde entered after the nurse finished cleaning her wounds. They'd probably spoken to the doctor, but she didn't ask. Clyde handed her a large cup of steaming coffee.

"I have no idea if you should drink it or not." His mouth remained tight. Eve knew he was trying to stay calm for her benefit. The front of his white T-shirt was smeared with blood.

"Drink." She took the cup, which warmed her freezing fingers, and immediately brought it to her lips.

She could only manage a partial smile and then her lips trembled. Everything that had happened swelled inside her then overflowed. She couldn't hold back tears.

Clyde took the coffee from her hand. He lay it on the metal table beside her, sat on the bed, and pulled her into his arms.

"I'll step out," Collin mumbled, and left the room quickly.

"I guess he didn't want to see his boss cry." Eve sniffed and burrowed farther into his warmth.

Clyde meant so much to her. He was her best friend. They had barely acknowledged their feelings for each other. His level thinking, sense of humor, and kindness attracted her. He was a good man and in Eve's life, she hadn't known many. He was divorced. Eve knew little about it other than he said he never planned to try again. Maybe that was why their feelings took so long to materialize. Or maybe they had always been there.

"You know I'm going to kill your brother, spend the rest of my life in a Utah prison, and run that place within a year. I'm planning the cellblock takeover while I plan his death," Clyde whispered gruffly, interrupting her clouded thoughts.

"He deserves it, but he's not worth it."

"Can you ID the men who did this?" he asked softly into Eve's hair.

"No. I don't think I was conscious when Aaron found me." She was lying to her friend. She couldn't prove it was her step-brothers but that didn't matter. It was them and they'd tried to kill her. She'd told Officer Gilbert everything and it would be in the police report. When she was ready, she would tell her team.

"Aaron's story is bullshit; he knew where to find you." Clyde's tone was soft though heated.

"Yes, he did." She leaned away and looked into his dark eyes, seeing his concern, his fear, and the anger he barely kept in check. "Say it," she told him. "You'll feel better."

He pulled back slightly.

"I. Told. You. So," he ground out.

Eve returned her head to his shoulder and circled her hands around his back.

"See, you feel better," she soothed.

"Actually, I don't," he grumped, and pulled her closer.

This was safety and caring wrapped into one. It was odd. Relationships and intimacy were both strange to her but right now, she was glad Clyde knew exactly what she needed.

"Why were you on the road?" she asked, because her thoughts kept jumping and this was the one that popped up.

"You didn't answer your phone and if you think I wasn't checking up on you, you were wrong."

"Free hugs and you didn't include us," Ray said from the curtain as Bina whipped it back and entered with him followed by Collin.

They were clearly relieved that she was okay. Ray pulled her in for a long hug after Clyde stepped back. Bina took her turn and sat on the bed doing the same. She gave Ray, who stayed close, a small push on his arm.

"This guy ran five miles to the van. He may have set a world record."

"Voilà." He pulled her phone from his pocket and handed it over. "It was on the ground inside the Walls' courtyard. Bina insisted we go by the Walls' house." His eyes turned cold. "We didn't find your gun but we did take photographs."

She groaned internally at the amount of paperwork in front of her. When a cop lost an issued weapon, it required a detailed report and multiple forms. Due to the circumstances, she would not stand in front of an inquiry board, but that was the only saving grace.

She turned the phone over and saw the missed calls from Clyde.

She fought back tears again. Her stepbrothers would never

understand what friendship was truly about. They'd made her realize the gift she had in these people. One even willing to run five miles simply to get to her. Throughout her career, she'd created a wall around herself like those around fundamentalist homes. Her team had been together for a year and still she'd pushed them away. She finally understood what had been missing from her life since she was a child. It was what she had now.

Family.

The doctor released Eve from the hospital two hours later. She didn't remember much of the first ride, but she stayed awake for this one. It was well after midnight when they came over the last twisting rise and saw the valley below, the three-quarter moon shining down on what should be a beautiful area.

The words "beauty comes from within" filled Eve. She shivered but not from the cold. An evil corruption that twisted the hearts and minds of over ten thousand people waited to stop Eve's team from discovering the truth.

What secret were they willing to kill for?

TWENTY-FOUR

They were all exhausted. Clyde said goodbye at her room after pulling her close. Bina turned away and busied herself, which made Eve's embarrassment worse, because this was not like the relieved hug they'd all shared at the hospital.

"Sleep," he whispered. "Check on her," he told Bina.

"Setting up the alarms on my phone." She lifted it to show she was doing as told.

Clyde kissed Eve's forehead and walked out.

She removed her nightshirt from a drawer and went into the bathroom with only a side look into the mirror at the vanity. She pulled her hair the rest of the way down, ran her fingers through the tangles and quickly braided it. They'd washed her injuries at the hospital and she was too tired to take a shower. She changed quickly and walked out so Bina could get in.

"I'll wake you every two hours," she told Eve before she stepped into the bathroom.

Eve had been given pain medication which she'd taken in the SUV and all she could think of was sleep. She closed her eyes and grumpily opened them each time Bina checked on her throughout the night.

She was alone when she woke up, a small bit of morning sun shining through an inch gap in the blackout curtains. She took a shower, allowing the water's spray to relieve some of her body aches. She washed her hair while thinking of what they had to get done. She added a thick handful of conditioner that had to be combed through. She detangled it carefully. There might not be open wounds on her scalp, but there were sensitive areas. Her headache was slightly better, but she still popped two ibuprofen so she could work. She had no intention of taking the pain medication again. She dressed in a pair of blue cargo pants and a lighter shade long-sleeved T-shirt to cover the bruises. She braided her hair without clipping it to the back of her neck. She didn't think her head could take it.

She found them in Clyde's room.

"You should be in bed," he said after answering her knock. He stepped back so she could enter. She took the closest empty chair and ungracefully slouched into it. They watched her closely and she smiled for their benefit.

Ray handed her coffee and Bina passed over a box of donuts.

"I'm rested and clean. We have work to do," she said after a long sip and a few bites from her selected sweet, managing not to groan in pleasure over the taste. "The doctor's recommendation was simply a guideline." She sat up straighter and stared them down, ignoring the sound Clyde made. "Hannah is in danger and we need to locate her. Ray, I want Family Services involved. Make the report airtight. I was assaulted while trying to check her welfare and she's also a key lead in a multiple homicide investigation. We've made numerous attempts to see her with no contact at all. Be sure to include that we've had no cooperation from the county attorney but he's told us he knows her location. We should have enough to get them rolling."

Family Services had their own list of rules to follow, but hopefully they could take custody of Hannah, even if it was only temporary. If they could find her, that was. They might also be able to keep Aaron busy and out of Eve's investigation for a day or two.

"On it." Ray turned to the computer bag resting next to his chair and pulled out his laptop. He was their best writer and knew the criteria that would get immediate action.

"We need to finish the interviews. How many homes are left?" Eve asked.

"Five," Collin replied. "We have no idea how many adults are in each family, but if we get an early start, this first round of interviews should be completed today, two days tops."

Eve started to rise, but Clyde's words stopped her.

"You will be in bed those two days." His glare made her sink back into the chair.

"That's not—" she tried to say.

He held up his hand, his dark eyes doing their best to intimidate. "The doctor's orders were bed-rest for two days minimum. It was not a guideline." She glared but Clyde wasn't finished. "I will go above you and Lieutenant Crosby will have you in the city recuperating so fast your head will spin. Don't push me."

Silence filled the room as Bina, Ray, and Collin found interesting things to look at on the walls.

From the stubborn set of Clyde's jaw, he would do exactly as promised. Her mind raced. Taking two days off in the middle of a homicide investigation was not in her mental vocabulary. She could, however, work the case by laying it out, adding a timeline, and filling in blanks while she did it. They had begun the process when Sheila arrived at the Tanners' and interrupted them.

Maybe she could shed light on the church's heavy-handed behavior. Whatever they were hiding would be trouble for them. Eve had to discover what they were up to. Putting a magnifying glass to the case was a good way to start. She glanced at Clyde.

His glare remained in place.

Eve shrugged off her ire, feeling guilty. She would do the exact same thing if their roles were reversed.

"I'll stay in my room and review the photo evidence."

"Does someone need to sit on you?" Clyde ground out, and Eve jumped.

"You should," muttered Bina, but she looked away when he shot her a frown.

"Unless someone stays here and does just that, I'll be working in my room. I will rest and even nap if needed."

"You don't know the meaning of the word 'rest,'" Clyde said firmly.

"No one on this team does, or do I need to remind you about Collin's ankle or Bina's eye surgery? If you ever opened your mouth to complain about aches or pains, we would know you're just as guilty."

"I think the rest of us should leave while the two of you work this out," said Ray.

Eve could see the grin he was trying to hold back. She began questioning a relationship between her and Clyde. The team's dynamic would suffer. She pulled her thoughts back to the case and left her personal life unsettled.

"I'll take it easy. I promise," she said to soothe Clyde's mind. "If I get a headache, I'll take a nap. My biggest problem this morning is aches and pains. I feel like I need to go for a run." She held up her hand at his furious glare. "I won't, I promise."

That was the best the team got from her. Eve wasn't happy about the forced time off but she was excited to lay out the case and look for things they'd missed. Ray sent the report to Family Services, giving Eve as the point of contact.

Her gaze followed Clyde as he carried the printer from the van into her room a short while later.

He placed it on the dresser and turned to her. She simply stood staring at this man who had become such a large part of her life while she wasn't paying attention. His arms opened and she walked into them. Her earlier doubts about the two of them not working went straight out the window.

"This is highly inappropriate," she said into his chest.

"I'm worried about you. This feud with your stepbrother has gone too far. You know he had something to do with your assault. At the very least, he knows who did it."

Eve's guilt shot up another notch. She knew who did it too.

"Be careful out there today," she said without responding to his statement.

Clyde pulled back and placed a kiss on her forehead before walking out.

Eve sat on the bed staring at the door. She couldn't deny her feelings and this was not the time to dwell on them. The case came first.

Her team would be back with lunch in a few hours and would catch Eve up on how the interviews were going. They would call immediately if new evidence came to light. Frustrating, but it was the best she had right now.

She began by downloading all the SIM cards she'd used in her camera to a new file. She didn't go through the images she had printed for the team the day before. She wanted a fresh perspective and a photo of each part of the house. While her computer did its thing, she connected the printer and printed a test page. She walked to her door and placed the Do Not Disturb sign on the outside knob. She then made her bed so she could build a timeline with sheets of paper and place them on the comforter in chronological order. She used a Sharpie for each main event, beginning with the original call from her brother.

It jogged her memory and she pulled out her phone and hit Tamm's number.

"I need you to pull the call log from the county attorney's first call on this case. I need it transcribed ASAP."

"I'm sorry, who is this?" Tamm asked in a fake sugary voice.

"Are you trying to be funny?"

"I was told you are on bed-rest and not to help you."

"Okay." Eve took a breath. "Who exactly pays your salary?"

"The great state of Utah," Tamm quipped back.

"That was not the answer I wanted and I don't want to argue over this. I'm working in my hotel room standing as close to the bed as I'm going to get and I need your help."

"I told Clyde I wasn't your watchdog," Tamm said with a faint laugh.

"How did that go over?"

"As expected. I will, however, monitor you. If you overdo it, I'll relay the news to Clyde and you can deal with him directly." She continued before Eve could get a word in, "This also comes with a condition: when this case is over, I want to know what's going on between you and Clyde."

"What do you mean?" Eve asked, trying to buy some time.

"You know exactly what I mean. Now, back to the case before you have a coronary."

"Can you get me that transcript?" Eve asked, and rubbed her temples. She shouldn't be surprised Tamm was the first to say something out loud. She wasn't exactly known for timidity.

"I'll need about thirty minutes and it's yours."

"Thank you."

The call ended and Eve sighed with relief. She finished downloading the SIM cards and started printing the pictures. She looked through them on her laptop and chose the best ones covering the entire area upstairs. She picked ones with and without Luminol. As they printed, she took the pillows off the bed and laid them on a chair so she had more room. She placed the photos in order, beginning at the stairs, as they rolled off the printer. She didn't use any from the attic. Though it was part of the backdrop to murder, it was not where the homicides took place.

She could lay the entire scene out on her laptop but this larger visual was better. She often used their conference table back at the offices. Her phone chirped with the email from Tamm. Eve read then printed it.

Her brother had been his normal terse self.

0820 hours

County Attorney Owens: We have a murdered family discovered by local law enforcement. Your team is requested at the crime scene.

Detective Sergeant Bennet: How many dead?

County Attorney Owens: Four. One man, two women, one child.

Detective Sergeant Bennet: Witnesses?

County Attorney Owens: No.

Detective Sergeant Bennet: When did it happen?

County Attorney Owens: Sometime within the past twenty-four hours.

Detective Sergeant Bennet: Do you have a suspect?

County Attorney Owens:—HESITATION—No

Eve appreciated Tamm noting Aaron's hesitation. She had asked a few additional questions but there wasn't much more in the conversation. She placed the printed text in the top left-hand corner of the bed and stepped back. She stared at the photos and the timeline she'd written on index cards with a Sharpie. Her eyes traveled left to right, down, left to right. She took a step closer and did it again. Something bothered her, but she wasn't sure what it was.

She read the timeline, which ended with the assault against her the evening before. Her eyes went back to the images. She lifted the first print from the bed, examined it closely, and went to the next. She was hoping whatever it was would jump out and scream "clue."

She knew she was a good detective, but this was actually her specialty. Since her mother had gifted her with the first camera, images spoke to her and had always been what she relied on most in her career.

One after the other she picked them up, studied the smallest details, and continued until she came to the partial blood print on Elijah's bedroom door. It was only a smudged remnant. This was the tricky part with prints: they had to be clear for the computer to identify a match. Something still bothered her. She finished examining each photo by lifting it for closer inspection.

She walked around the bed and reexamined the scene upside down. It did no good and she was growing frustrated that her brain wouldn't click whatever was bothering her into place.

The images showed the drops of blood going to Hannah's room. She lifted the picture of the bloody partial prints found at her closet door. Again, they were smudged and they didn't have enough to make a match. She turned it sideways then upside down. Her eyes went back to the photo of the one on the master bedroom door-jamb. She lay them down, side by side, and reviewed them again. The ache in her head grew worse.

She picked the photos up once more and walked to the door. She stared between the photos and the hotel doorknob.

The bright blue glow from the Luminol was caught perfectly in the camera's lens for both images. She examined the Luminol's contrast to the walls, floor, and carpet. Spray on the walls came from the actual murders. Blood drops on the carpet had fallen from the weapon and/or the person carrying the knife. Lower areas of the doorframes and doors themselves had the blood smears.

She had Collin's video footage and she pulled it up on her laptop and watched the entire file. Again, her brain zeroed in on the blood prints on the doorframes. She shook her head in frustration because whatever was bothering her would not let go. She decided on an old trick showed to her by a professor in college from a crime photography class she took.

She placed the pictures back on the bed and examined all the photos in backwards order. She was prepared to walk around the bed and repeat the process upside down again. Then, she realized what bothered her. Eve's heart dropped into her stomach, her mind not wanting to see the truth.

She reexamined three photos. Two were the smeared prints on the doorframes. One was spatter in the hallway. The pattern of the blood seemed to bother Collin and now Eve knew why.

It was more terrifying than she wanted to believe. She walked to the chair in the corner of the room and sank into it, rubbing her temples, trying to find a way out of the thought in her head. She wanted to dismiss the evidence. She wanted to scream. When she was able to stand, she stepped to the bed and chose another image of Hannah's closet taken farther out.

She looked at it again with clearer eyes. The placement of the smears. She turned and looked at her hotel room door once more. She sat on the bed in the only empty spot available.

The partial bloody prints on the doorframes were low. Too low. The blood spatter in the hallway came from blood dripping off the knife approximately a foot from the floor.

She didn't need to look at the photos again because they

were now frozen in her head. Her stomach turned queasy and it wasn't because of the assault.

The puzzle pieces clicked into place. She tried to deny what the evidence showed but she couldn't. It explained so much. The case was screwed from the very beginning because the church had something major to hide.

Those in power knew who killed the Tanners. Aaron and the Walls knew. Hell, all her stepbrothers more than likely were in on whatever twisted plot the leaders had come up with to hide the truth. They were sent to stop her from discovering it. Maybe they were only supposed to scare her or maybe—she hated the thought—they were sent to kill.

She had no idea why Aaron helped her. Chances were good that it was part of a bigger plan. Evil permeated this community, but it wasn't an evil designed by the devil, it was one designed by men.

An abused ten-year-old child—*that child*, as Aaron and Howard Wall referred to Hannah—had brutally murdered her family. The polygamist church could not afford for the world to find out.

TWENTY-FIVE

Nine-year-old Eve looked down at the blisters on her dry, red hands. She had swept and mopped the entire bottom floor of the house before the women prepared dinner. The mop was heavy and she had a hard time lifting it from the water and wringing it out. She was in trouble because Aaron had found something to mark the walls that she was responsible for keeping clean. Her punishment was mopping the floor. When she was finished with half of it, Aaron knocked the water over and she had to start again.

"I hate you," she said, even though she knew it was a sin and that she could get into more trouble. No matter how hard she tried, it was difficult to keep sweet.

Aaron knocked her down and kicked her leg after she hit the floor. This was nothing new. He enjoyed kicking her.

"You will be punished when you belong to me. Father said I could have you when I was older and he would speak to the prophet about it. My father is important and he will make sure they choose you as one of my wives."

Eve did not want to marry her brother. It made her afraid and caused her to lay awake at night and fear for the future.

The women and most of her siblings were mean to her. She didn't understand. Her mother, who she could barely picture, had left a year ago. Her other brothers stayed away because of Aaron. They were afraid of him too.

Aaron's father always took his side. His mother also believed him when he spoke against Eve. They told her she was not keeping sweet. Her job was to follow Aaron's direction even at nine years old. She didn't know why his direction hurt so much.

The night after the mop incident, she woke to find Aaron standing over her. She was in a room she shared with three of her sisters, but they were asleep. Aaron hit her in the stomach with a sock. It had something in it and hurt. She curled to her side and he hit her hip. He covered her mouth when she cried out and hit her again.

His low whisper rang in her head through the pain.

"Abomination."

Eve's eyes flew open, her heart racing as she found her bearings. She'd fallen asleep in the chair beside the pictures of the homicides. Her head pounded, which was why she'd taken a break. She grabbed the bottle of ibuprofen and took two of them before she leaned back in the chair.

Aaron hadn't changed from the vicious bully he was as a child. His position as county attorney made him more dangerous.

A ping on her laptop dragged her from the chair. It was an email from Aaron with two attached files. It was hard to read his official email address as the county attorney and think of him and his corruption as a part of law enforcement. A short message gave an overview of the two lists he'd sent.

Aaron had come through with the names of the wives removed from the Tanner home as she'd requested. He was generous enough to include their current addresses. One was out of state and two out of the country in Canada. Candace was the only wife removed from Bart Tanner who remained in Utah. Four in total, with Marcella and Tracy making it six wives. Five children had left with their mothers. They were victims, just like Elijah and Hannah. Eve had no idea why the church had allowed Bart Tanner to stay in the community and might never learn the reason. Hiding crime came naturally to the polygamist sect. The women, controlled by extremist doctrine, would remain silent if they were told to.

During college, Eve had studied the hows and whys of cults to try and grasp some semblance of understanding. The class did the opposite. She came away with a sense that the people who followed them were disturbed to begin with. Even though it was before she went to college, fundamentalist Eve had fallen for the lies fed to her, struggled with her sins, and desperately wanted to go to the Celestial Kingdom. She'd been young and still couldn't forgive herself. Clyde knew that was her biggest problem and he was right.

Unwanted memories filled her thoughts. After the incident with the sock, the prophet visited their home with his favorite son in tow. Her father made it clear it was a huge honor. They'd cleaned the house from top to bottom, making everything more pristine than usual.

The wives lined up in the gathering room wearing their newest prairie dresses, color-coordinated to show they belonged proudly to their husband. The boys and girls stood in front. Even the youngest daughter's hair was piled high for Christ's return. The prophet slowly passed them while his tall son looked over his shoulder. His arrogance even as a teenager was just the beginning of his immorality. The prophet asked a question here and there of Eve's mothers. Eve remembered her terror that he would see her unworthiness.

Aaron's continued bullying had caused severe doubt in her mind. He cornered her alone whenever possible to whisper of her tainted blood. According to him, she would not be granted a place in heaven because Aaron, when he was her husband, wouldn't pull her up by his side. Eve tried to keep sweet but when he said those horrible things, she broke the covenant placed on women and was punished. Even when she managed to control her feelings, he read the fear in her expression. He used that fear to terrorize a young girl with no defense against him.

"We don't know how pure your blood truly is but God knows and you will be cast into hell for your sin."

It was Aaron's favorite monologue. She wasn't born of a priested father. That and a pure bloodline were needed to enter the highest tier of heaven, or so she'd been taught. During the prophet's visit, he never looked at or spoke to her. After he inspected the wives and the older daughters, he walked around and checked for dust on the cabinets and furniture. He gave Eve's mothers a nod of approval for keeping a righteous home. He then told them to get on their knees and pray with him. They gathered around in a half circle with the prophet standing, his son beside him, and prayed. Eve remembered her knees hurting by the time he finished the long-winded version of what was expected of women according to God.

With a shake of her head, she dispelled the memory and returned her thoughts to the homicides.

She examined the list of Bart Tanner's wives again. She made a note to inform the jurisdictions where the women were located and have local detectives handle interviews. She would discuss the plan with Judge Remki when she spoke to him. Eve hoped the children would receive some type of counseling for what had happened inside the Tanner home, but she wasn't the person who would make that decision.

The second list included the names and addresses of the families close to the Tanner's home. Her team had most of that information now and she knew the delay in sending the list was a tactic to slow the investigation down.

Her team would return for lunch in about thirty minutes. Eve reviewed the evidence against Hannah again and walked through the crime scene with new eyes. It made more sense now.

She didn't plan to say anything until they finished their work today. She wanted to give them time to conclude the same thing she had. The evidence didn't lie, even if she wanted it to. Once her team opened their minds to what the photos showed and the one thing that would cause this kind of cover-up, they would need time to absorb the information. Yep, she would wait until they concluded today's interviews.

The height of the blood print on the master bedroom doorframe and Hannah's closet doorframe would be difficult for an adult to unconsciously leave behind. Other anomalous marks of blood could be explained if the murderer was no taller than an average ten-year-old. The blood on the sleeves of the dresses now made sense. The killer was not looking for Hannah. It *was* Hannah.

The phrase *that child* kept running through Eve's head.

The church's response and everything that had occurred since the team arrived in town made more sense now. Her brother had known who murdered the Tanners from his first phone call. The church had been unable to cover the crime and dispose of four bodies. They didn't think Eve and her team would figure out the truth. They forgot that Eve knew what monsters they really were and, after a year, so did her unit. They may even have hidden the knife and Hannah's bloody clothing. Yet proving their involvement would be hard unless she could interview Hannah.

When the media discovered the truth, it would be bigger news than if one of the plural wives had done it. Only in very rare cases had children committed crimes like this. Her team would have trouble seeing the truth, just as she did, but they would come to the same conclusion. The evidence didn't lie.

Bina and Clyde arrived first, while Collin and Ray fetched platters of Mexican food from a restaurant twenty minutes away.

"I'd like to move to your room to eat if you don't mind. I have the timeline laid out on the bed," she said, and nodded toward the photos.

"Which means you didn't take a nap," Clyde accused.

"There you're wrong, Mr. Detective Man. I actually did nap and I feel much better now." She smiled and saw a slight tilt to his lips at her response.

They changed rooms and Bina texted the guys to let them know where they were.

They dug into the food after it arrived. Thankfully, she was starving and had no problem eating an entire entrée.

Eve's thoughts centered on Hannah and the crime scene. She wanted to walk back through the house with her new assumptions and see if they had missed anything that would help the case. Once they talked it through, she knew her team would agree.

They also needed to know why Kathryn Wilson was not at home the night of the murders. Though it was a small possibility, maybe she had helped Hannah or given her the idea. They had to tie up all loose ends. Every step they made in this case would be closely analyzed by Eve's superiors. The media was another story entirely and she knew the public would have a hard time understanding what could possibly bring a child to murder her family in such a gruesome way. Bart Tanner was dead and people wanted someone to punish. A law enforcement set up that placed the blame on a child was an easy out.

Eve hoped, for Hannah's sake, that they could find an adult such as Kathryn to share the blame.

"We should have the first round of interviews wrapped up today," Collin said, and caught Eve's attention.

She nodded. "We'll have a meeting this evening. Be

prepared for a late night. I have something you need to see. Don't worry," she said after Clyde gave her a hard glare. "I have another nap planned and I'll be rested."

Clyde grunted. He was still indignant that Eve was working. Her aches and pains were better with the help of ibuprofen. After their meeting tonight, he would have something else to think about.

They cleaned up and left to finish the interviews.

Eve had something to do before she took a nap. Being in this town and the memories of her childhood always made her think of her mother.

Maggie worked at the front desk of a small dental office. She had never remarried. She lived in a one-bedroom apartment within walking distance of work. She called Eve periodically and checked in. Eve rarely called her because their conversations were so stilted and she dreaded them.

Her mother had always been standoffish and still Eve didn't doubt her love. Maggie rescued her. She could have left Eve inside the cult, but she hadn't. These thoughts had her pressing her mother's number. She was tired of running from the past. Her mother had answers, but Eve understood Maggie had to have help before they could move forward in their relationship. Right now, Eve really needed to hear her voice.

"Hi, Mom," she said when her mother answered her cell phone.

"Eve?"

"I know you're at work but is there any chance you could talk for a few minutes?"

"Of course. Hold on."

Eve heard her mother's muffled voice and then the line crackled twice and a door closed.

"Are you okay?" her mother asked.

"I'm working a difficult case and needed to speak with you."

Maggie hadn't wanted Eve to take the oversight job. She'd

given one objection and then never brought it up again. Maggie and confrontation did not go hand and hand. Her mother lived a quiet life and preferred it that way.

"I'm not sure how I could help with a case," she said, doubt in her voice and also a touch of fear. Eve recognized the response after years of seeing her mother back down and hide away from things that bothered her.

"It was a long time ago, but I wanted to thank you again for Whiskers and the camera. I know we didn't have much money. You had to pay a deposit so I could have a cat. You need to know how much these two gifts helped me."

Today, with the realization of how bad the church was and the devastation it caused, Eve could clearly see what Maggie's rescue had done for her. She'd saved her from years of terror at Aaron's hands because Eve knew he would have married her. Her mother also saved her from becoming Hannah.

"Oh, honey." Her mother started crying.

"You don't like talking about your past, but I think you should. You made sure I saw a therapist and you need to do the same. I'm in Aaron's jurisdiction right now and it's brought up a lot of memories. Maybe someday we can talk honestly about our time here."

"I've thought about a therapist. I just don't know." She sniffed.

"You made the best choices you could. What happened was not your fault. You thought you were keeping us safe. You rescued me when you understood I was in danger. I don't hold what happened in my childhood against you." She had blamed her mother for long enough. If it weren't for Maggie, Eve's entire life would have been one nightmare after another.

"Thank you, Eve. I will find a therapist, I promise."

"I'm glad. I'll let you get back to work."

"I love you, honey. Never forget that."

"I love you too." It felt good to say the words.

Eve disconnected. Her emotions were raw. She should have done this years ago. Her mother never gave herself enough credit for the strength she instilled in Eve. She had demons Eve couldn't imagine. Maybe one day, Eve would have answers to some of the many questions she'd had since childhood.

Maggie needed to forgive herself first.

Eve lay down on Bina's bed. Her eyes grew heavy and finally her sleepy brain let go. She didn't dream, at least not anything she remembered.

She checked the time when she woke up and two hours had passed. She decided on another hot shower to help her body aches. It felt great and she was a new person by the time she got out. Her headache was gone and hopefully would stay that way.

Bina arrived at the room. She looked at the bed and the photos a few times but didn't ask what Eve had found.

"The interviews were uneventful," she said. "The women wanted their husband present but talked to us after we told them it wouldn't happen. I swear they're almost relieved."

"They are," Eve agreed. "They know if they mess up and tell you something they shouldn't that they will be in trouble. Easier to misspeak and get away with it if their husband isn't there. Most walk a fine line. It's difficult to be as perfect as what's expected of them. They're also scared about the homicides. They've been told God punished the Tanners. They don't want the same punishment."

"That's sick."

"I completely agree."

Clyde knocked and Bina let him in. He glanced at the photos and timeline cards on her bed.

"Collin and Ray have sub sandwiches in their room," he said after glancing from the bed to Eve and looking her over thoroughly. "You look better than you did earlier."

"I napped as promised and my head no longer hurts. I know you want me staying put tomorrow but it won't be easy."

"Nothing is easy with you," he grumbled, and Eve bit back a smile. It was nice having someone care about her.

They left the room and joined Collin and Ray.

"Anything new to report?" Eve asked, thankful she was hungry again.

"Nothing exciting," Collin said between bites. "One houseful of women were convinced the murderers were long-haul truckers spreading evil throughout the country. When we asked why, they told us the truckers carried the deeds of Satan with them."

"Yeah," Ray added. "I expected someone to mention aliens. Collin is convinced they exist."

Collin threw a pillow at him, which Ray tossed back.

"What's going on this evening?" asked Bina, ignoring the guys.

"I need to show you something and see if you find what I did."

"Like an actual clue?" Ray grinned. "Those have been few and far between on this case."

"Maybe more than a clue."

"Are you sure you're up to this?" asked Clyde.

"Promise. I feel a lot better. Are we ready to start?"

The team followed her from the room. She didn't plan to spell it out; she wanted them to see it themselves. When the church didn't protect women and children from the monsters they created, the loss of innocent lives was the consequence.

TWENTY-SIX

She sat in the chair farthest from the bed so they had room to move. "I walked around the photos and mixed the order," she told them. "Take your time." She thought about the media and the hype this case would generate once the reports were public record. Hannah would ultimately be the one hurt. In Eve's opinion, she'd been through enough. She wasn't letting Hannah off the hook. She was a very emotionally disturbed child. Fundamentalist doctrine said the age of accountability was eight. That, Eve did not agree with. Hannah was a product of everything wrong with their beliefs.

She checked her watch. They'd been examining the timeline and photos for twenty minutes. Ray was staring at the images from the opposite side of the bed. His eyes went to Eve and then back down. He grabbed the two door prints and held them side by side. His gaze snapped back to Eve's. He shook his head, his gut having understood what his brain hadn't caught up with. Slowly he laid them on the bed and moved to her side.

"Let's go to your room and we can talk about it while the others keep working," Eve told him.

"Smarty-pants," said Collin, engrossed by the photos.

Ray didn't say anything until they were in his room. He dragged his fingers slowly through his hair.

"Christ," he said. "It makes sense but I'm having trouble wrapping my head around it."

"What makes sense?"

"It was the daughter. Damn, I can't believe this."

Eve was relieved. She'd needed to hear him say it out loud.

"Hannah killed four people," she said softly. "I didn't want to believe it either."

"I'm struggling here. The brutality. They were deliberate, planned assassinations. I can't picture a child doing something so horrific." He began pacing.

"Do you think she had help?"

He shook his head. "The evidence doesn't show it."

"Not in the way you're thinking. What if someone incited her hatred? They told her how to do it and put everything into place. The family was drugged. Would Hannah have the mental ability to come up with the idea, wait long enough for the drugs to work, know what knife to use, and then deliberately kill them?" These were questions that had been running through Eve's mind and it felt good to share her thoughts.

"You're right. Rationally, it would be hard for a child to plan it alone. The brainwashing that goes on here is beyond anything imaginable. It's not too much of a leap to think someone could push a child into doing something like this."

"Let's check on the others," Eve said now that she and Ray were on the same page. They walked back to her room and she used her keycard to open the door.

Collin and Bina were sitting on the bed, the stacked images pushed to the side. Their expressions were almost identical. Clyde left without meeting her eyes.

"A very short man or woman?" Bina asked. She was serious.

"I'm not counting anything out at this stage," Eve replied. "The fact Hannah was the only one alive does not prove she killed them. Circumstantially she had motive. We don't know if she even went to her aunt's house for the night. Fundamentalist children do not do sleepovers. I should have questioned that from the beginning."

"I have daughters her age," Collin said, staring at the floor. Bina placed her hand on his shoulder and squeezed.

Eve hadn't considered the ages of his twins. She could see the hurt in his expression.

"Why did they call us to investigate?" he asked in frustration. "Why not hide the murders, hold one of their late-night funerals, and cover the deaths up completely?"

"Too many people knew about it," Eve said. "With law enforcement oversight they couldn't take the chance of being caught covering it up. In their minds, the only thing worse than a child killing four people is the church being seen as the bad guy that caused it." Eve looked at them and took a breath. "We need to reinterview everyone as soon as possible. I need everything we have for Judge Remki. He will be key. Until I speak to him, we build our case. First up, Ray readies a warrant for the Wall home. I'll need to use someone local to get it signed. That could cause even more trouble and let what we know out of the bag."

She could practically see their minds clicking on the logical conclusion that they had overlooked earlier. She'd chosen them because they weren't just good at their jobs; they were the best.

"Bina, go through the photos again with me," Collin asked, already positioning the images again. "I need to get this right in my head."

"I've had longer to think about it than you," Eve told them. "We knew the killer had an emotional attachment to the victims. The mother and father's joined hands, the hand propped beneath Tracy's chin, her hair arranged over her shoulder. Collin, you noticed something off with the blood spatter in the hallway and bedrooms. It bothered you. There was little spread, which would have happened if the blood fell from higher up. Even with the knife held low at a person's side, the distance from the floor was too small for it to have been an adult. I looked it up. The average height of a ten-year-old ranges between three feet six inches and four feet. That would place the bottom of her hand, extended straight down with the tip of the knife at about ten to twelve inches."

Collin nodded and Eve continued. "Hannah wouldn't think twice about using the towels in the bathroom. Like I mentioned before, children don't spend the night at relatives' homes. I shouldn't have missed that."

Her gaze traveled to each of them, knowing how hard this was. "We'll never feel *right* about this case. We shouldn't; but maybe we can prove Hannah was somehow coerced."

She gave them a moment to absorb what she'd said.

"I'm going to grab my laptop from my room and I'll come back here to get started on the warrant," said Ray.

"I'll check on Clyde," she told Collin and Bina after Ray stepped out.

"He didn't say anything before he left. Walk gently." This came from Collin.

Clyde didn't answer her knock so she walked out to the vehicles. He was leaning against the back of the van, staring into the darkness.

She moved shoulder to shoulder with him and did the same.

"I know what the evidence says, but I'm having trouble accepting it," Clyde said softly.

"I don't see a way around it being her. There's a possibility someone smudged the prints on the door. Law enforcement would know it's hard to get rid of blood evidence completely. The best way to throw us off would be to make sure there was no viable print."

Clyde was in his own thoughts.

"How could she do it, physically? Elijah was almost the size of a grown man. He struggled. I just don't see how it's possible."

"He was drugged. Hannah was also a very determined child. I received the toxicology report a few minutes before you returned today. It was Benzodiazepine. Elijah didn't have as much in his system as the others but there was enough. It also makes more sense if you add the strange vibes we've had since the beginning. We knew they were covering something. They don't want the world knowing that they allowed a monster like Bart Tanner to get away with his crimes. Leaving two wives and two children in that home is the biggest reason for the cover-up. The church may not be responsible for Bart Tanner's crimes but once they became aware, they are just as guilty for everything that came next." She took a breath and allowed the clear night air to fill her lungs before exhaling. "I don't think they knew about the attic. When I brought it up with Candace, she mentally lost control. The church knew what he'd done, but they didn't want the specifics. I'm sure they didn't even interview the women. They got them out before they could make bigger waves."

"Every case uncovers more about the sick minds of these people. It never fazes you; you're never as surprised as the rest of us. You expect this level of evil before we arrive. I think about what your childhood must have been like. I don't like where those thoughts take me."

Clyde had never liked Aaron and Eve didn't blame him. He knew the fundamentalist doctrine concerning the color of his skin. In their eyes, he was as big an abomination as Eve. It never stopped him doing his job but then again, it didn't stop her either. Now that the evidence sank in, she wasn't surprised Hannah had murdered her family. The corruption, control, and absolute power in the area were nothing new to her.

"I was a child and they groomed me to be an old man's bride. I looked forward to marriage because that was my duty to

God." She took a moment. "I was one of the few to get away. Who knows what my life would have been like? I could have easily been Marcella or Tracy. I could have been Hannah."

He took her hand and turned his body so they were facing each other.

"No. Even without your mother's help, you would have gotten away. I'll never doubt that. You have a sense of justice that rivals all of ours."

She shrugged. "Maybe you're right. I'll never know for sure. Ray is writing a warrant for the Wall home. We're hoping to find evidence that Hannah did not act alone. Kathryn Wilson was missing that night. We'll get a warrant for her home if we need one."

"Maybe," said Clyde. "I don't see it."

"Neither do I. This will be a media storm and we either prove someone helped or we disprove it. We need the case airtight."

"I'll accept that Hannah possibly had help as a theory. Until now, they've been in short supply." The moon cast a glow in his dark eyes. "Your stepbrother didn't think we would solve this case."

Clyde was right. They were set up for failure from the beginning. The church held women and dark skin in contempt. That covered four out of five of her team.

"Underestimating us was their biggest mistake. If he would had admitted the truth from the beginning, it would have been better for them. They've opened themselves to a media nightmare made larger because they lied. Now we need to prove the lie. That could be difficult." She took another slow breath. "They tried to kill or seriously injure me to hide the truth."

"Yeah, they did." His thumb rubbed over her fingers.

Eve fixed her gaze into the darkness again. "He told me when we were young that I would be one of his wives."

Clyde's thumb stopped moving for a moment and then

continued its gentle stroke. "I've never liked the way he looks at you."

Eve's face heated and she was glad he couldn't see it. "Aaron isn't a good person and I need to open my eyes to who and what he really is. Monsters are grown out here."

"After what we've discovered in this case, I agree with you."

"Are you ready to go inside and get this organized? It's possible the Walls have the evidence tying Hannah to the murders. We need to get this rolling and we can't do it without you."

"My room," he said. "I don't want to stare at the photos again tonight."

She understood how he felt.

"Come here." Clyde opened his arms.

It was the easiest invitation Eve had accepted in her life. She slid into his warm scent. He was her rock. She pulled away after several long moments.

"Thank you. That helped."

He smiled gently with a flash of white teeth.

She squeezed his hand then sent the text to the team.

Eve shivered before they walked back inside. Hannah was out there somewhere. She was a danger to others. Even if someone did coerce her, she could kill again.

TWENTY-SEVEN

They gathered in Clyde's room a few minutes later and settled into chairs. Ray continued clicking away on his laptop.

Eve looked at the time. It was late but she decided to try Tamm's cell anyway.

She picked up on the third ring.

"Are you okay?" were the first words out of her mouth.

"Much better," Eve replied.

"That's not good enough. You're up late. Did you take a nap today?" Tamm was stubborn and Eve wouldn't get anywhere without answering.

"Two hours and even nodded off for a short period before that. Bina and the guys have been watching me closely and they are right here with me. No headache this evening at all. Now can we get to the reason for my late-night call? I have a huge favor to ask."

"You've got it. I've been worried about you and couldn't sleep. I just boiled water for chamomile tea. I'll change it to green for a caffeine boost."

Now that she'd settled Tamm's concerns, Eve got straight to the point.

"Judge Remki is still in the hospital and we haven't heard from him. We need a judge to sign a warrant; one who is not involved with the church. Could you find out if there is anyone in the county we can trust? Contact info would be great, if such a person exists."

"Give me thirty minutes and I'll have someone for you." Tamm ended the call.

Ray spoke before she could mention the next step they needed to take.

"The warrant is almost finished." He didn't look up.

Eve glanced around the room and her mind slid from the case for a moment. Bina was deep in thought, no gummy bears in sight. Collin stared at Ray, his attention far away. Clyde made furtive glances in her direction.

"How is everyone mentally?" she asked, and met each pair of eyes when they looked over.

"I'll survive," Bina said. "I'm running possibilities through my head and they all lead back to Hannah doing this on her own."

"I can't stop thinking about the twins," Collin admitted. "This goes against human nature. Unless the evidence is planted, it rarely lies, but I don't need to like it."

"What are your feelings about the case?" Clyde asked her.

If they were sharing their thoughts, the least she could do was add hers.

"I'm on the same page as all of you, but my mind is going far past that. I want to take them down. I've wanted that for a long time." She shrugged. "I don't like the personal baggage I carry interfering with a case, but it's time to admit it's my driving force."

They turned their full attention to Eve. She'd never admitted this out loud to them before.

"I'm on board with that," Collin said. "If we can't do it this time, we keep going and prove their corruption in the next one.

I'm sick of them running us around in circles. If we don't stop them, no one will."

Bina searched her pocket and took out a gummy bear.

"If we do that, we'll be out of a job. I for one could use a simple gambling debt and murder with a side of money laundering." She popped the gummy bear into her mouth. She was back in work mode.

They smiled and some of the tension eased.

"Can you review what I have?" Ray asked, and turned the laptop in Eve's direction.

She made a small change to the probable cause statement and made the outside description of the Walls' home clearer. Ray and Collin went to Eve's room and moved the printer back into the van. They needed it set up for the next day. They printed the warrant and returned to Clyde's room. Eve signed so it was ready to fax if Tamm came through.

The call came in five minutes later.

"He's new, he's Mormon but not fundamentalist. I think he's a good bet and I have a home number."

How Tamm managed it, she didn't know.

Judge Nelson didn't answer the phone so Eve left a message, hoping he would get back to her quickly. If not, she would try again in the morning.

The call came through as soon as she'd finished the thought.

"Detective Bennet," she answered. "Thank you for calling me back," she said after he gave his name. "I wouldn't have called, your honor, if it wasn't important."

"What do you have for me?" he asked, his tone neither accommodating nor angry.

Eve told him everything. She outlined the interference from the church and her belief they were covering the crime because it was committed by a child. The judge listened without interruption.

"Is there another possibility?" he asked when she finished.

"Someone coerced her. Either the evidence holds up with additional information or it won't. The warrant is crucial."

"Send it and if everything is there, I'll sign."

"Thank you, your honor."

"You'll need to get it to the courthouse within twenty-four hours for the official time stamp. I'm high on discretion in my office so make sure you deliver it to my personal secretary. I can't promise word won't get out, but you have a better chance this way."

She appreciated the heads-up.

"We're doing a grid search from the Walls' home to the murder scene at noon tomorrow. They'll possibly figure it out when they see the route." They discussed a few more particulars before the call ended.

Finally, Eve caught a break in this godforsaken county.

The warrant was electronically signed an hour later and Eve sent it to the printer.

Tamm answered before Eve heard the phone ring on her end.

"Thank you, you came through again. We're serving the warrant in the morning and then doing an involved grid search. Could you work another miracle and see if a team from the lab could meet us at noon?"

"Consider it done. You need sleep. I'll call you in the morning."

"Thank you." They disconnected and Eve looked at her team. "Whether we find something at the Walls' home or not, we need to track the route Hannah would have taken. I'm not sure she went to the Walls' at all, or that she's been there since we arrived. It hasn't rained and if she made the walk, maybe we can locate a print. We'll stop at the Tanners' and measure the boots in the entry room and I think I remember a pair of shoes in her closet." Collin nodded his head in the affirmative that they were still there. "That will give us an approximate size."

"Lucky we all love grid searches," Ray said with a groan.

"Stop your whining," Clyde told him.

Ray was joking. They all hated the monotony of grid searches and there was a lot of ground to cover. It would be easier with the added bodies from the state lab if Tamm could pull it off. Not that Eve doubted her. The woman could rule the world if she set her mind to it.

She knew her next statement would not go over well.

"I need to borrow a gun."

TWENTY-EIGHT

"You're not going." Clyde's expression had turned hard. They needed her and he had to see reason. She didn't doubt Lieutenant Crosby would order her home. She'd sent him a quick email, being truthful about the doctor's orders and telling him she would take it easy. She hadn't checked her messages since.

"I can hang back. Let me go in on entry and then I'll wait in the van until you're ready for photos. You need an extra body."

"No to the entry team. We'll worry more about you than danger inside. You wait in the van until the home is cleared and then you can take photos." His eyes did not match his expression. He was concerned. Warrants were his specialty when it came to entry and keeping everyone safe.

Eve looked at the others.

"I need help here," she implored. Her only chance was backup on this.

"All in agreement with Clyde, raise your hand," Ray said, and looked at everyone but her.

Four hands went up including the brief fan of fingers Clyde gave. He bit back a smile.

"Thanks for nothing." She scowled but gave in.

"We love you." Bina looked directly at her. "This is our way of showing it."

Pressure built behind her eyes. *Family.* The word ran through her mind again.

"I have a confession." She was tired of worrying about their response, especially Clyde's. They needed to know the truth and she had to get this over with.

She told them about her stepbrothers waiting for her in front of Aaron's office.

"There were five?" Clyde asked, his eyes hard pinpoints, his body rigid.

"Yes." She wanted to duck her head but she deserved this and kept her gaze level with his.

"And five men attacked you?"

"Yes."

"Did you give this information to the officer who took your statement?" He barely opened his mouth, his teeth clenched so tight.

"I did."

His eyes continued drilling into hers. She could feel his anger but she also knew there was hurt mixed in.

"When it happened, I didn't think it was important. I was wrong. I was threatened my entire childhood with the word abomination and I'll simply admit it: I was ashamed that they had confronted me."

"But you didn't think you should mention this last night?"

Now Eve was annoyed.

"Last night I was still in shock and when I left the hospital, I took medication for pain. I wasn't in any condition to have this conversation. That doesn't mean I shouldn't have said something about what happened outside Aaron's office directly after the confrontation. It was a mistake."

Clyde gave her a long look then backed off, his body losing its fight mode. Eve turned to the team.

"I owe everyone an apology. When we're back at the office, I'll give you an overview of my childhood. The attack made me realize you shouldn't be in the dark and we should all know what we're up against. Tamm will be included."

"Was there anything you could identify to prove your brothers did this?" Ray asked.

"No, they weren't wearing the same clothing. Their height was similar but it happened quickly. If the same stepbrother spoke the word abomination, I might have been able to match it to the first incident, but they spoke in unison. I told everything to the officer and hopefully the detective assigned will have some ideas. It's not our investigation and we need to concentrate on the warrant and our case."

Clyde walked with her and Bina back to the room. He didn't say anything and she was worried, but there was nothing she could do. His hurt had replaced the anger.

"Those men are not your family," Bina said as soon as their door closed behind them.

It took her a moment, then she nodded.

"They were never your family."

Bina grabbed a shower while Eve prepped herself for bed. It was hard to keep her eyes open. She needed sleep. Even with her worry over Clyde, she barely stirred when Bina came out of the bathroom.

Dreams didn't wake her.

They ate a quick meal of fruit and cereal she and Bina had stored in their small room refrigerator. Ray and Collin stocked the van's cooler with items for lunch from their room. The warrant and grid search could take hours.

Tamm called at seven and let Eve know a team would be there at noon.

"I feel great," she told Clyde when she caught him assessing her while he ate one of his protein bars.

"You're sure?"

She didn't know if he was still upset with her and it caused a tightness in her gut that she hated.

"Yes, positive, and I'm good to go. You should change your mind on entry."

"Not a chance." His genuine smile relieved her mind.

They were okay. He might not have forgiven her completely for keeping the confrontation with her brothers from him, but he was moving forward. This was one of those relationship quandaries she knew nothing about. She would learn, Eve told herself.

She hadn't needed ibuprofen this morning and movement, even though it was just walking, would help the aches in her arms and back where she had taken the brunt of the blows. The area around the sutures was sore and there was a dark multi-colored bruise that made it look worse. She also had discoloration beneath her eye. The bruises only hurt if she touched them and it brought up a memory of her mother.

"Well, don't touch it then," Maggie had said when Eve had complained about an injury after being hit by a softball during physical education in her first year of high school.

She didn't usually have normal everyday memories of her mother.

They picked up a tail a block from the hotel. Two black lifted trucks followed them to the Tanners' home. The squad cars were outside the crime scene tape as usual. The officers, sitting inside their vehicles, ignored them. Ray jumped out and lifted the tape and they drove through. Collin carried an evidence bag. Eve got out and Clyde didn't object.

They found Hannah's boots in the mudroom. They were the smallest of the five and easy to identify. Eve took photographs of the tread and they measured the size before packaging them. She remembered the prints they'd found on the search around the outside property. Blowing dust was a problem then and it would be one now, but they had to be sure. They climbed the stairs and entered Hannah's room. It hadn't changed, but their opinion of the crime scene had, and they looked at the room with different eyes.

Sadness swelled inside Eve. All she could hope for was someone pulling Hannah's strings. If it had happened, they would prove it. She wanted to interrogate Kathryn and get the truth out of her. That would need to wait and anytime they had to wait on interviews, people disappeared in this community.

Eve took pictures of the shoes before they measured and bagged them. Like Hannah's dresses earlier, they were now needed as evidence. They were covering all bases. With Hannah as their suspect, they had to collect anything that could possibly tie her to the murders, or even disprove she did them. If they looked for shoe prints, they collected shoes. A defense attorney would eat them alive on the small stuff.

They returned to the vehicles. Eve got into the van this time. Collin drove with her and Ray inside. Clyde handled the SUV with Bina riding shotgun. The God squad trucks followed along with a few members of the media.

Ray had security detail and would handle media or church personnel outside if they approached. Eve would watch from inside the van and would call the others out of the house if Ray ran into trouble.

Collin parked to block sight to the inner courtyard. Eve, in the passenger seat, could see inside and see Ray's position through the driver's window. The God squad drove past, turned around, and parked half a block away. The media parked a bit closer. Two journalists walked up to Ray and he told them to get back in their vehicles for safety reasons. They weren't happy but they complied.

Her team's refusal to speak to the media was widely known. Not one word had ever leaked from her office. The state attorney general decided on dissemination of their reports. They didn't need to be given out on public record's requests until an investigation was concluded. Speculation was all the press had right now.

Clyde grabbed the door ram from the back of the SUV. It would be used if no one answered quickly.

"Children in the home," Eve reminded them. They'd discussed not pulling their firearms but decided after the attack on her, they couldn't take chances.

She watched from inside the van, thankful she could at least see what was going on. Her hand gripped the butt of the gun and she was ready to jump out if she heard shots. The weapon was one of Clyde's. He packed more firepower than the rest of them combined. The Smith & Wesson M&P 40 caliber felt almost like her Glock.

"Safety here, and on the other side, here," he'd told her. "It has a slightly bigger kick than your 23c. Be prepared."

The state issued them 40 caliber Glock 23s with compensated barrels. Their safety was located behind the trigger, which was really saying there wasn't one. They'd all been trained to have a bullet in the chamber, ready to fire. Clyde didn't want her getting hung up on releasing the safety if there was trouble. She'd pulled the slide and made sure the gun was tactically ready before pushing it into the Serpa holster, which was the same brand she carried for her Glock. She'd added an extra magazine clip to her belt even though the most likely scenario was an empty house. It didn't matter. They had to be prepared for anything. Her adrenaline kicked in and she kept her hand on the butt of the gun, her finger on the release.

No one answered after a series of loud knocks and shouts of "police" and "search warrant." Bina wiggled the door's handle then moved back so Clyde could get in position. It took him three strikes before the wood splintered completely and the lock gave. Bina had fitted them with earpieces and they each had a radio on their hip. They also had their vests on beneath their shirts. They were as prepared as they could be.

The shades were pulled and Eve couldn't see inside. Each minute seemed like an hour.

"First floor cleared," crackled over the radio.

A few minutes after that, the second floor was cleared.

Bina came out and approached the van's window.

"It looks like they packed for an extended vacation."

"Or forever," Eve grumbled.

"Yeah, that too. We're going room by room for anything that could possibly be related to the crime scene, but it's not looking good. They even took all their shoes. Garage door is locked and we're looking for keys."

"I'll just sit here and twiddle my thumbs," Eve complained.

"That will make Clyde happy."

Eve received a sympathetic smile before Bina went back inside. She rolled down the driver's side window when Ray walked up to the glass.

"God squad just took off like a bat out of hell and the media followed them."

"That doesn't surprise me. Hold your post. We can't trust they stay gone."

"Got it." He walked over a few feet and turned his back to the van.

Bina came out carrying keys and started working them into the lock on the garage door. Several tries later, it clicked open. Before she lifted the door, Eve got out and crouched down, ready to cover if someone were inside.

"Collin, get out here," Bina called over the radio thirty seconds after the door slid upward.

The garage was angled so Eve could only see inside about five feet into the right front corner. Collin jogged out and stopped, covering his lower face with his hand, indicating something smelled foul.

Eve walked over. The garage was a hunter's paradise except for the smell. A deer carcass had been left rotting in the back corner. Heavy sheets of black plastic were draped under it to catch the blood.

The family had left in a hurry. Chances were good that they had gone shortly after Eve and Collin had spoken to Howard Wall. Eve wondered if they had been packing while they were there.

Clyde came out of the house and joined them.

Their attention turned to the wall opposite the carcass, which held more than ten knives displayed in a large wooden frame. It contained two empty spaces that were waiting to be filled, or could have housed the missing murder weapon.

Collin stepped closer. "He's got a Wicked Edge Pro. Expensive and a really good knife sharpener." He pointed to a piece of equipment mounted to the counter below the knives.

"What are we taking?" he asked, continuing to stare at the assortment of hunting gear.

"Can you point out the skinning knives?" Eve questioned.

He stepped closer. "There are three that fit what the expert said. I can't entirely rule out some of the others, though."

"We're packaging them all. I'll get pictures first." She turned to Clyde. "Anything to collect inside?"

"No, but I think we should dust for prints and collect DNA samples. What if they try to say Hannah was here and she hasn't been in town since we arrived?"

The thought had occurred to Eve too. The worst-case scenario was that Hannah was dead. If she had never been in this home, Eve might have enough recorded audio to implicate Aaron and Howard Wall for obstruction. Murder would be harder to establish, but if Hannah wasn't found, Eve would do everything she could to prove exactly that.

"Do you want my help?" she asked Clyde. It wasn't her favorite job, but she could handle it.

"No, get photos of the garage. Do you think we should take photos inside to show the family cleared out?"

"Good idea. I'll grab my camera."

"Are you okay?" he asked, once again visually checking her over.

"Yes, just tired of the van."

"It's been twenty minutes." He chuckled softly.

"Too long."

They got back to work. The blood in the garage appeared to come entirely from the carcass. Collin bagged the knives after Eve took photos.

Eve felt impending doom deep in her gut. The church was notorious for moving its members to other communities when there was trouble. Eve didn't know if they would bring the Wall family back here. They had not heard from Family Services though this wasn't unusual. In the report, Ray had stressed the need to keep their case information from local law enforcement. Theirs was an ongoing investigation and Family Services dealt with this area a lot. In most circumstances, they could be trusted to keep quiet.

The evidence, which consisted of knives, prints, and DNA, was moved to the van. They did not have a positive on a knife or bloody clothing and they might never find them, but this case would be handled methodically, one step at a time.

They ate a quick meal standing up while waiting for the state techs to arrive for the grid search. When they finished lunch, Eve gave her team the bad news.

"We can start walking the grid around the outside of the house before the other team arrives. It will cut down on time."

"You need to stay here," Clyde said.

"I can walk and squat down. If I feel the slightest bit sick, I'll stop." She covered her heart. "Promise."

"The idea of sitting on you is looking better and better." His eyes flashed.

"I didn't even need ibuprofen this morning. I'll go crazy in the van." She planned to be stubborn and insist if he pushed it.

"You're walking next to me and I'm keeping an eye on you."

"I'll take her other side," said Ray.

Having got her way, Eve was not going to object.

They searched the interior of the courtyard carefully. There were several child prints, but none matched Hannah's shoes or came close to their size. Eve snapped a few photos to add to the report. Once the inside area was complete, they spread arm's length apart and started walking slowly outside the wall, Ray positioned on her left and Clyde on her right. Circling the house, they established a twenty-yard perimeter. No further shoe prints were located. They then began searching the most direct route from the Wall residence to the Tanner home.

The techs arrived early. Eve didn't want to admit it but she was tired. The sun was brighter, with no clouds. The temperature was somewhere in the high sixties. Her vest made her warmer and the extra weight didn't help. Usually, she barely noticed it, but she wasn't at one hundred percent, even if she hated admitting it.

They marked their location and walked back to the van where the other team waited. A large man with short red hair wearing tactical pants and a collared shirt with the state seal on it identified himself as Alex Taylor. They shook hands, grabbed water, and explained what they were looking for.

"All shoe prints. Another possibility is a knife. It doesn't matter if it's a pocketknife: mark it and we'll bag it after I take photos. Also, any sign of clothing. We're looking for things that don't belong."

The God squad and media had not returned. Someone had called them off.

Eve grabbed a baseball cap she kept in her evidence equipment bag to help block the sun. She managed another thirty minutes before she knew she wouldn't make it. Her head was aching slightly and she needed to rest. She was angry that the assault was stopping her from doing her job, but she had to trust that if something was out here, they would find it without her.

"Halt," she called, and turned to Clyde. "I'm done. I'll take the SUV back to the hotel." She took a sip of water. "You need to take over."

"What's wrong?" he asked with concern.

"Only a slight headache but I'm tired. I'll just slow things down. The sun is getting to me. I promise I'm not on the verge of collapse."

"Bina can go with you."

"I can drive myself. I'll go straight to the hotel and rest. I'm not nauseous or anything. I'm also doing as promised and playing it safe."

"Okay, but call me when you get there. I'll give you thirty minutes."

Collin turned over the keys to the SUV. The line moved in after Eve started the hike back. They were about two hundred yards into the search. She removed her collared shirt and then her vest once she was at the vehicle. She wore an undershirt, which protected her modesty. Not that she cared right now. She put her outer shirt back on and tossed the vest into the passenger seat beside her. As soon as she leaned back and turned on the air, she felt better. A minute later, she rolled down the window and waved at the line, which had stopped to watch her. Clyde probably called a halt to make sure she was okay. He lifted his hand and she took off.

She felt like a failure for returning to the hotel, but Clyde would never forgive her if she passed out. She adjusted the air conditioning so it blew straight on her face.

She was a block from the Tanners' home when she realized the officers in charge of scene integrity were gone, along with all the media that had stayed behind when they left this morning. A text came in on her phone.

Tamm.

County attorney holding a press conference. It's on the news. He's blabbering about nothing.

She would kill Aaron for the press conference and pulling the officers from the Tanner home. The church must have figured out that they knew about Hannah and even their semblance of cooperation was at an end. It was the only explanation. She rolled to a stop and parked next to the outer crime scene tape. She needed to check the front door to make sure it was locked. She didn't trust the officers.

The cool air had helped with her headache and she felt better. She walked to the door and turned the knob. The door opened and her anger rose to new levels.

"What the actual heck," she muttered to herself. She pushed the door wide and looked inside. The officers must have had another set of keys and they had purposely compromised the scene's integrity.

She thought about calling Clyde. She stepped inside the mudroom then moved farther into the house. She felt well enough to check things herself and decided to let the team finish the grid search. A report would need to be written stating that the house had been left unsecure for up to five hours. Law enforcement had probably cleared out at the same time the God squad took off.

Picturing Aaron in a prison jumpsuit did little to calm her anger. She locked the door behind her and quickly walked through the lower floor. She stopped at the staircase. The hair on the back of her neck stood up, but she shook it off.

She placed her foot on the first stair and disregarded the sense of foreboding that ran through her.

TWENTY-NINE

The house was silent. It seemed strange after being here so many times with her team. With five of them, there were always small noises and talking. She turned at the landing and stopped at the top, peering down the hallway. She decided to start at the rooms closest to the stairs instead of the master bedroom.

Her head shook slightly over the ridiculous apprehension she felt. After checking the utility closet and bathroom, she stepped carefully around the dark spots on the wooden planks and entered Elijah's bedroom. The blood on the walls and floor replaced her unease with sadness. He didn't deserve what happened to him. Marcella and Tracy could be held accountable for not leaving when they had the opportunity, but Elijah's decisions were made for him. He had nowhere to turn. His father had gotten away with horrible crimes, supported by church doctrine.

God, prophet, father.

That was their hierarchy. Even Aaron and her other stepbrothers were the product of the twisted indoctrination. But the crimes they committed and were now accountable for happened as adults. They no longer had the excuse of brainwashing. Control over women and children drove them to seek more power regardless of the consequences. Their prophet placed them above the law.

She backed out and moved to Tracy's room. The stains on the mattress had her walking closer. She should be using her new knowledge about Hannah to look at the scene with her detective's eyes, but she couldn't bring herself to do it now. The team would come back here and put their thoughts together. She just needed to check the house and get out.

She entered Hannah's room and looked at the twin bed that had belonged to her. If she was located, maybe a psychiatrist or therapist could unweave the horror she'd suffered along with what had brought her to commit the murders. She hoped Hannah eventually found peace.

Eve checked the closet that still had several dresses hanging inside. Now was not a time to cry but that was how she felt. She turned and walked out, her heart heavy.

The unused room containing only the three beds was exactly as she remembered.

The master bedroom was last. After she moved around the bed, she noticed the attic stairs. They were pulled down, sticking six inches outside the closet. Her team had not come into this room earlier. She remembered them securing the ladder on their last visit. This meant officers had invaded the family's secrets. To Eve, it was a violation of the victims and her investigation.

She walked over to the stairs and looked upward. She considered simply closing them. She was being stupid, she told herself. She had to check the attic.

The house creaked above her but she'd heard the sound while they collected evidence. She remembered it from her childhood too. Large, two-story homes were like that. She climbed the stairs and stepped a few feet into the room. The sun was brighter today and it wasn't as dark as it had been the last time she was up here.

"Who are you?"

Eve spun around so fast she stumbled back a step. Her left hand went flat against her chest and her right hand to her gun.

Hannah stood about three feet from the bottom corner of the bed, partially behind the chair. Her face and the top of her pale green prairie dress were cast in shadows by the slope of the ceiling.

Eve slowly lowered her left hand from her heart, slipped it into her pocket and flipped on the recorder. Her right hand remained firmly on the butt, her forefinger on the holster release. She tried to bring her breathing under control.

Hannah didn't notice her left hand; her eyes were on the gun. Eve dropped her arm loosely to her side, inhaling deeply then exhaling.

"Hannah?" It wasn't really a question but her mind was racing as she tried to grasp that the ten-year-old was standing in front of her.

"I don't know you," the child said in a tiny voice that sounded incredibly innocent.

For a moment, Eve's conviction that Hannah killed her family faded.

"I'm Eve. I came here to make sure the house was locked." She spoke softly, hoping Hannah wouldn't be afraid.

"Why do you have a gun?"

"I'm a police officer," she told her with a gentle smile.

"Are you going to shoot me?" Hannah asked.

"No. I wouldn't hurt you. I've been looking for you to make sure you're safe. I'm glad you're here."

"Why did you come up the stairs?" Hannah asked accusingly. It was in sharp contrast to the tiny voice from a moment before. "No one is allowed here unless Father permits it." She took a step from the shadows but her face was still hidden. Her hands were partially covered by the full skirt of her dress.

"I saw the ladder pulled down and wanted to make sure no one was here before I closed it. I'm glad I did. Would you like to go downstairs and we can talk?" Eve's heart beat double time.

"I don't like your clothes or your hair."

No, she wouldn't like them. Women in Hannah's world didn't dress this way and Eve's hair didn't show righteousness.

"These are my work clothes." Her thoughts were scattered as she tried to think what to say. "I wore dresses like yours when I was your age."

Hannah took one step closer and came fully out of the shadows. The front of her hair puffed only slightly and stray wisps stood out here and there. It was her eyes that momentarily halted Eve's thoughts. Piercing, ice blue. They were starker than the photograph. Her pupils were tiny dark pinpoints of intensity. Eve would never forget the way they looked. There was no feeling in them. Hannah was a child but her eyes said differently.

"My father liked it up here. This was his chair." She pushed it slightly with her foot. "He won't sit in it again." Her left hand came up and she ran it over the top of the chair's high back. "Did you see how God punished him?" Her head cocked to the side. She didn't blink. She appeared curious and showed no signs of fear.

Hannah turned slightly and sat in the chair. Her skirt billowed out then flounced down. She adjusted herself to get comfortable, her back against the wooden slats. Her feet didn't quite reach the floor. Her little black boots swung back and forth, the laces making a clicking noise when they hit the shoes.

"My father sat here." She studied Eve's clothes all the way down to her shoes. "I can sit here now and he won't get mad." She lifted her eyes to Eve's.

How much time had passed? Clyde expected her to call

when she arrived at the hotel. He would check on her soon. Her cell was in her back pocket.

"Do you want to sit down on the bed?" Hannah asked. "I think you do."

It was an odd thing to say. A cold sweat broke out on Eve's skin. She was allowing fear to get the best of her. Hannah would see it just as Aaron had when she was young. This child behaved like a predator. Eve was the prey.

"We should go downstairs and sit at the kitchen table. We can talk for as long as you like. How does that sound?"

"Why won't you sit on the bed? Does God's retribution scare you?"

"No, I'm not scared." Eve wasn't lying. Neither God's retribution nor the bed bothered her. Hannah, on the other hand, terrified her, even if the reaction didn't make sense.

"The bed is for atonement. You're an apostate. It should be your bed."

Okay. Eve had to gain control of her fear. From the few interactions she'd had with ten-year-olds, Hannah was nothing like them and spoke like she was much older. None of this mattered. Eve would never have an opportunity to talk to her again. Lawyers would step in and not allow her to be interviewed by law enforcement.

She took a slow steady breath then jumped slightly when her phone rang.

She pulled it quickly from her pocket, hit the speaker switch and set it to silent mode. She clicked on the answer button then tossed it on the bed. This was all done in seconds using mostly muscle memory. She barely took her gaze from Hannah.

"If you want to talk to me, I won't speak with whoever called," Eve said, a very slight rise in her voice. Her legs felt unsteady, her heart in her throat. Eve sat on the bed. "I'm still not sure why you're in the attic." She was telling Clyde her location.

"This is God's retribution room. Do you like it on the bed?"

Eve's dread spiked.

"It's not very comfortable. What would you like to talk about?"

Hannah looked slightly over Eve's shoulder at the wall. She brought her left hand up and scratched her nose then wiped the sleeve of her dress across it. It was a childish gesture but Eve couldn't relax.

"Did you see all the blood?" Hannah asked. Her eyes appeared soulless, completely devoid of empathy.

If this was what Hannah wanted to talk about, Eve wouldn't stop her, but the need to escape was hard to hold back.

"I saw the blood in the bedrooms," Eve told her.

"I think it's pretty. Did you know red is the color Jesus will return in?"

Yes, Eve knew that, but he would be wearing it, according to polygamist doctrine, not bleeding it.

"You won't go with Jesus because of your sins." The soft lilt of her voice had disappeared; it had dropped an octave. Hannah examined Eve's clothes again.

Clyde would need to get to the van. They would be farther along the grid search now. He wouldn't be at the halfway point but he would be close. It might be faster if he ran straight here. She'd locked the front door. The keys to the Tanner home were in the van. That wouldn't stop anyone on her team from getting inside.

Eve wasn't sure why she wanted them here, but her gut said she was in danger. She wasn't disregarding it this time. She should have listened to it and not entered the house alone. She could stand against a ten-year-old, she reassured herself. She inhaled and exhaled slowly to stay calm.

"Do you know why my father and mothers suffered a

penalty for their sins?" Hannah's eerie voice was completely monotone, devoid of inflection.

Eve's full attention locked on her again.

"No, I don't," she lied.

"My father said I would never be married and he would pull me up to the celestial kingdom to live with him for eternity. I didn't want to be there with him." Her eyes moved to the gun holster before she looked up and continued speaking, "He punished me for my sins and God didn't like that. My mothers and Elijah were part of his atonement. They deserved Father's punishment too." Her feet continued kicking back and forth. "God tasked me with their retribution. Now they are together in heaven, like they should be."

"I'm sorry your father hurt you." The sound of the laces messed with Eve's psyche.

Hannah innocently shrugged her small shoulders. The creepy response heightened Eve's dread.

"Father lied. He wasn't the true prophet." Hannah cocked her head to the other side. "Did your father hurt you because of your sins?" she asked.

The question startled Eve. Everything he did was because of their sins. Her father's punishments caused backaches, dry, chapped hands, and sore feet. He was severe in his convictions, but his actions didn't compare to the tragedy done to Hannah.

"Yes, my father hurt me," she said. It wasn't on Bart Tanner's scale, but it was child abuse all the same.

"Did you have a punishment room?" Hannah asked curiously.

"Not like this one." Eve had never considered her childhood pleasant, but compared to the life Hannah had, the abuse was mild.

"God told me what to do so they could be together. I practiced cutting the animals at Uncle Howard's house." She gave that small shrug again. "He was angry that I punished Father.

Uncle Howard didn't understand that God guided my hand." Her gaze went to the wall behind Eve, lost in memory. "I put pills in their dinner. It was easy. I stirred the pot so the stew didn't burn. Elijah had a tummy ache and he didn't eat all his food. God wanted him to suffer."

"Did you punish your Uncle Howard?" Eve asked. Could he and his family be dead by Hannah's hand?

"No. He might marry me when I'm older."

Did he abuse this child too? Eve was having trouble processing her thoughts. Each time Hannah spoke it was more chilling than the last. The small feet kicked faster and she suddenly appeared agitated.

"Are you okay, Hannah?"

This brought her attention back to Eve. Hannah stared into her eyes, capturing her in their trance. Eve couldn't breathe.

Very slowly, Hannah smiled.

Eve wanted to run down the ladder and escape the house.

"Father told my mothers to take the pills sometimes. He would make Elijah cry after they fell asleep. My brother had to suffer more because he cried." Something in Hannah's words reminded Eve of Aaron. "God told me it wasn't a sin to punish them. He said it would help me keep sweet. Maybe you should take the pills and God's retribution won't hurt so much."

"We should go downstairs. Are you hungry? I could make you something to eat." Eve had to get her out of the attic. Her senses continued screaming that she was in danger.

Hannah looked upward and stared at the vaulted ceiling, her neck stretching, eyes almost rolling back into her head. It was the eeriest movement she'd made since Eve heard her voice. Slowly Hannah's head lowered and her eyes settled on Eve.

"God told me you must atone for your sins." Hannah stood and took a step toward the bed.

Eve barely noticed the flash of the blade in Hannah's right hand before she lunged. Eve rolled to the side, drawing her gun as Hannah stabbed the knife down, slicing the mattress with a vicious stroke. Eve gained her feet and shuffled back, putting space between them.

Hannah smiled again.

"Drop the knife," Eve ordered sternly. The gun was shaking in her hands. The knife in Hannah's was steady as she turned. The smile hadn't left her face.

The blade lowered. Hannah moved it in a small figure eight motion, running it back and forth across the side of her dress.

"Aunt Linda brought me here. She didn't want me to hurt the baby in her belly. It doesn't have sin now but maybe someday it will suffer God's penalty."

She stopped moving the knife and lifted it slightly. Her left hand rose and she pressed her forefinger on the sharp side of the blade and sliced. She watched as the blood slowly appeared on the cut. She turned her palm to Eve.

"Jesus is coming for me. He doesn't want you."

Eve heard a sound on the stairs. She took a step to the head of the bed, closer to the wall so Hannah didn't notice someone coming up the steps. Hannah watched Eve's movement closely. She paid no attention to the gun, which remained pointed at her.

From the corner of her eye, Eve saw Clyde's head rise several inches above the attic floor.

"Hannah, put down the knife so we can keep talking." Her voice was calm even though she didn't feel it.

"Why?"

"I need someone to talk to. Maybe you could help me."

Hannah lowered her hand. Blood ran down her finger and spread to the dress.

"Do you want me to help you atone for your sins?" Hannah asked. "I don't think you have anyone to pull you into heaven."

Clyde stepped on the next ladder rung and his head rose six inches higher.

"Let's sit back down," Eve told her, trying to get Hannah's back fully to the stairs.

"Are you going to shoot me now?"

Eve's breath caught. Did Hannah want her to shoot?

"No, Hannah, I don't want to hurt you. I just want to talk." Her shaking fingers belied what she said. Her fear became centered around shooting a child. "I met your uncle Howard. Would you like me to call him?" She was thinking of anything that would keep Hannah's attention on her.

"I like cutting things," she said, and sliced another finger, barely looking at it. "Uncle Howard let me cut the deer and show him how I performed God's retribution. He let me touch the blood." Her hand went to her head, smearing red into the blonde. "I need to fix my hair."

"I could do that for you. I know how to make it high."

Clyde took another step. His body was half into the room now, his gun trained on Hannah.

"You don't have yours fixed properly either. Jesus won't like that." Hannah lowered the knife slightly.

"It's long like yours." Eve scrambled for the right words. "You could help me fix it and I'll help you."

Please put the knife down. Please don't make Clyde shoot you, Eve recited silently.

"Jesus would like that." Her voice was once again innocent. Hannah turned to the steps suddenly and she saw Clyde. She jumped back and put the chair between them then turned her attention to Eve.

Clyde exploded the rest of the way into the room, Ray behind him.

"Don't shoot," Eve shouted.

THIRTY

Hannah stumbled backwards when Eve yelled. Eve jumped between her and Clyde.

"Satan came to get you," Hannah said, her voice breathy, showing strain. She leaned to the side so she could see around Eve and keep her eyes on Clyde. "I'm waiting for Jesus," she told him. "He will make you leave the atonement room."

"Hannah," Eve said sternly, bringing the child's attention back to her. "Put the knife on the chair. You will be punished if you don't."

"You can't punish me," Hannah said angrily, her face reddening. "Only God or the prophet can do that."

"Eve, move back." Clyde was prepared to shoot. Eve knew him. He wouldn't be able to live with killing a child.

Hannah lifted the knife. Eve prepared to fire.

"It won't hurt," Hannah said. "Even Elijah didn't scream. I like watching the blood."

Eve lunged forward, grabbing the chair before Hannah moved. She swung and hit the girl solidly in the chest, knocking her over. She threw herself on top of her and grabbed the hand holding the knife. Within seconds, Clyde had Hannah's other hand secured and Ray took control of her legs, which were kicking with enough force to drive her body off the floor.

Hannah continued fighting, her head twisting jerkily as she squirmed, making it hard to keep hold of her. Eve holstered her gun, switched hands on Hannah's wrist and used the other one to take the knife.

"Hand it over," said Bina, from her right side.

Once Bina had it, Eve pushed down on Hannah's shoulder to help control her flailing body.

Clyde and Ray managed to holster their weapons and now they had three sets of hands holding her down. Hannah fought for another minute, hissing and spitting. Suddenly, her body went lax. Clyde flipped her to her stomach and Bina handed him flex cuffs. He secured her hands and turned her to her side. Hannah stared straight ahead, her breathing harsh, her eyes locked on something they couldn't see.

"We need to carry her out of here. Collin, take Eve's place. Bina, help Eve and make sure she isn't cut."

She wasn't sure when Bina had come into the attic. Her brain was having trouble processing.

"I'm good," she said, but didn't resist when Bina took her arm and pulled her gently away.

"You are on bed-rest and Clyde is my acting supervisor. What he says goes." The harsh words barely penetrated Eve's racing thoughts. Bina checked her over quickly, looking for blood. "She's good," Bina said when she finished.

People were stabbed and shot without knowing it due to adrenaline. Clyde was right to have her checked.

They lifted Hannah and carried her carefully down the steps. Eve went to her knees and looked at her hands. Her fingers shook uncontrollably.

"It's okay," Bina said beside her. "Hannah is okay. Breathe."

Eve suddenly gasped for air, unaware she'd been holding her breath.

"I'm good." She inhaled and exhaled deeply again. "I'm good," she repeated. "Call an ambulance for Hannah."

"You are not my supervisor right now. Clyde will handle it. Keep breathing."

Eve reached into her pocket and turned off her recorder. She sat back on her legs and looked at Bina.

"Hannah may have been staying here for a day or two. Check the attic, see if there's any place she could hide."

"You don't listen very well. Get out of detective mode and stabilize yourself. You're in shock."

Eve leaned back and her butt hit the wooden floor, her legs curled at an angle and her head tilted down.

"I feel sick."

"No bucket up here. Slow deep breaths."

"Your bedside manner sucks," Eve told her a minute later after she felt calmer.

"Promising you would go straight to the hotel wasn't so hot either."

"Really, now?"

"Now is better—you'll be my boss again tomorrow."

Ray climbed back up the stairs and squatted by Eve. She heard sirens in the distance.

"We've notified Family Services," Ray said. "They have a two-man team in the area working our earlier report. Clyde asked me to come up here and check on you."

"I feel sick but it's getting better. How is Hannah?"

"Catatonic. She hasn't moved and she hasn't blinked since we got her down there. She's breathing and has a pulse. Am I allowed to be freaked?"

"Yeah," Eve said between breaths. She raised her head and looked at him. "Thank you for calling the ambulance."

Bina sat beside Eve and started taking deep breaths with her.

"Clyde had you on speaker the entire drive over. She's one messed-up kid." Bina lowered her head.

Ray didn't say anything for a moment. They were in some semblance of shock.

"I'm going back down. I'll give Clyde a heads-up that you're okay. You are okay, aren't you?"

"Yeah. I just need a moment and I'll come down." She smiled at Ray. She needed to prepare herself to see Hannah again.

Her phone suddenly popped into her head. Eve started to rise. Bina placed her hand on her arm when she wobbled a bit. "I'm good, thanks," she assured her once she was upright.

She walked the few feet to the bed and grabbed it. The sirens drew closer and she knew the ambulance was at the house when the wail stopped.

"Where's the knife?" she asked, trying to remember what happened to it.

"In the back of my pants. We need gloves to remove it." Bina turned and Eve saw the butt sticking out.

She remembered Bina asking for it. She inhaled deeply.

"I want to check on Hannah before they take her," Eve said. "Family Services also needs to make the ride or one of you will need to go with her."

"Agreed. I'll go down first and catch you if you fall."

"Yeah, that'll work." A small grin escaped Eve. Bina was smart and would move out of the way no matter what she said. The humor helped calm her.

Hannah was on one of the couches in the gathering room. Her hands were no longer in flex cuffs. The paramedics were taking vitals. Clyde, who stood behind the couch, glanced at Eve, and nodded grimly.

A man and woman dressed in casual clothing walked in. Bina intercepted and they showed identification. They were from Family Services.

Eve walked with them into the kitchen area and gave a brief overview of what had happened in the attic. Her hands had finally stopped shaking. She told them that Hannah killed her family. Eve wasn't sure they believed her but they agreed to take custody.

"I have her recorded confession," Eve told them. "She's dangerous. Don't allow her out of your sight."

One of them would ride in the ambulance.

Ten minutes later, everyone had cleared the house but Eve's team. No one from local law enforcement came.

Eve needed to notify Judge Nelson to clear the way for law enforcement where the hospital was located. They had to oversee Hannah if she wasn't placed in a locked facility at the hospital. Family Services could not put her in emergency foster care and she wasn't sure if they understood that.

"Someone needs to glove up and get the knife from Bina," Eve told her team. "Hannah may have been staying here. We should check for someplace she could hide. The attic first."

They looked at Clyde, not Eve.

"Take photos of the attic and give us a moment," he told them.

Ray walked out the front door and came back with an evidence bag. He removed the knife from the back of Bina's pants and packaged it.

Eve's brain was finally processing again. She called Judge Nelson before Clyde could stop her. Thankfully the judge immediately took her call. He said he would personally notify law enforcement after she explained the situation.

She dared a glance at Clyde after the conversation ended. The others were upstairs.

"Do you want to have our conversation in the van or on one of the couches?" he asked.

"Van." She wasn't getting out of this discussion but she wanted out of the house.

After they sat down on the bench seat inside the van, Clyde listened to what had transpired before his phone call.

"You shouldn't have stepped between us. She could have killed you."

"I know. I wasn't thinking straight. I didn't want you to be the one to shoot her."

He ran his hand over his bald head.

"You should have called us when you saw that the officers were gone."

"Yes," she nodded. "I should have."

Clyde was the one having trouble processing right now. He wasn't yelling. Eve might have felt better if he were angry. She would have been furious if their roles were reversed.

"How is your head?" he finally asked, taking her hand.

"I need ibuprofen."

He released her and stood to access the first aid kit located in the cabinet above the bench seat. He dug around and handed her two pills, along with a bottled water from the cooler.

"You need food," he said after she swallowed the pills.

"Are you going to lecture me now?" she asked.

"Would it do any good?"

"It might make you feel better."

"It might. I'm worried about you."

"I'm okay. Shook up, but okay. I'm worried about the Wall family."

"Your stepbrother hasn't called. Local law enforcement hasn't shown up even with the 911 call for an ambulance. They're in this up to their eyeballs. If anything has happened to the family, it's too late to do anything about it now. I think we need to finish what absolutely needs to be done and clear out. Judge Remki can sort this mess when he's back on the bench."

Eve thought about it. Clyde was right. Judges and lawyers needed to review what happened here. She had a full recorded confession from Hannah.

Clyde's phone buzzed and he looked at the screen then typed a quick reply.

"The forensic team that helped with the grid search just finished and they're taking off. They didn't find anything."

"Thank you for getting here so quickly."

"You scared the hell out of me. Don't do it again." He smiled for the first time.

"I'll do my best."

THIRTY-ONE

"Chuck Wilson watches you at church," Sheila told Eve while they swept the back porch. "Do you like him?" Sheila had just turned thirteen and Eve was eleven.

He wasn't mean like Aaron and Eve thought he was cute, even though recognizing worldly beauty was a sin.

"He's nice," Eve told her sister. Chuck had never spoken to her but he did smile if he caught her eye. He didn't push or kick her like Aaron.

"What do you think it's like to be married?" Sheila asked.

"I'm not sure." Eve shrugged. "Maybe our husband would have ice cream day twice a month. That would be wonderful."

"Yeah, it would. Why do you think all the young girls marry old men?"

"They don't." Eve shook her head and thought about it. "Well, some of them don't."

"A lot of them do," Sheila said stubbornly. "I don't want to marry someone old. I think they're nicer when they're young."

She could be right. The older men didn't smile much. They watched the girls all the time but rarely said anything. The boys didn't get much chance to talk to girls outside their families but they did smile when no one was looking. Eve's brothers got to play with other boys but girls didn't play with anyone.

Aaron walked onto the patio. "What are you gossiping about?"

Eve opened her eyes and glanced around the hotel room. Bina was at the sink brushing her teeth.

The previous evening had been hectic. Ray and Collin took the warrant to the courthouse and had it timestamped to keep it valid. She finally heard from Judge Remki. It was a short phone call and he sounded tired. She didn't go into detail but told him a full report would be submitted to his office in the next seven days.

She wanted to have a meeting with the team but Clyde refused.

"I'm going to work out and you're going to bed." There was a very small gym in the hotel that consisted of a treadmill and a set of weights.

She hadn't argued. She and Bina ate dinner in the room together and went to bed early.

Her dream about her childhood left her frustrated. Aaron had been angry at her and Sheila but Eve couldn't remember how he retaliated. His many cruelties were jumbled in her head.

She had to contact him today.

By now he would have an explanation concocted for why the officers left the Tanner home, why no law enforcement answered the 911 call that brought the ambulance, and why there had been no contact at all since her assault. She wanted to hear what he had to say and then he could explain it again to Judge Remki.

Aaron's press conference had drawn the media away from the Tanner and Wall homes. Eve didn't have a timeline for when Linda dropped Hannah off. Their actions were highly suspicious.

She couldn't help thinking the confrontation with Hannah was a set-up. Had they planned for her team to find her? One of them could have been killed. It frustrated Eve that there were so many questions and few answers.

She was tired of Aaron invading her dreams. It was time to stand up to him and get some things from their childhood out in the open. Past time.

She sent a text to Clyde.

I'm heading to the guys' room for breakfast.

See you in ten, was his immediate response.

Bina went with her. Collin and Ray had gone out and picked up breakfast from a local deli. They needed to decide on a plan for today. Clyde knocked and Bina let him in. He grabbed a chair and sat down to eat the yogurt he carried.

"Don't you ever get tired of that crap?" Ray asked him.

"I think you need to look up the definition of crap," Clyde said and grabbed the spoon next to Ray's Styrofoam box that held eggs, bacon, and toast.

"My stomach disagrees. Your food would keep me in the bathroom full-time."

Clyde ignored him and turned to Eve. She spoke before he could ask.

"My head doesn't hurt. I had a good night's sleep and I'm ready to take back over command."

"Uh-oh," said Bina, and the guys looked at her. She shrugged. "I may have been a little bossy yesterday about Clyde being the acting supervisor."

"He was," Eve told her. "I'll try not to hold a grudge." She smiled. "Has anyone heard a word about Hannah?"

They all shook their heads.

Collin grabbed his phone and called the hospital. He gave his badge number and agency then hung up.

"They wouldn't give me info," he said.

"Family Services probably read them statute and threatened penalty if the media got wind of what happened from medical staff," Clyde told him.

"I don't think we need a final walk-through at the home," Eve said. "It's been compromised and we know Hannah committed the murders. Her confession will stand up in court. Everything she said was voluntary. Anyone disagree?"

"I'm okay with never going back to that house," said Ray.

Bina raised her hand. "I second that."

Collin and Clyde both nodded. Eve was relieved. She didn't want to return to the Tanners' home either. She never wanted to enter the attic again.

"I need to go to Aaron's office and talk to him in person. He'll have some explanation cooked up or will know nothing about law enforcement leaving. I want his defense on record."

"You're not going alone," Clyde told her.

"I was hoping Bina would come and wait outside while I speak to him."

"I'm coming in with you," Clyde insisted.

"I'll pull rank if I must. I'll record the conversation but he won't talk with anyone else there."

Clyde crossed his arms.

"I agree with Eve," Collin said. "He can't do anything at his office and she knows him better than we do. Let's all go. We'll take the van and wait outside. I'm hoping her other stepbrothers decide to pay a visit."

"I like that idea," Ray said. "I'm in."

Eve knew how lucky she was.

. . .

Denise looked up when Eve entered the building. The door to the offices clicked open and she pointed in Aaron's direction without saying a word.

It was strange and most definitely different from their last meeting.

Aaron sat at his desk. When he saw her, his face reddened and he stood.

"You fucked this up," he said, placing the blame on her and using a word she never thought would leave his mouth. "I may never unravel the damage you've done," he continued. "Did you even read Miranda?"

"Read who Miranda?" Eve asked softly, and placed her recorder on his desk. She would do this part professionally and completely by the book.

He dropped into his chair, realizing what he'd said, and stared at the recorder. She could see his mind clicking for a way to backtrack.

"I've been informed you have a ten-year-old child in custody. Is that true?" He came up with it quickly, his eyes leaving the recorder and finding hers.

"No, who told you that?"

"You're playing games. You arrested Hannah Tanner yesterday." He hesitated. "It's all over town."

Clyde had removed the flex cuffs before the ambulance arrived. Her team had temporary custody of her while the cuffs were on but no arrest was made. Aaron was digging his hole.

"Why would I take a child into custody?" she asked, her expression full of pretend innocence.

"Don't play games with me," he said, his face growing redder.

"I'm only here to ask why my crime scene was compromised. The officers watching the premises were gone and the door was left unsecured. That's all I came to ask about." She didn't mention the ridiculous press conference that she'd listened to on the television this morning. He'd basically said the investigators had leads and were following up on them. His only accomplishment was drawing the media from the two homes.

"You're telling me you didn't place Hannah under arrest?" he sneered, much like he'd done as a juvenile.

"Again, why? I'm very curious."

His frustration was obvious. He had to step carefully with the recorder going.

"Do you have a suspect for the homicides?" He'd decided to try another tack.

"I do. It will be in my full report once I've written it. I'll be more than happy to send you a copy."

He inhaled sharply. His eyes turned into small pinpoints of anger.

"Do I need to remind you I am the county attorney? This is my jurisdiction."

"Do I need to remind you a judge put me in charge of oversight for your jurisdiction and I am not under your command?"

"No, but you are under God's." He simply couldn't help himself.

"I was assaulted by members of your church. I don't answer to you, them, or your God. I answer to the state of Utah and Judge Remki."

"You're proud of being an apostate. Your filthy arrogance drips off you."

He was one to talk. Eve also noticed he didn't defend his church against the assault.

"Can we get back to the case and why law enforcement left the crime scene unsecured?"

"You would need to ask Chief Jackson that. I am not in control of his men."

Eve didn't bother reminding him he had just said this was his jurisdiction.

"I need the address of the Walls for interviews on the entire family including children. Hannah is not in good mental condition and she may have said something to one of the children in the home. Since her aunt took her to the Tanner home, the Walls must be staying locally."

This was conjecture. They had no idea how or when Hannah was taken to the home. They found no keys and no forced entry so it was very possible she was dropped off after the officers left.

"I don't know where they are, nor do I know how to reach them," he said. "Now you're saying Hannah committed the murders. Make up your mind."

"I didn't say that. You did. Hannah is a lead in our investigation and always has been. I haven't interviewed her, even after telling you how important it is that I speak with her. The children in the home might know something." She bit the inside of her cheek to keep from smiling. "Do you think the phone number you previously used for the Walls still works?" she asked calmly.

Aaron's eyes burned with fury which the recorder couldn't see. He had no way out of this without giving away his corruption. Family Services had said nothing to the paramedics or ambulance crew. Eve had spoken to one of them before leaving the hotel this morning. They said Hannah never uttered a word the entire drive.

"Mr. Wall has not answered my calls. If he does, I will let him know you want an interview."

"Next question," Eve stated. "My assault, which you've made no mention of. I gave leads to the responding officer at the hospital. Could you let Mark and Patrick Owens know a detective should be in touch? They can provide the names of my other three stepbrothers."

"Your mind is twisted. They had nothing to do with your assault." His eyes went back to the recorder.

She knew it would throw him off balance if she placed it on his desk. She was right.

"I wanted to thank you for the list of names of Bart Tanner's previous wives. That was very helpful."

"Are you going to tell me who the suspect is?" Aaron demanded.

"It will be in my report," Eve repeated. She reached forward and shut off the recorder.

He'd bullied her long enough. This fight had built for years and it was time to get it over with. She was no longer the child under the church's rule. Aaron had no control over her. She needed him to understand a few things.

"A ten-year-old child killed her family for Bart Tanner's sins. You and other members of law enforcement knew about it. I plan to prove you interfered with a felony investigation."

"Is that a threat?"

"You'll know when I make a threat." She leaned forward. "I know in your opinion, Hannah is of marital age but—"

Eve jerked away from the desk when Aaron stood and slammed his chair back several inches so it hit the bookcase behind him with a solid thud.

"How dare you?" he demanded, his face reddening even further.

The look in his eyes was wild and for the very first time, Eve knew she'd hit a major button. She stood and took a step around the desk so they were almost toe-to-toe. His blue eyes glared but Eve gave as good as she got. It was time a woman stood up to him.

"I'll tell you how I dare." She held up her hand between them, ready to shove him backwards if she needed to. "I was raised with those disgusting rules where young girls are prepared on the altar of sexual gratification for men such as yourself. Don't you dare lecture me on the sick ideology of your church. I will fight with everything I have to make sure your control is cut short and you and the men of the church are punished. The Tanner family is only one of many such tragedies. Their deaths are on your head and that of every man who belongs to your cult. Those children were abused to the point a young girl took the law into her own hands because no adults would help her."

His rage high, he inched closer.

"I," he spat, "have never abused a child."

She took a step back and tipped her head. Her next words were crystal-clear. "You abused *me*." She let that sink in before continuing. "If I had stayed in the family, you know exactly what you would have done."

The fact she said it out loud startled him. It had always been the elephant in the room.

"You would think of it that way," he said through gritted teeth. "I had a crush on you and it was like a little boy pulling a girl's hair." Shame showed in his expression and he didn't meet her eyes.

It was such a giveaway and Eve wasn't backing down.

"I can't even count the number of dresses you ruined, the bruises from each time you kicked me, or the bloody knees I suffered at your hands. You knew your feelings were sinful and you took that sin out on me. You had every intention of carrying out your threats and making me pay for your wickedness. You're a grown man now and still you harbor lust for someone who isn't your wife."

There. She'd said it.

"Get out," he shouted, and pointed to the door, his breathing the loudest sound in the room.

"I know who pelted me with rocks and caused a concussion. Do not insult me by playing dumb. They would have killed me."

Her stepbrother glared.

His silence said everything.

"Hannah needs help," she told him, standing her ground. She would make sure Aaron understood his role in this and she would push it down his throat if need be. "This isn't a case of find killer, put killer behind bars. This is a young girl who had no recourse and used the teachings of the prophet to condone her actions. The sin belongs to you and the members of your brotherhood. She needs mental help, not prosecution. If you go after her to save your high and mighty male society, I won't keep quiet and will scream from the highest mountaintop to every media outlet in this country."

He lifted his hand and pointed at the door, again.

"Go after Hannah and I'm coming after your job. I won't stop until you lose it. You will be disbarred and once you can't give all your money to the church, we'll see how soon they reassign your wives and throw you out." She scooped up the recorder. "That, dear brother, was also not a threat. It was a promise."

She walked out. She'd said what she needed to.

Denise was standing ten feet from Aaron's door.

She smiled.

THIRTY-TWO

"I don't know what will happen but Judge Remki won't be happy," she said. She would play her audio recording for them later. "We need to interview Kathryn Wilson and find out why she wasn't home the night of the murders. Bina, I want you with me. We'll pick up the SUV and go straight there."

"I can do that," said Bina.

"Clyde, Collin, Ray, pack. I want out of here. Bina and I will throw our clothes in a suitcase as soon as the interview is finished. We'll meet you at the hotel after we speak with Kathryn."

They headed straight to the Wilson home after grabbing the SUV. Kathryn answered their knock.

"We need to interview you again," Eve told her without smiling.

Kathryn looked down and took a deep breath. When she lifted her head, Eve saw guilt. "We can do it here or in the SUV."

"The car would be best."

Bina sat in the back seat.

"Do you want me asking questions or would you rather tell me about that night?"

Kathryn started crying. Eve reached over and opened the glove box and handed her a tissue.

"Take your time," she said.

Kathryn never looked up.

"Sister Linda called me. She is Hannah's aunt. Hannah went there after she murdered her family. She told Linda what happened. I was called to the house but there was little I could do. Hannah fell asleep on the couch after she took a shower. Killing her family didn't bother her."

"Linda Wall?" Eve needed to be sure.

"Yes."

"Have you spoken to Linda since that night?"

"No. My husband told me to forget what I knew."

"Did you tell anyone other than your husband?"

"No, but Candace saw me when I came home at around three."

"Did you go to the Tanner home?"

"No, I've never been inside."

"Did you speak to law enforcement or Aaron Owens, the county attorney?"

"No. I was told never to speak of it again."

"Do you know what happened to Hannah's bloody clothes?"

She nodded and Eve waited for her answer.

"I hid them."

Eve hadn't expected this.

"Where are they?" she asked.

"I buried them in our backyard."

Eve glanced at Bina who picked up Eve's camera and handed it to her. They had an evidence bag in the back.

"Will we need a shovel?"

"No, I'll show you where they are."

The clothing was buried in loose dirt a few inches down. The blood on the dress and undergarments was easily identified. Hannah's shoes and socks were buried with them. They also discovered an empty bottle of Benzodiazepine. The prescription information was torn away.

"Does your husband know you had them?"

"No one knew but Linda. This could have been stopped if someone had gotten Hannah out of that home. I was afraid. I'm sorry I didn't say anything sooner." She glanced at Eve for the first time. "Is Hannah okay?"

"Hopefully, someday, she will be." Eve hoped it was the truth.

She asked Kathryn a few more questions before they drove away. She didn't know where Linda and her family were staying. Eve believed her.

"She obstructed us during a felony investigation," Bina said, her words tight. "If she'd told the truth, Hannah wouldn't have had a chance to attack you."

"We'll turn in our reports and leave it to the attorneys to fight over. The wives will always do what their husbands say. I don't want to be here right now and an arrest would be more paperwork than it's worth. I'm ready to go home. We all need a vacation."

"I couldn't agree more," Bina said, relaxing slightly.

They drove to the hotel and had the room cleared within ten minutes.

They were on the road a short time later. Eve didn't look behind her. They would be back and she would face her stepbrother again. He would find a way to wheedle out of this mess but she wouldn't stop. He would eventually go down. She just wanted to be home. After the mountain of reports were finished, she planned to take that vacation.

* * *

Daisy's sorrowful meows greeted Eve when she opened her apartment door. She scooped her up and brought her close for a hug. Daisy purred and purred, along with giving a few pathetic whimpers to make sure Eve knew she was to blame for leaving her.

The team was meeting bright and early the next morning to start typing their reports. Eve wanted to sleep in her own bed and cuddle Daisy all night.

Hannah's eyes still haunted her. Family Services notified her on the ride home that the first hearing before a judge was in two days. Eve and her team had to be there. Hannah needed to stay in custody. For now, it would most likely be a juvenile facility. Hopefully the wheels of justice would go faster than usual and they would place Hannah in a mental health facility quickly. She'd meant what she said to Aaron. He would not be prosecuting Hannah unless he wanted Eve making a deal with a major network. She didn't care if it cost her job.

Opening the refrigerator, she saw its dismal contents and was reminded she needed to pick up groceries and restock. These mundane thoughts were welcome. Placing Daisy on the floor, she made the cat's dinner first while Daisy wrapped in and out of her legs. She added wet food to the dry kibbles exactly as her spoiled highness preferred.

While Daisy devoured her food, Eve heated a can of soup and sat at her small breakfast nook to eat. This was her lonely life. Little on the walls, sparse furniture, and no style whatsoever. Not a real home. It needed to change.

After she finished, she decided to watch the news and possibly find a show that would allow her to relax. The evening edition had stories of the Tanner murders but they didn't yet know about Hannah. That would change sometime before the hearing.

Her cell rang and she glanced at the screen. Clyde.

"Hi," she answered.

"I'm checking on you."

She smiled and sank into her couch cushions.

"I appreciate it. I just finished eating and so did Daisy."

"How are you doing mentally?"

"Exhausted, wired, sad. I'm sure we're all going through it. How are you?"

"The same."

"It's hard to grasp but we'll push through," she told him.

"Are you giving me a pep talk?" he asked.

She chuckled, so glad he had called.

"Maybe. Now it's your turn."

"Any chance you'd like to come to dinner on one of your vacation days, if you're not out of town?"

She'd told them all to schedule time off and that she was going first.

"I'd love to."

"I'm heading to the gym to work out and then getting some rest. I'll see you in the morning."

She hung up with a smile. Daisy jumped on her lap and she rubbed her soft fur.

THIRTY-THREE

Hannah's first hearing was a media circus. They swarmed the area and Eve and her team had trouble getting into the courtroom. The judge slapped a gag order on everyone involved in the case so leaving the courthouse was easier.

Hannah was remanded to juvenile detention awaiting psychological testing. Two separate psychiatrists were ordered. Three weeks later, Hannah was sent to a mental health facility. Eve's recording showed more about Hannah's instability than any doctors could write in a report.

The prosecution and defense worked together, which was almost unheard of.

The story of a ten-year-old committing such a heinous crime remained a top news story. Hannah's attempt to kill Eve placed her team in the limelight. A month later, Eve had still not taken her vacation.

The media went after the fundamentalist church with no holds barred. Eve's team was seen as the avenging angel of justice. She would have preferred they remain anonymous. After the judge lifted the gag order, it was worse. Eve's past was scrutinized and someone discovered she'd been part of the polygamist sect as a child. She worried it would be hard for the team to do their job. Her boss disagreed.

"This will die down," he said during their one-on-one meeting. Lieutenant Crosby was in his fifties. Clean-cut, graying hair, and hard eyes from his years of handling high-profile cases. If anyone knew how the media worked, it was him. "Do your job like you've always done and the media will be bored of your work quickly."

"I'm requesting a week off."

"Granted. Please tell me you're heading to a tropical setting and I'll allow two."

Eve hadn't really planned anything but downtime. She wasn't a beach-type person.

"One will suffice."

"Call when you return."

Eve had one thing on her plate for the time off and then she would relax. She had to jump through hoops to get it.

Her team was handling an extortion case without her. Clyde was in charge and most of the work was done from the office. He'd called in a state accountant who was wading through mountains of paperwork. It was a good time for Eve to take a vacation.

She pulled up outside the facility. She'd worn a long-sleeved pale pink blouse with a three-quarter navy skirt. Her hair was higher on the back of her head than she wore it for work. Her navy shoes had one-inch clunky heels. She carried a paper gift bag with no tissue paper inside. It was examined by security personnel.

Eve was led through a long, well-lit institutionalized hallway. No outside windows. The heavy doors solidly snapped into place after they walked through them. The destination was a small area outside with surrounding walls on all four sides. There was grass, a stone picnic table, and trellis against the walls with vines weaving in and out of it.

Hannah sat at the table. She was wearing a blue shirt and khaki pants. Her hair was cut short and it made her appear younger.

"Hi, Hannah," she said. "I'm Eve."

"I remember you." Hannah's eyes grew larger. They had the same intensity but not the maniacal gleam Eve remembered. "I tried to hurt you."

"I simply wanted to visit and make sure you were okay." Eve didn't know if she should sit down. She'd been nervous since the call came that her request to visit Hannah had been granted.

"Do you want to talk to me?" Hannah asked.

Eve was sure that was all Hannah did. Every psychiatrist in the country probably wanted to get their hands on her and talk. She shook her head.

"I wanted to visit. It's up to you though. I'm not here to ask questions."

"You can sit down. What did you bring?"

Eve sat across from her and placed the bag on the table.

"When I was young, my mother gave me something like this so I thought I would return the favor. It's for you, if you want it."

"Like a gift?" Hannah's curious gaze stayed on the bag.

"Exactly like a gift." Eve pushed it closer.

Hannah lifted her body slightly and looked inside. She reached her hand in and pulled out the white-and-brown stuffed kitten with soft animal-like fur. It had a flat face resembling a Persian.

Hannah's eyes lifted to Eve's.

"It's for me?"

Children in the polygamist community did not receive gifts.

"If you want to keep it, it's yours."

Hannah pulled the kitten close and dipped her head so her nose ran over the fur. She smiled and glanced up again.

"It tickles."

"You can name it if you want. I named my first one Whiskers."

Her childlike giggle sounded so normal. Eve was able to read the psychiatrist reports from the court file. Hannah was diagnosed as a sociopath and a psychopath. The combination of the two was rare. The report stated Hannah would kill again if given the opportunity.

Eve was upset that Hannah had no family to represent her in court. Howard Wall could have gone or even sent his wife Linda, though Eve knew he wouldn't. It bothered her that Hannah had no one.

No matter Eve's mother's problems. She'd rescued Eve from the cult. She'd given Eve Whiskers and a camera.

"I don't have a name," said Hannah.

"You can think about it. If you want me to visit again, you can tell me what you decide."

"You want to visit me?" Hannah's head cocked the same way it had when they were in the attic, but her eyes stayed neutral.

"I would like to, but it's up to you. I like your hair," Eve told her. She hoped it had been Hannah's decision and not the facility.

Her small hand reached up and touched the ends.

"My roommate has hair like this and I wanted to be pretty like her."

It would be up to the psychiatrists if Eve could come back, but if this visit went well, there should be others. She'd had to get special permission from Lieutenant Crosby too. He'd been against it. Eve pushed until he surrendered.

"I like it here," Hannah said. "I get to watch television and cartoons. I like *Care Bears*."

"I like *Care Bears* too, though I haven't watched them in years."

Hannah told her all about the latest adventure she'd seen

the night before. They spoke for about forty minutes before a woman stepped in and told Hannah she had to go to class.

Hannah objected. For a split second, the little girl who murdered her family showed in her eyes. Eve shivered and then left, walking out to her car.

She would never forget what Hannah had done, but she would come back.

THIRTY-FOUR

Sitting at her vanity, Eve inhaled deeply. So many thoughts ran through her head. She'd allowed her childhood to control her for too long. Her anger and resentment were okay. She accepted them and would fight to see other women and children had a chance. If her mother hadn't come for her, she could have been Hannah. Clyde disagreed, but Eve couldn't help thinking it. She wasn't sure what she would have done under Aaron's full control and abuse. Eve's stepfather was important in the community when she was a child and he would have paved the way for Aaron to marry her.

She examined the scissors in her hand. She would get the ends shaped but she needed to do this alone. If a ten-year-old could leave this fundamentalist dogma behind, so could Eve.

Lifting her ponytail, she took a breath. Her hands didn't shake. She cut through the first section. She released the sheared strands and watched them fall to the floor. She made another cut. Then, another. A million pounds of memories drifted down with them. She thought about the way Aaron always stared at her hair and couldn't help smiling.

She removed the plastic band and shook her head until the

uneven ends rested on her shoulders. It felt different in a good way. She shook her head again. The weight she'd carried for so long was cut in half. She brushed the shorter length and enjoyed how it swayed. She had made a huge stride in defeating her demons. She glanced in the mirror again and liked what she saw.

A survivor.

She tossed the hair in the garbage and took the bag to the dumpster on her way to her vehicle. She left her apartment and drove to a place that took walk-in appointments. The stylist had little to say after Eve told her she chopped the ends herself. They were tidied and looked great by the time the professional haircut was finished. Eve was glad she was the one who did it originally.

She had more to prove.

She took a selfie in her car and sent it to her mom. Her cell rang a minute later.

"I like how it looks on you."

"Thank you. It was time."

"I think it was too."

So much lay between them. Her mother had found a therapist and she was going regularly. Eve wanted Maggie to have peace.

She left the parking lot and drove to the store. She felt self-conscious with her purchase and laughed at herself in the car. She was tired of sitting on the sidelines, allowing her past to rule her decisions. She steered the car away from her apartment. She had one last stop to make. It was now after seven and dark outside.

His vehicle was in the driveway when she got to his house. She gathered her courage. She hadn't called. This could be awkward. She would get over it if her plan backfired. With a mental kick, she opened the car door, marched to the porch, and rang the bell.

Clyde's shocked expression was almost worth her nervousness. He wore soft gray sweatpants and the same color T-shirt. His feet were bare.

His gaze stayed on her hair. She lifted her hand and tugged a small section.

"You'll get used to it." It curled in different places and somehow worked. Or so she hoped.

"You look great." His eyes went from her hair to the bottle of wine in her hand.

She held it up and he smiled. They both remembered his first visit to her door. The only difference was that Eve hadn't taken a cab.

"I came for information and I decided it might be easier if I got you drunk first." They were the same words he'd said to her years ago. "Are you going to make me stand out here or may I come in?"

Clyde stepped back.

He knew much of her story, and more since she had told the team about her life as a child. He was her rock. She didn't know much about his past. She wanted to. She was interested in anything he was willing to share.

"I know I'm drinking alone so I'll dispense with the wine glasses," he said with a grin, finally letting her know he was okay with her visit.

"Get the glasses. I've decided to try alcohol for my midlife crisis." She smiled back.

"You're not old enough for a midlife crisis." His charming grin included a full flash of teeth.

Eve was not immune to how good he looked. Maybe it was why she'd pushed him away more than let him in. The attraction scared her. Clyde knew her secrets and still wanted her in his life. She was ready to take the next step.

His grin turned serious.

"I'm not sure drinking alcohol is wise so soon after cutting your hair. Too many changes too fast. I'm the one ready for a midlife crisis and I might take advantage." The smile flashed again but he was also asking a question with his eyes.

There was one last thing she had to get out before she could relax.

"You've never kissed me."

"Come closer." He opened his arms.

A LETTER FROM HOLLY

Thank you for reading *Only Girl Alive*. Oh wait, let me shout that: THANK YOU! I've been so excited to finally share Detective Sergeant Eve Bennet with the world of crime-thriller enthusiasts. Click below if you would like to join the email list for future updates. Your email address will never be shared and you can unsubscribe at any time.

www.bookouture.com/holly-s-roberts

Only Girl Alive was a work of blood, sweat, and tears that included imagination, research, and my background as a sex crimes and homicide detective (retired). My work in law enforcement took place several hours from a large polygamist community on the Utah and Arizona border. Research took me through the founding of the Mormon Church in the 1830s to the current day fundamentalist polygamist movement. I had no idea it would eat four years of my life and drive those around me crazy with anecdotes, documentary enthrallment, and months of writing to turn my thoughts into a novel. My family is hoping I'll find a new distraction, umm, obsession, but as of now, I'm contracted for two additional Eve Bennet books and still obsessing.

Eve and her crew are a work of fiction although much of the information surrounding them is based on eyewitness accounts, investigative articles, and digging deeply into the criminal cases that have plagued the polygamist movement for years. Stay tuned for more chilling adventures as Eve and her team turn up the heat on the fundamentalist brethren.

I love hearing from my readers—you can get in touch on my Facebook page, through Twitter, or my website.

Sincerely,

Holly S. Roberts

https://wickedstorytelling.com/

 facebook.com/hollysrobertsauthor

 twitter.com/HollySRoberts

 goodreads.com/hollysroberts

ACKNOWLEDGMENTS

I want to thank my daughter Amanda for her belief in me as a mother and writer. Her dedication to my grandchildren and the many challenges facing a single mom of four inspire me daily. To the wonderful Bookouture family, I could not have done this without you. My amazing editor, Helen Jenner, your encouragement and brilliance turned my words and ideas into a novel. I've learned so much from you and look forward to our next adventure. Readers and book bloggers, you are motivation personified. Thank you for your support.

Made in United States
Orlando, FL
10 March 2023

30912375R00168